2415

The Final Game

– JASON MICHAEL –

An environmentally friendly book printed and bound in England by
www.printondemand-worldwide.com

Mixed Sources
Product group from well-managed
forests, and other controlled sources
www.fsc.org Cert no. TT-COC-002641
© 1996 Forest Stewardship Council

PEFC Certified

This product is
from sustainably
managed forests
and controlled
sources

www.pefc.org

This book is made entirely of chain-of-custody materials

i

To Martin

Simon Reichert

ii

www.fast-print.net/store.php

The Final Game
Copyright © Jason Michael 2013

A catalogue record for this book is available from the British Library

ISBN 978-178035-568-9

First published 2013 by
FASTPRINT PUBLISHING
Peterborough, England.

Thank you

Janet and Darrill

*Janet, for her helpful advice which led me to
rewrite the original story.*

Darrill, for continually drinking my finest whisky.

*Maggie, for making the thousand and one cups of coffee needed
to keep me going during the whole process.*

Kirsty, for providing the inspiration for the part of 'Sasha'.

Chapter One

Cartagena, Colombia

They'd watched Paul Ford for a long time before approaching him to act as one of their representatives in Europe.

They liked his brutal way of dealing with people who appeared to offer resistance to his determined plans to make a great deal of money from importing drugs into the United Kingdom: it was something they understood and appreciated.

They could do business with someone like that and they wanted him on side, so they baited him, slowly over a period and then reeled him in, just like a fisherman reeling in a salmon on a hook.

Because he was, in their eyes, now their man in the UK, Ford had a lot of flexibility when he visited Cartagena. He maintained an opulent flat in a tower block in the centre of town and was never short of glamorous females at his beck and call.

He became something of a socialite after dark in Cartagena city centre, often drawing attention to himself because of his generous way of keeping his friends happy with regular supplies of cocaine.

When his dealer suddenly moved away, Ford felt his immediate inability to continue maintaining his status as a supplier to friends was not something that he could allow to last. He had noticed that already some of the beautiful girls he normally associated with were avoiding his calls and, as far as he was concerned, having no cocaine meant virtually a stop to his parties!

Ford then had a brilliant idea.

His influence with his employers in Cartagena extended to free access to the offices and underground stores inside the walled city, why not use that to his advantage in the short term?

Business meetings with the Cartel took place in offices next door to where millions of pounds worth of cocaine, sourced from across some of the most productive parts of the country and donkey-packed into Cartagena, were stored awaiting shipment to Europe. They would not miss a little bit. And anyway, once he got a new supplier he could replace what he had taken and no one would be any the wiser.

At first it was simply a few grammes here or there, nothing large or noticeable. He was able to wander past the guard on duty into the stores and secrete some of the smaller packages inside his jacket. On leaving the stores, he always stopped and talked to the guard just to front out the possibility of suspicion.

Ford got away with it every time, thus increasing his confidence. The amounts of the cocaine that he was pilfering began to increase in size as he regained his popularity on the party scene. The parties began again and he was soon enjoying having his pick of the girls and enjoying life to the full once more.

In order to maintain the level of his supplies, Ford soon began driving in to the walled city in his car so that he could load a kilogram sack into his boot. He planned such visits when the guard left the stores unattended for a few minutes to change shift. He reasoned that he would not be suspected because he was such a regular visitor to the walled city. Anyway, they had so much cocaine there they would probably never miss the comparatively small amount that he was taking.

Of course his luck eventually ran out. Although Ford did not realise it, all of his visits to the stores had been closely monitored by cameras discreetly hidden within the stores.

The Cartel discussed the matter and decided to act. It wasn't so much the quantities that worried them, it was the principal. The gringo had been caught stealing from the hand that fed him. If he was allowed to get away with it, then others might try to do the same thing. Why, even the local Chief of Police might think that he could steal from them!

★ ★ ★ ★

A few nights following the meeting of the Cartel, Ford took home a particularly attractive young blonde woman who had excited him when he saw her hanging off a chrome pole at the local lap dancing club. Within minutes of entering his flat, she glanced around and went immediately to the glass table in the centre of the room and began laying two generous lines of cocaine out on the glass table.

When Ford returned from the kitchen with two large glasses and a bottle of champagne they made a start. It was not long before both of them were devoid of any clothing and enjoying the cocaine and the champagne.

They soon graduated from the floor to the main bedroom where Ford lost no time in exploring the girl's body. His tongue was soon running along her vagina and back again, his hands cupping her tight bottom. The sweat was dripping from his body and mingling with the perspiration from her body.

She lay on her back and using both hands was manipulating Ford's penis in a way that he had not experienced before. He was ecstatic.

He knew he could keep going for days without a break such was the level of excitement caused by the alcohol and the designer drug. Ford considered he was unstoppable. She would do his bidding whatever was involved. She had no choice; she was his guest and plaything.

★ ★ ★ ★

At three in the morning Ford became dimly aware that the door to his flat had parted company with both the door locking system and the hinges. The door hit the passageway wall and came to a stop as four employees of the Cartel rushed into the flat and made straight for the bedroom.

Two of the men grabbed Ford and dragged him off the bed. They slammed him back against the bedroom wall and held him upright. A third man then began to punch Ford solidly about the face. Ford felt his nose break on the second punch. Blood began pouring from his wound and dripped down his front. The man then changed his attack to Ford's ribs and chest.

The fourth man, a huge man for a South American, watched his friends dealing with Ford for a few moments before turning his attention to the girl, now sitting up in the bed and looking with horror at what was happening to Ford. He seized her by the hair and dragged her struggling from the bed and draped her over the bedrail.

He spread her legs, unzipped his fly and forced his penis into her anus. She screamed with the pain as he forced himself deeper into her and began a rhythmical motion backwards and forwards.

When he had finished, the man who had been punching Ford, clearly bored with his task, crossed the room and after speaking to the big man unzipped and dropped his trousers and forced himself into the girl.

When he had finished with the screaming girl, both he and the big man dragged her to the open window and threw her out. She plummeted still screaming to her death five floors below.

Without hurrying, the four men, carrying Ford in much the same way as natives would carry a dead beast, left the flat and made for the exit. There was no one to complain. No one would dare complain, not if they wanted to carry on living another day.

Chapter Two

Ford slowly recovered consciousness and found he was lying on a cold concrete floor inside a small cell. The cell door was metal with a small inspection hatch set in the middle. There was no sign of a door handle on the inside of the door. On the outside wall and placed above head height was a small metal barred window that had been closed for years. A smell of dampness and human waste prevailed. When he tried to move, every muscle in his body ached and felt swollen. Ford found he was unable to stand up easily if at all, so he sank back to the ground and stayed there.

He knew why he was there, and the thought of what was going to happen to him filled him with terror! Ford knew that the Colombians had savage and permanent ways of dealing with those who offended them. If they were lucky a single bullet would rectify matters. If they were unlucky, then dying for them was a long, slow, painful process. In spite of the cold, Ford began to sweat and panic.

★ ★ ★ ★

During the first week of his imprisonment, Ford's captors visited him daily at varying times. Sometimes he was simply forced into a standing position and then beaten about his body with a wooden club until he collapsed onto the floor. He was then kicked about the body until he lost consciousness.

There was no point begging them to stop, he was there to be tormented until they decided to kill him.

Ford screamed in pain and lost consciousness all too quickly. He was often revived simply by a bucket of his own urine being thrown over him and the routine then repeated. Often, as an added pleasure for his tormentors, they applied electrodes to his body and then cranked up the generator, laughing as he screamed in agony.

Each session was unhurried and designed to inflict as much pain on Ford as possible. He was shown no mercy.

Throughout his ordeal Ford was never questioned about his misdeeds. It didn't matter. He had offended the Cartel and was now being punished. Ford expected to die: he just hoped it would be soon.

In his more lucid moments away from the torture sessions Ford realised he could not carry on for much longer. His food intake during his stay was so uncertain that it appeared to be sometimes days between meals being supplied to him. When they did arrive, both the quality and quantity left much to be desired.

Ford reckoned that he had lost about two stone, which left him in a weakened state. Furthermore, his drug problem which was directly responsible for him being a prisoner was having a serious withdrawal effect on him. He had the shivers and stomach cramps most of the time and it was getting worse on a daily basis.

As he lay there contemplating his sad state, the door of his cell suddenly opened and in rushed two of his torture team. They simply began kicking him about his body until he felt himself slipping, once again, into that pain free zone.

Ford had a faint memory of being dragged by his captors into the back of a large car and of being kicked and pushed until he lay across the well of the car. Two people got into the car and kept their feet on his back, kicking him from time to time. Ford by now was past caring. Please God, he thought, let it be soon. Again, he experienced that all-over warm feeling replacing the shivering and the hurt. He slowly slipped into a welcome unconsciousness.

★ ★ ★ ★

Ramos Gonzales left his office and walked slowly across the cobbled courtyard and up the stone steps that led to the battlements of the walled city. At the top, he stood and stared out at the deep blue of the

Caribbean Sea. The day was perfect. The sky was blue with not a cloud in sight. A warm breeze gently blowing in off the water caused him to perspire. Gonzales felt pleased with himself that morning. Matters were going well, so well in fact that he thought the time was right for him to act and apply pressure on the Englishman. He stayed for a few moments more and then made his way slowly back to his office. Gonzales loved the intrigue of the city, his city, for that is what it was. He was now the number one main man in all of Cartagena.

★ ★ ★ ★

Built in 1533 by the Spanish, Cartagena soon became the major sea link to Spain. Treasures, donkey-packed from across the entire nation, were stored in the hundreds of small warehouses that littered the shoreline.

The popularity of the port soon came to the notice of marauding pirates, who simply waited for the small ships to leave the shores before attacking them and taking the treasures for themselves. The ships were easy pickings and their demise was often watched from the shore.

Greedy for more, the pirates began blocking the sea lane entrances and preventing ships from moving out to the sea lanes. It became easy then to board the many ships waiting to leave and take the treasures. Setting fire to the ships afterwards became a frequent practice of the pirates. From the ships it was a short step to invading Cartagena itself and stealing the gold and silver artefacts direct from the many stores by the shoreline.

Francis Drake brought the situation to a head when, in 1586, he applied a massive siege to the area and plundered the treasure reserves of the people for the last time.

The people of Cartagena fed up with the savagery of the pirates, who not only stole their livelihoods from them but also raped their women, killed thousands of their people and burnt them out of their houses, organised themselves and built the wall and the ring of outer forts around Cartagena, making the city impregnable against sieges from the sea. From then on the city flourished and grew in importance to become the major trade centre for the Spanish empire.

★ ★ ★ ★

Standing there shading his eyes from the glare of the sun, Gonzales frowned as he looked out to sea. The ship had left port and was now clear of local sea traffic. Its ultimate destination was Portugal, where the cargo of Colombian ore would be unloaded. The ship's other cargo, of one thousand kilos of the finest quality cocaine, would be unloaded after dark, away from the prying eyes of those with no need to know.

Yes, Gonzales thought, it is most definitely time that I spoke to the Englishman. With that thought, he returned to his office and ordered his car to be brought around to the front door.

En route to the small airport and close to the outskirts of the city, Gonzales leaned back against the leather seats of the converted London taxi and examined his fingernails. He smiled to himself as he thought over his plan to deal with Ford. It had taken him some time to convince other members of the Cartel of its merits.

He had been helped enormously, of course, when one of the early objectors to his plan, a senior member of the Cartel, had been paraded on US television showing off a variety of bugs, cameras and other surveillance equipment that he had used to infiltrate both government offices and the American embassy in Bogotá. Perhaps the worst offence he had committed was to listen in on Cartel meetings and then sell the tapes to the Americans. Such treachery by a respected and senior member of the Cartel was unheard of. It would not have occurred in the days of Pablo Escobar.

The resounding crackdown by the authorities, prodded by the US State Department, had succeeded in making life very difficult for the Cartel after that. Firstly, it had caused them to look inwards at their own structure and reassess those who were loyal to them and those not so loyal.

They were forced to continually move their processing plants and their chemists to deep in the jungle to avoid the activities of the army and Special Forces squads sent out by the Americans. It was at this point, following a number of successes by the various agencies, that the calls for revenge to be inflicted on the aggressors came to fruition and his plan had been accepted.

Gonzales had smiled at the look on their faces as he suggested to his masters that the way to attack the Americans, and hit them where it hurt, was to simply cease sending drug supplies to that country. As they were responsible for eighty percent of cocaine being imported into the United States it followed, like night followed day, that stopping supplies would have an immediate and catastrophic effect upon all of the suppliers and users in that country.

Once the shortage of cocaine importation became apparent, it would cause panic. A massive crime wave would ensue as dwindling supplies would attract a higher price that had to be funded by the users. They in turn would increase their efforts to pay by increasing their criminal activities. Then the Americans would come to understand just who their masters were.

Of course, in the short term, the Cartel had to understand that there would be a shortfall, but it would last only as long as it took the Americans to come to heel. In the meantime the Cartel could use that intervening period to reorganise their European adventure by increasing their supplies to the developing markets there and replacing the existing Colombian director of supplies in Europe with a trained Englishman who better understood the needs of his home market.

The frowns on their faces had turned to smiles as they began to appreciate the wisdom of his long term plan.

At the conclusion of the meeting Gonzales was promoted to the office of European Consultant, with the directive to pursue such measures as he thought necessary to develop new business in what was seen by a number of those present as the New World.

Yes, he, Ramos Gonzales, was about to unfold the beginnings of his plan and get the respect of the Cartel, which he so richly deserved.

Chapter Three

The small, twin-engine Cessna aeroplane was waiting for Gonzales at the airport. The airport was small and little more than a single runway operation. It was operated by those with sympathies to the organisation and any other groups who wished whatever it was they were transporting to travel with some degree of security and anonymity.

Both engines were turning over with gentle revs as Gonzales arrived and boarded the small aircraft. The pilot waited for his passenger to seat himself and lock his seatbelt before taxiing onto the dirt strip and taking off. It was a daily run from the airport to the villa on the hilltop, usually taking little more than fifteen minutes unless there was a prevailing headwind or the mist was down which made it a bit hazardous trying to identify the flares put out for the landing.

On the odd occasion, the pilot would fly as low as he could, pick out the flares and then turn and come in to land from the other end of the strip. Either way he would always come to a stop as close to the white line stop sign as he could. There was no point making the boss walk halfway down the runway to get the taxi. He would not like that.

The waiting taxi would then drive as close as he could to the aircraft and pick up its passenger and his bodyguard, Carlos. Security in the hills was just as important as it was in the town. It was always possible for a team of Special Forces to be waiting on the hillside ready to attack either the taxi and passenger or the villa on top of the hill. There was always somebody ready to even the score and celebrate the death of Gonzales.

Once he arrived at the villa, Gonzales walked through to the vast patio that overlooked the valleys below. The views were magnificent and, perched as it was on top of the cliff, the villa offered considerable protection from any attack from below.

He sat at a table laid for breakfast. A young Colombian girl dressed as a French maid came from within the main building and offered him his usual cold orange juice. He nodded and she poured out the liquid in a tall thin glass.

No more than about twelve years old, the girl fussed around the table and made a great show of bending over the table at various points to display her French knickers and pert bottom which appeared to be desperately trying to force itself out from either side of the thin gusset that ran between her legs.

Gonzales looked at the girl and thought that perhaps later he might have the girl to join him on the patio for drinks minus her uniform and see where it took him!

Carlos, the bodyguard, appeared at the doorway. He walked across to Gonzales and waited for instructions. Sipping from his glass, Gonzales looked at his man.

"Carlos, is the Englishman here yet?"

"Yes sir, the gringo is downstairs. He arrived here an hour ago."

Gonzales smiled. "Bring him to me. It is time for him to begin working for us again."

Carlos picked up the nearby telephone and spoke into it for a few minutes.

Ford appeared in front of Gonzales supported under each arm by two of his torturers. He was unable to stand up by himself and was still naked and showing the body scars of his recent maltreatment. Ford was squinting through bloodshot eyes and found some difficulty in focussing. Gonzales sipped his orange juice and looked at the broken and pitiful wreck before him. He smiled.

"Mr Ford, you abused the hospitality of our family. Why should I not kill you?"

Ford's jaw had been broken and some of his teeth were loose. His lips were split and dry and his nose had also been broken. Speech did not come easily to him, yet he knew that for some reason he was being given a second chance.

He had to make the most of it; it might be his last chance to save himself. He tried to straighten up and present the best image of himself that he could, but failed. The pain from his injuries made him wince and buckle, he thought he was going to collapse.

"I am so sorry for taking advantage of your hospitality. I can only assure you that it will never ever happen again. It was a one-off and I have learnt my lesson." Ford stopped as he felt blood begin to ooze from his mouth. He was unable to continue.

Gonzales turned to Carlos.

"Carlos, show Mr Ford what happens to those who abuse their position."

Carlos half-turned towards Ford and suddenly struck Ford's torturer nearest to him with a knife-hand strike to the throat. The blow ruptured the man's carotid artery. He blinked and his mouth opened, as if he was unable breathe, then he fell backwards on to the floor, dead. Carlos reached down, picked the man up without effort and raised him above his head. He then strode to the edge of the patio and threw the man out and over the top of the patio wall. Carlos paused for a moment before looking over the edge. He grinned and turned towards Ford.

Gonzales smiled at Ford, who was now visibly terrified and waiting his turn to be cast over the parapet to oblivion. "You see what happens to those who abuse us Mr Ford?"

Ford wondered why it was taking so long. What more could they possibly do to him? Why prolong talking to him? They could see the effect they were having on him, why not throw him over the top and have done with it?

"Carlos, bring Mr Ford closer to me!"

The huge man pushed the remaining bodyguard to one side and seized Ford by the hair. He dragged him in front of Gonzales and forced him onto his knees. With his free hand Carlos reached down and grabbed Ford's testicles and began squeezing them and twisting them from side to side. The pain was excruciating, and Ford screamed in agony. It was all he could do not to vomit. Gonzales sipped his orange juice and waited for Ford to recover.

"Carlos, show Mr Ford the other side of the balustrade, and what awaits him should he ever choose to abuse our hospitality again."

Carlos again seized Ford and bent slightly and then straightened up hoisting Ford up above his head. He marched to the edge of the patio and hung Ford over the top. He then dropped him onto the top of the patio wall so that he was upside down. Ford looked below him and saw the broken body of his torturer lying on the rocks. Already the birds of prey were pecking at the carcase. Ford vomited.

At a signal from his employer, Carlos dragged Ford back and to his place on his knees in front of Gonzales.

"Mr Ford, I have decided to let you live. Soon you will leave my country and travel to Portugal where a task awaits you. Are you agreeable to this?"

"Yes sir," Ford gasped, unable to believe his good luck. "I'll do whatever you want."

"Carlos, take Mr Ford to our place in the town and ensure that he understands his instructions."

Turning to Ford, he said, "Mr Ford, do not let me down again. If you do, I will let Carlos have his way with you and you would not like that at all. Is that understood?"

Ford felt himself begin to cry as much from the pain still coursing through his body as from the sheer relief that he was not going to join the guard already on the rocks below. He was unable to respond and passed out.

In the taxi and on the floor in the back, Ford felt both of Carlos's feet on his back pressing him into the well, but he was alive. The taxi stopped after an hour of driving down the mountain roads into the small town and to the hotel. Ford was dragged out by his hair, around the rear of the small building and into a small room.

Carlos took out a document from his jacket pocket and dropped it onto Ford's chest.

"You will read this now and understand it."

Ford, still in a dazed state, picked up the paper and tried to focus on it. When he had finished, he went to pass it back to Carlos. The bodyguard gripped all of the fingers on Ford's hand and began bending them backwards.

"Listen to me gringo. If you fail us again, I will kill you very slowly, do you understand me?"

There was a distinct cracking noise from two of his fingers as he passed out.

Chapter Four

John Ridge sat in the office and contemplated his return to front-line intelligence work. Not much had changed in the three years that he had been away from the office; it was still staffed by the same people. The only real difference that he could put his finger on was the supervisors now seemed permanently office-bound as if going out into the world was no longer a requirement.

He glanced out of the window and took in the view west, over the spectacular minarets of the Royal Pavilion. He recalled that during the autumn and late in the afternoon, the setting sun would cast the most glorious views out over the rooftops. Because his office was on the first floor of the E-shaped building, Ridge was privy to views of the royal love nest that few others had. His phone buzzed. He glanced at the display and read the text with some excitement. Putting on his coat he cadged a lift to the railway station.

Ridge presented the travel warrant that he had earlier obtained from the whinging admin clerk who appeared to think she was paying for it out of her own money, to the clerk behind the glass window.

He saw the spotty-faced clerk look at the warrant then at him as if he was going to argue over it. But after a brief pause the youth conjured up a ticket and threw it on the turntable and spun it around until it faced Ridge. Picking up the ticket, Ridge then walked out onto the main concourse, buying a daily newspaper and a large *Starbucks* on the way to the platform where his train had just pulled in.

Arriving at Victoria Station, Ridge left the carriage behind a group of chattering foreign students. He stayed behind them until they passed through the control point and spread out over the concourse. Ridge saw nothing that caused him concern as he checked for people in the wrong place at the wrong time. He continued walking and watching for signs as he went into *Smiths* the newsagents. Going to the magazine counter he picked a *Men's Health* magazine and opened the pages as he looked over the top of the shelf, through the main window and into the station bar a short distance away. He watched for about ten minutes until he was satisfied that all was in order. Replacing the magazine back on the shelf he squeezed himself past people and left the shop, making in the direction of the station bar.

He tapped the man on the shoulder. "Hello Charles, it's been a long time."

The tall man dressed in a light beige suit turned and smiled at Ridge. He shook hands with him as if they were long lost friends rather than two people with potentially separate agendas.

"What would you like to drink?" he asked.

Ridge settled for a lager and Charles Ford did the same as he frantically tried to attract the attention of the barman. Once the drinks had been obtained, they moved to a table and chairs where they could both watch the comings and goings in and out of the bar and onto the concourse.

Ford sipped his drink. "It took me some time to get here because I am being looked at. It's not your lot is it John?"

Ridge showed surprise.

"No, it's not my lot I'm sure of that. Maybe it's the Customs?"

Ford shrugged. "Maybe you're right. If it is, they are not very good at it."

Ridge looked at him.

"Why should anybody be looking at you, are you up to something?" He grinned at Ford.

Charles Ford smiled as he sipped his lager. "I really don't know. I have turned over a new leaf!"

Ridge almost choked over his drink. Both men talked pleasantries asking about each other's family and making the sort of small talk that friends who haven't seen each other for some time do. They continually scanned the doorway looking at those customers coming and going.

When they had finished their drinks they left the bar and walked across the concourse looking into shop windows at the reflections. At the escalator they hesitated for a few moments and then stepped onto the moving belt. Ford carried on talking continually to Ridge who was half-turned watching others moving onto the escalator. At the very top of the escalator and off to the right-hand side was an open plan coffee shop. There was plenty of room to sit and enjoy a coffee, watching the escalator and stairway as they talked.

Ford said, "Would you like to recover a load of cocaine coming in from Portugal?"

"Yes, of course I would." replied Ridge, feeling his heartbeat increase. "When will it be available? And what sort of quantities are we talking about?"

"About sixty kilos, I think!"

"What's the street value of a load like that?"

"The way your lot count, it is probably somewhere in the region of several million pounds."

"What's the story with it?" Ridge asked, a little surprised by the offer. "I can't understand why after all this time you make me an offer like that. We haven't met for just over three years and here you are offering something that will make my lot wet their knickers."

Ford looked at him and smiled.

"I owe you something from the last time. I know it wasn't easy for you when your lot gave you grief over that importation. I also know you kept your mouth shut, because I was never arrested or even followed. I just wanted to say thanks."

Ridge recalled the job where he had arranged for one hundred kilos of Amphetamine Sulphate to be recovered from a caravan site in France. Simple enough really, except that instead of doing the job themselves the Crime Squad had passed the job over to the French Customs who had made a complete hash of it. A Customs officer had been badly injured in the shootout that had followed their intervention.

The French got upset and aggressive when they questioned the gunman but he refused to tell all. They then tried to work backwards from the informant stage and not unnaturally asked the English Crime Squad for the name of their informant. The Crime Squad Chief Superintendent then became embarrassed because Ridge had declined to name Ford. At his refusal to assist the French officers, Ridge's supervisors became enraged because they also were not in the loop about the informant. It appeared to them that a mere detective constable was holding them all to ransom.

A few weeks later at Ridge's annual appraisal time a disingenuous report about Ridge's behaviour was presented at the meeting and rubber-stamped without discussion. Ridge was thrown out of the department and returned to uniform duties where he stayed until his recent and unexpected return to the same department.

Ridge smiled. "So, you old tart, you have a heart after all!"

Ford grinned. "I want to settle a few scores on my side. I'm sure you want to do the same with your lot?"

Ridge looked serious for a moment.

"You are sure that this will work? I don't want a repeat of last time."

Ford, also serious, said, "I will give you what you need to make it work. It is up to you to bring it all together. I know you can do that."

Ridge said, "I have less than a year to do before I retire, something like this will really get up their noses. But I will be working with some of the same people involved last time, so I will need to be careful."

Ford smiled. "Trust me. I know of nothing at this time that can go wrong. It's a piece of cake. I just want the people importing this lot to lose it: simple as that."

Ridge picked up a slight tension in Ford's voice.

"Who is importing this lot of drugs?"

"You know the rules John, both of us have our secrets, but the important thing to remember is we can both win. While I am talking about winning John, I want twenty grand for this lot. I want paying. Is that okay?"

Ridge thought Ford had as much chance of getting twenty grand as he had of flying to the moon.

"I don't see any reason why you should not get that. Just wait until I recover the total amount of drugs, then I will whack in for that amount," he lied.

Ford stood up and offered his hand. "John, it's been nice doing business with you again. The moment I have more details I'll buzz you, okay?"

Shaking hands with him Ridge noticed that Ford's hand was damp with perspiration. He wondered why.

"Speak soon Charles and take care."

Ridge sat down again and allowed Ford to leave. At the bottom of the escalator, Ford turned slightly and glanced up the way he had just come. His eyes met Ridge's eyes and they both grinned at each other, both pleased at being back talking to each other again.

Finishing his *Starbucks*, Ridge made his way to the terminal and back to Brighton.

Chapter Five

Seated on the train heading south Ridge had time to go over in his mind the time spent with Ford. It was good that so soon after his return to the office and to the type of work that he enjoyed, Ford had popped up with his offer of a job that, let's face it, on the surface appeared to be the chance of a lifetime.

From the conversation with Ford it was obvious that the job was ongoing in a sense and not lying dormant waiting to be brought to life. If he was to be believed, Ford was able to monitor the job throughout and be in a position to advise Ridge when to raise the cavalry and intervene. It all sounded very straightforward but, as Ridge knew, life wasn't like that and, what is more, Ford's sweaty handshake was an indication that there was something he was not being told.

Why had Ford reappeared? How did he know that Ridge had recently returned to intelligence work? Was

Ford so full of the milk of human kindness that all he really wanted to do was to repay an old mate for services rendered? The more he thought about it the more he knew that there were other factors going on of which, at the present time, he was unaware.

Ridge mentally revisited the jobs over the years when Ford had supplied such accurate intelligence information on large scale drug importation that his supervisors wanted to take over the running of Ford as an informant and oust Ridge from his role with Ford.

They thought, in very simple terms, that if the man was talking to him then instead he could talk to them, but there was more to it than that. When you are dealing with people who give information their feelings have to be taken into account. With an informant supplying really good information they were always paranoid that if it became known that they were giving information, then they would suffer some form of retribution from the very people they were informing against. Their lives would be at risk. In short, they had to like and trust the officer they were dealing with.

He had managed to thwart these attempted takeovers by saying that Ford was a nasty bastard who would not deal with people that he neither knew nor could trust. So far that argument had prevailed, but the day had to come when he would be overruled. Professional jealousy was a continual problem and he knew that his supervisors were simply watching him, awaiting their opportunity.

Jason Michael

The train eased into the station and glided to a stop. Ridge got out and made his way out of the station via the main concourse.

The main thrust of passengers using the station had passed although it was still a busy time. Glancing at his watch face he decided it was too early to go back to the office.

He a made quick telephone call from a nearby kiosk and then caught a taxi to Norfolk Square, by the old Police Box. Ridge walked south from the square towards the sea, turning right at the end of the square. He wandered northwards to the top of the road and then turned left again making sure that he was not being followed. He followed the Western Road for about two hundred yards before suddenly turning down under the arch and making for Oriental Place where he looked for a particular house number. Finding what he was seeking he walked up the steps and knocked on the door. Almost immediately the door was opened by a petite Thai girl.

She greeted Ridge as if he was a long lost friend and bid him enter the premises. Inside the house Ridge was offered refreshment. He declined; it wasn't a drink he was in need of. A door opened and he saw his friend standing waiting for him. She was dressed in a traditional manner and, clasping her hands together, bowed in Ridge's direction. Ridge noticed that her jet black hair was freshly combed so that it cascaded over her shoulders. Her dark brown eyes, complete with that heavenly almond shape to them, sparkled as she looked at him; she was beautiful and physically flawless from tip to toe

"It is so good to see you again, please come with me," she said, with just a soft oriental lilt to her voice.

Ridge walked over to her, stopped and bowed to her. He could see from her reaction that she was surprised and pleased to be accorded this level of politeness from a customer.

They entered the room together. The moment that the door was closed Ridge took her in his arms and gently kissed her on both cheeks in another sign of respect, which delighted her. She took his jacket off his shoulders and placed it on a chair before leading him into the large shower room. "I will return in a moment!" She then left him alone in the room closing the door on her way out.

Ridge undressed and entered the shower. Within a few moments, the Thai woman returned to the shower room completely naked and joined Ridge. Placing her hands on his shoulders she gently turned him, so that he was facing the wall as she increased the water temperature and began soaping down his back with soap especially imported from Thailand. Reaching his lower back the woman gently played with his buttocks before moving her hands around to his front. Ridge shuddered at the effect on him that she was having as she began rubbing her body against him.

Turning Ridge around once more so that he was now facing her, she slowly dropped to her knees and took him in her mouth and began a gentle rhythm, until Ridge could not stand it any longer. She dried him off using gentle swirling motions with the soft white towel, taking care not to rub him too hard with the towel in case it provoked an early finish!

When he was dry, she led him into another room and onto a massage table. Lying face down, Ridge felt the gentle electric massage begin to work in waves up and down his body. Immediately in front of him on a small table was a chilled glass of white wine. He picked up the glass and sipped from it. The woman selected a number of aromatic creams from her dressing table and returned to Ridge. Leaning across his back so that her breasts touched him she began massaging cream into the nape of his neck and shoulders.

The combination of the wine and aromatic oils was beginning to make Ridge feel drowsy. He felt the warm glow spreading across his back as the woman moved her hands in ever increasing circles eliminating some of the stiffness in his shoulders. Eventually, she straddled him and bent forwards and introduced the points of both elbows in the tense area and slowly reduced the inflammation.

Ridge could feel her soft, silky pubic hair pressing into the small of his back. With that, and the uncomfortable massaging of his shoulders, Ridge was starting to lose his drowsiness and becoming very aware of what was happening to him.

The smiling woman turned him over and saw his level of excitement. Climbing back onto the table she positioned herself so that she was able to gently lower herself slowly onto Ridge before sitting up straight and watching his reaction. By using her muscles she coaxed him to a point until he urged her to stop. She paused remained where she was until Ridge asked her to continue. Massaging his chest brought together all his feelings as he watched her body and felt her above him. Her lithe body rippled with perspiration as she tormented Ridge. He reached the point of no return quite quickly. Reaching up he pulled her down towards him and increased his momentum as he felt his body entering the very centre of her being. When he had finished she covered him with a warm blanket and allowed him to lie and relax.

In the quietness of the semi-dark room, Ridge decided that from time to time there was some compensation for being a police officer, not much mind you, but this was definitely one of those compensatory moments!

Twenty minutes later, he showered and dressed, paid the woman and left.

Chapter Six

The following morning, Charles Ford left his north London home at 10am and caught the Tube to Liverpool Street .He wandered in and out of the railway station bookshops employing basic counter surveillance techniques looking for a tail. Like Ridge, he was a very cautious man who knew that attention to detail decided whether you became a short term player, a long term player, a prop for a concrete flyover or worst of all, a long term guest of Her Majesty. His career of theft, burglary, assault on police and three successful years as an across the pavement robber had all helped to mould him into the man he now was. Like his brothers, he could be a very nasty bastard.

Satisfied that he was not being followed, he went into one of the bars and ordered a light lunch of chicken and a small side salad. He sat watching the door as he consumed his meal. When he had finished, he paid for his meal and left the bar. Ford looked at the railway station clock and decided that he had spent enough time playing silly buggers. He crossed the concourse and found the ticket machine. Masking the screen so that he could not be watched by someone using binoculars from an upstairs office window, he bought a ticket. Ford again resorted to a walkabout before making his way to the Tube and catching the train to the Queensway.

He was certain that he was not being followed. At Queensway, Ford got off the train and crossed to the other side of the station and checked the times of the train going to Havering railway station. He then strolled over to the counter and bought a ticket afterwards walking into the newsagents and buying a daily paper. He remained in the shop looking out of the window as the train arrived at the station. Ford left it to the last minute before dashing out of the shop and jumping aboard the last carriage. At Kings Cross station he changed for the last part of his journey. At Havering, Ford deliberately walked slowly from the carriage to the exit with four other passengers. Nobody seemed to be paying him any attention or was threatening in any way.

He saw the environmentally friendly green-coloured Range Rover parked in a no waiting area. Peter, his brother, had collected a newspaper from the station news-vendor and was walking back towards the car.

Peter Ford was a former student with a degree in chemistry. He also possessed a licence to fly fixed-wing aircraft and helicopters. In 1972, he had been convicted of illegally flying into the United Kingdom six very small and very sick Pakistanis. He served five years for that. On his release from his custodial sentence Ford furthered his flying experience by importing twenty-five kilos of cocaine into the United Kingdom. Unfortunately for him, while coming in over the fields of Kent, engine failure forced him to ditch the lot in a farmer's field, much to the consternation of the farmer in the field at the time!

By the time Ford had circled around and landed nearby, hoping to recover the jettisoned load, the local policeman was on the scene, and waiting for him to land. He was captured without fuss.

At Maidstone Crown Court nine months later, His Honour Judge Michael Crown, described Ford as a menace to society and gave him four years imprisonment for his trouble.

Peter Ford drove the Range Rover away from the no waiting area and towards the farm. Turning to his younger brother, he said, "Paul rang in from Portugal last night. The ship has arrived in port and is waiting on being unloaded. He thinks tomorrow is D-day for unloading. He says the sooner he can get the gear away from the port the better. He's going to ring again tomorrow, when hopefully it will be on the road towards France."

Charles looked at his brother.

"Good. It's beginning to come together. My friend bought the whole story. It was so easy." He paused. "In a way I'm sorry I've had to involve him: he has been fair to me in the past and got nothing but grief for it. There was a time when he gave evidence on my behalf and according to my brief, it knocked five years off the top."

Peter glanced at him.

"What you have to remember is we may not need to use him. He is an insurance policy if the job goes pear-shaped. Forget him for the time being, Paul will sort out that side of things when he gets back over here, in the next few days."

Chapter Seven

R idge drove into the underground car park and left his car in one of bays allocated to his department. He noticed that both his immediate supervisors' cars were already parked in their nominated spaces. He climbed the back stairs, walked across the yard and punched in the number on the lock on the back door of the police station and let himself in. Back in his office he found his coffee mug and washed it out in the small kitchen near his office.

As he waited for the office percolator to fuse the hot water with the freshly ground coffee beans, Ridge silently cursed Joanne, the office secretary. She was a good looking tart of about nineteen years of age who, in spite of a good many O-levels, found it extremely difficult to maintain any standards of hygiene in the office. Coffee cups from the previous day were littered about the office. Some, for whatever reason, lay on his desk. He cleared the lot away and sat down.

Ridge could hear conversation coming through the thin partition wall between his office and his supervisor's office. Sipping his coffee, he wondered how much of Ford's information he could put into the system. He had to account for some of the information if only to get the job registered as a live job and justify any further time spent moving it on. The problem was that if he put it all down on paper then his supervisors might try to interfere with what they saw as supervision and he saw as interference and the day-to-day running of the job would be cocked up.

At one minute past nine the small wooden hatchway halfway up the wall linking the two offices was opened with some force and his detective sergeant, Emil Kimber, peered through at Ridge.

Kimber was about thirty years of age and in spite of an aggressive front lacked the confidence to perform much of his day-to-day work without upsetting people. Ridge noticed that he was again dressed in the same clothes as yesterday, a multi-coloured rugby shirt and jeans. Both items of clothing appeared to be in need of a wash. Kimber topped the lot with a trendy spiky hairstyle and two days' worth of designer stubble.

"Doing surveillance, are you?" asked Ford, grinning from ear to ear.

"My office, now!" snapped Kimber.

Ridge got up and walked next door to where Kimber was now sitting behind his desk.

Kimber glared at him.

"I want to know, and the detective inspector wants to know, where you got to yesterday? We believe you went to London without either of us being aware just where you had gone."

"London?" queried Ridge, as if he had never heard anything so ridiculous. Kimber, easily annoyed by a stroppy, secretive and sometimes arrogant detective like Ridge, started to go red at what he knew was the start of what was going to be a difficult conversation.

"If you persist with this attitude Ridge, you may well find yourself biting off more than you can chew. Now please explain!"

Ridge put his empty coffee cup down on Kimber's desk. At this, Kimber suddenly flared up.

"Take your fucking coffee mug off my desk and go and see the DI, I don't want to know. Save your explanations for the boss."

Picking up his coffee mug Ridge left the office and walked along the corridor to the office marked: Detective Inspector Johnston.

Ridge knocked on the door and waited. Eventually there was a crisp, "Come," from within.

Ridge offered a mock bow to his inspector and said, "Sire, I come from Antioch with good news from the goat herders!"

Johnston looked at him. He did not appreciate Ridge's humour.

"Sit down and shut up!" He sat back in his chair and looked at Ridge with something approaching distaste.

"I could not reach you at all yesterday. I understand that you, without my authority, travelled to London to see the sights or whatever. Please explain."

Ridge, sensing that the conversation was likely to become difficult, kept a stony face.

"It wasn't quite as you suggest sir. I was, as always, working myself to the absolute limit!"

"Doing what?" Johnston asked. "I have nothing from you in writing, accounting for your activities in town. No bloody explanation at all. Please share your thoughts with me!"

"I had a late call from an informant who asked to see me that evening. I had no option but to go and see what it was that he wanted," Ridge replied.

"What did he want?"

"He offered me the chance to recover a very large quantity of cocaine when it is imported into this country from the continent and prior to its distribution."

"He offered you a large supply of cocaine? No prisoners? Just the drugs?" asked Johnston, disbelievingly. "Why on earth should he offer you anything? I don't swallow this. Who was it who called you?"

Ridge took his time replying. He was now on very dangerous ground and he needed to be careful.

"It was someone who I have successfully used in the past but who dropped out of sight a few years ago. The man has reappeared on the scene, at just the right moment. I do not want to let the opportunity of using him again pass me by, simply because I am not allowed to pop up to town as and when. I need that flexibility to do my job and get a result."

"Who?" asked Johnston, now suspecting he knew the name but wanting it confirmed by Ridge.

"Charles Ford," Ridge replied, maintaining a stony, inexpressive face.

Recognising the name but still believing that he was not getting the complete story Johnston pursued the issue.

"Are you seriously telling me that this fucking man telephoned you, met you in London and then offered you a large haul of drugs with no strings attached? Why would he do that? Better still, why did he do it? What does he want?"

Ridge smiled at the man's complete naivety. If he said Ford wanted twenty thousand pounds for supplying accurate information leading to the capture of the biggest amount of drugs in the whole known world, the Force would look for any reason not to pay out. They saw paying criminals money as something morally wrong and almost indefensible. It was far better to lose the job than pay money to a criminal. He thought it wise to await the endgame before mentioning money to this man.

"Sire, I remain amazed at your lightning grasp of a very complicated drama now beginning to unfold amongst us!"

Ignoring Ridge's sarcasm, Johnston continued, "Okay, this is the bastard who was at the centre of all the problems you had before. It's all coming back to me now. Why should he ring you when there are any number of senior officers in the Metropolitan Police who could service his needs, what's special about you?"

Ridge was finding difficulty keeping his patience with this man.

"Trust, is the reason! You may recall from your past attempted dealings with Ford that he is allergic to senior officers from whatever Force they come. He prefers dealing with people on the ground. Working police officers! That's why he has come to me. His previous dealings with me have shown that I can be trusted even if I have to wear a funny hat from time to time."

Johnston bridled at this reference to the enquiry into Ridge's dealings with Ford that he instigated and that caused Ridge's return to uniform duties.

"Ridge, you must understand that, as your senior officer, I must have a complete and frank understanding with you over your use of this informant. In fact I want you to put down on paper the full details of what has happened so far and my name is to be included as joint handling officer. Do you understand?"

Ridge again took his time.

"I think you must recall from the last time, that Ford indicated quite clearly that he did not want to talk to you under any circumstances. I could put it stronger than that but I won't. Didn't you learn anything from that time? If you want to interfere again then the chance of getting a positive result is almost zilch!

"You can make your own arrangements to meet the man but, believe me, his reaction will be the same as last time. It is just not going to happen! But I can guarantee you that what will happen is that Ford will go elsewhere. He will not risk being involved with your type. He will see it as being too dangerous to him."

Johnston sat back in his chair. Although Ridge was unaware of it, he and Kimber for that matter had been heavily criticised at the enquiry into the shooting of the French Customs officer. Lack of supervision and leadership they had called it.

He did not want a recurrence of that on his CV again. He backed away slightly and said to Ridge, "I will take advice on the matter; in the meantime, I want you to keep Detective Sergeant Kimber in the loop on a daily basis. I want no excuses. Keep him briefed."

"Right," said Ridge. "Let's get it sorted out once and for all." He got up and walked out of the office and back to his own office.

After he had gone, Johnston sat back and carefully reviewed his options. He knew he could not go to his immediate boss and complain about Ridge so soon after Ridge's arrival back in the unit. It would be seen as a conflict of personalities. He wanted to avoid any suggestion that he was not impartial. No, he would just have to wait and watch for the right moment. It wasn't going to be easy. On the one hand he knew that of all the staff under his control Ridge was the one who was most likely to keep turning in a good result. He had an uncanny ability to be able to almost sniff out big jobs and had provided work for the Regional Crime Squad and other squads over the years. Ridge was a useful man to have on the unit because his success rate also reflected on him and helped boost his reputation. The trouble was Ridge could be such an annoying and secretive bastard.

Chapter Eight

Ridge parked his car in the garage and walked into the house via the back door. He could smell the dinner cooking. Going through and into the kitchen he silently walked up behind his wife and put his arms around her waist and pulled her back into him. He began nuzzling her neck as he felt her start to squirm in a very half-hearted attempt to disengage. Continuing to tease her he felt her hand pushing gently back into his groin and begin stroking him. He let her go and said, "What's for tea?"

Marie, his wife of twenty-five years, grinned. "You are so romantic! All you ever think about is eating or sex!"

Ridge smiled. "I haven't thought about sex yet, but once we have had dinner I will try and focus on it."

"You won't have to focus for long if I know anything about you." She laughed.

Ridge loved his wife with a passion not diminished in anyway by the years. He loved the stability of married life. He loved coming home to a warm house where there was always a welcome awaiting him whatever the time of day or night. Now that the kids had left home, they were on their own. He had his job and she had hers lecturing at the local college of knowledge as he called it. Because of their almost separate daily living arrangements they always had something to talk about in the evenings. She with her strong views on the economy in so far as it affected the local council of which she was staunch member. He with his passion for things oriental: in particular his consuming interest in Japanese martial arts.

"Pour me a drink and I will serve dinner," she said.

As they ate he told her briefly of his meeting with Ford, his day at the office and his meetings with Kimber and Johnston.

Even talking to the one person in his life whom he trusted completely, Ridge still left out bits and pieces. Over the years he had learnt that open secrets were of no use to anyone. Things, in his view, didn't just happen. They were made to happen and the more people involved in the decision process of trying to make things work the less chance they actually had of working. It was his experience that the fewer people involved the better; just one person pulling the strings was all that was needed. Forget the crap of all people being on the same team with the same objective. The buck stopped with him and no one else!

Marie looked up and he saw her eyes had moistened up. "John, we are not going to have a repetition of what occurred last time, are we? I don't want to see you go through that or anything similar again. It was awful watching people who were supposed to be your friends trying to destroy you. Can't you just coast your way through the next eleven months until you retire next year?"

Ridge raised his eye level off the tablecloth and looked directly at his wife.

"You know that asking me to coast for nearly a year is not possible. I just cannot coast along paying lip service to the job and simply get a wage. There is more to the job than that. It's what I enjoy doing, and getting well paid for it at the same time. Besides, it was Ford who approached me. I have not been chasing him. He has something very big on offer and I want to collect on it."

Marie studied him. She knew him so well and would not try to change him. Better than anyone she knew him to be stubborn and inclined to be irritable with others whom he thought to be attempting to change his direction. Talking to him now in their home where over the years they had between themselves resolved the usual problems that most families have, she felt warmth and a desire for him.

Although she was not sure, Marie guessed that there had been other women in his life. No direct evidence, just the occasional feeling that once or twice when he had cried off making love with her it wasn't because he was tired, as he said he was. He was fit as a flea. And of course there were those times when she had smelt just the merest whiff of perfume on his shirt. Nothing significant, but it was there nonetheless.

"John, just be careful. Don't set yourself up as target."

He was about to respond to her comments when the back door opened and their eight-year-old granddaughter Sasha rushed into the kitchen with mum, Tamara, following closely behind her.

There was a big show as Sasha went round and kissed Ford's wife and then moved on to him.

Once satisfied that the greetings had been completed Sasha scraped a chair across the floor and sat on it looking at the food remains on their plates. Sasha then looked around the room to see if any changes had taken place since her last visit. When she had completed her inspection she turned her attention to Ridge and began talking so quickly that Ridge lost the thread of her words.

He raised his hand and slowed her down.

"Slowly, slowly," he said, "I can't understand you!" As he spoke, so he spoke just a little slower than normal and took the trouble to enlarge his lip patterns.

Sasha was deaf. In fact, to be precise, she was profoundly deaf. That meant that she could not hear a jumbo jet if it taxied alongside her.

At the age of two, when she was already talking well, Sasha had contracted a virus that led to meningitis. Fortunately for her, at the early onset of her symptoms, Tamara had called in a bright young doctor from the surgery who quickly realised what the symptoms meant. He had Sasha taken immediately to the Children's Hospital where she underwent treatment. Sadly, there wasn't a lot the hospital team could do for her, and when she left hospital after two weeks treatment she remained profoundly deaf.

The trauma was almost as bad for the family as it was for Sasha, taking them all a long time to adjust to the day-to-day problems of communicating with their favourite grandchild.

Sasha, however, bit by bit began fighting back in her own inimitable way.

One of the side effects of meningitis was that, amongst other things, it could affect the body's balance. Sasha was like a little drunk. Particularly bad first thing in the morning, she had a job to sit up straight let alone walk. When she walked, it was like watching a little drunk staggering about. Her condition improved with time as did her general demeanour, but it was slow work. Periodic visits to the hospital were continued in the hope that in some way or other the damage to Sasha's hearing could be reversed but nothing appeared on the horizon.

The day came eighteen months later and Sasha was enrolled in a Hearing Unit within a local infant school. It was heartbreaking, watching her trying to come to terms with the complete loss of hearing. Many times in the school day it was possible to see her standing in a corner crying, unable to fathom out why she was so different from the rest of the children. Why she could not hear anything going on around her.

Sasha was nearly five years of age when a perceptive audiologist at the Royal Sussex County Hospital suggested to her mother that Sasha might be a suitable person to have a Cochlear Implant. That simple suggestion was the start of an idea that eventually led Sasha and the family to the world famous Addenbrooke's Hospital at Cambridge for tests.

Much to the delight of the family Sasha was accepted as a child who could possibly profit from being number six on the Cochlear Implant Programme.

It was explained by the leading transplant surgeon that an implant device was a miniature hearing aid containing twenty-two electrodes implanted into the cochlear or inner ear and direct to the auditory nerves. Once implanted, it was hoped that stimulation of those auditory nerves would occur and enable the recipient via a small processor to hear some sounds that with training would be understood as speech. A three-year course of speech therapy given by experts within that field would, it was hoped, enable the implantee to return to the hearing world. It was a massive challenge for Tamara to agree to on behalf of Sasha; the family wanted a miracle and saw the operation as the best way of getting one. Tamara agreed and made the life changing decision to go for it.

Sasha spent five days as an inpatient in Addenbrooke's where the device was fitted inside her inner ear. At that time Addenbrooke's was one of only two medical centres in the country capable of fitting the Cochlear Implant. Not unnaturally, Sasha's family thought they were the best.

Six weeks following her operation Sasha was switched on. It was clear to see right from the start that the implant was working. Although she did not at that stage appreciate precisely what was going on, Sasha could hear sounds that she previously could not. One of her early pleasurable exercises was to sit in her granddad's car and continually turn on and off the car radio and CD-ROM listening to the sounds that came out it. On one weekend alone Sasha turned the device on an off so many times it drained the car battery. Her life had changed for ever.

Teaching Sasha to talk again was, as expected, going to be a protracted affair. It meant weekly visits to Addenbrooke's Hospital where the A Team, as they became known to the family, weaved their magic. It was awe-inspiring for the family to watch the team and Sasha at work. Where there had been total silence now there was laughter and speech of a sort. Thinking back on those times, Ridge was still amazed that so many people tried so hard to give one child the joy of sounds and speech.

Chapter Nine

Detective Sergeant Emil Kimber of the Force Intelligence Unit (Development Team) made his Detective Inspector a cup of coffee and walked along the corridor towards his office carrying the offering before him. With his free hand he knocked on the door and waited for the command to enter. The heat from the hot coffee was beginning to filter through the polystyrene cup and burn his fingers when the short sharp command to enter was given.

Kimber entered and quickly placed his boss's cup of coffee on the desk top in front of him doing his best to hide the fact that his fingers were now stinging from the burn. He sat down in front of his boss and looked at him, waiting for him to start the conversation.

Detective Inspector Roland Johnston glanced at Kimber in his usual supercilious way when talking to lower ranks. It was a cultivated look that Johnston felt enhanced the quality of his position.

Certainly with Kimber he tried his best to use the look at every opportunity. He did not much like Kimber but realised, as a senior officer, that he could not always hand-pick his staff. Sometimes he just had to make the best of what was given to him.

Johnston had noticed Kimber's pain as he placed the hot steaming coffee container in front of him but said nothing. He gingerly put the cup to his lips and gently tried the contents.

"Emil," he said, "what's the word on Ridge since I last spoke to him?"

"In what way Guv?" asked Kimber, who sensed that he might be led into saying something that exposed him in a way that he didn't want to happen.

Johnston looked up at the ceiling and pursed his lips as if he was trying to find simpler words to use when talking to someone of limited intellect.

"Come on, Emil, you know what I mean. Since Ridge has returned to intelligence duties, how is he performing?"

"Well Guv, it's like this. He has made a good start with this job involving the drugs. Remember, he has only been back on the unit for a few days and already he has turned up something which, if it comes off, will be good for those of us in control of the unit. He is of course a very different person to deal with than all the rest of the team put together. For example, his job is the only big job that the unit has on the go at present. The rest of the team seem content to talk about various jobs which they have on the go, but nothing amounts to a job with substance. There isn't a meaningful job amongst them.

"This unit unfortunately needs someone like Ridge to boost the monthly report figures! His main problem is that he is a loner and not a team player. That's the bit that gets right up my nose. In spite of that, he has always had the ability to keep pulling jobs out of thin air like a fucking magician. Why do you ask?"

"I suppose you are aware that I had to lay the law down to him yesterday about his recent visit to London. I am not going to have one man running about all over the country doing what he wants to do and me not being aware of it. It has got to stop and I told him so."

"Quite right, boss," Kimber said, showing his support for Johnston's handling of the discussion with Ridge.

Johnston looked at Kimber.

"You say that," Johnston said, "but really Emil, it's your fucking place to keep him in order, not mine. I have enough on my plate without doing your work as well as my own!"

Kimber swallowed hard. He recognised the warning signal when he saw Johnston glance at the ceiling and start to shake his head in that annoying way that he had.

"Boss, I was just letting Ridge run a bit, letting him find his feet, so to speak."

Johnston put up his hand as if he was stopping traffic.

"Emil, were you aware that Ridge had gone to London off his own bat and was already talking to this man Ford?"

Kimber knew he was being sucked in by Johnston.

"No, not really I knew he was up to something," he lied, "but, no, not the precise details."

Johnston again looked at the ceiling and then at Kimber.

"Exactly my point, Emil. Like you, I am aware that Ridge is a determined investigator, but he needs to be watched if only to ensure that when he turns up something we are there as the guiding hands so to speak. Do you understand? Furthermore Emil, this man Ford was at the very centre of the French complaint when we managed to blame Ridge for all the problems associated with that job. I do not want that bastard sneaking up on us. Do I make myself clear?"

"Yes boss," muttered Kimber, who felt that once again he was being blamed for his boss's failures.

Johnston noticing the sullen response from Kimber, weighed in with his pièce de résistance.

"When I spoke to Ridge, I insisted that he completes an intelligence log on a daily basis giving a full account of his activities with Ford. I also said to Ridge that I would be named as the joint handler whatever his views on the subject were and that you were to check the log every day." Johnston paused. "Unfortunately, Ridge threw a tantrum and appeared reluctant to endorse that instruction causing me, I might add, to seek advice on the matter." Johnston shuffled his position so as to give himself a slightly higher chair position. He placed his fingertips together and glared at Kimber.

"The chief inspector is of the opinion that if Ridge runs true to form and is successful with this job, then the success of that job is something that will reflect on all those taking part. He has therefore instructed that I be nominated as joint handler with this informant to ensure a smooth passage and successful conclusion to the enterprise!"

Kimber, sitting about five feet away from Johnston almost choked.

The arrogant bastard, he thought, talk about jumping on the bandwagon and trying to snatch the job. He straightened up and appeared to be giving some thought to the matter. "I concur with the detective chief inspector's viewpoint, sir," he intoned with a small degree of reverence, "but in the circumstances which now confront us, do you think it the wisest course of action to declare your hand to Ridge?"

"What do you mean?" asked Johnston, sitting forward and looking intently at Kimber. What was this moron about to say!

"Well sir, you and I both know that Ridge is something of a prickly character to deal with. He will probably draw back from simply doing as he is told. He will only want to do as he wants to do. I know he is only a detective constable but the fact of the matter is that at the present time he is holding all the aces. Why not let him control the job as he wants to until we need to step in and take over?"

Johnston again placed his fingertips together looking as if he was about to deliver a sermon.

"Emil, I like your thinking but, if we let Ridge run, we will not know what is happening, because as sure as eggs are eggs, Ridge will not confide in us. That is why you have to keep your finger on the pulse, so that we do know what is happening. Got it? That is my decision. I want a daily briefing from you as to what that bastard Ridge is up to."

"There is just one point I was going to mention," Kimber said. "A friend of mine on the Proactive Unit has been watching premises in Oriental Place. As I understand it, it's basically a brothel they are looking at but, and here is the interesting bit, Ridge was observed going into the premises. He was then observed leaving on his own about an hour later. Fortunately the lads were using bino's to look at the premises from some distance away so Ridge, sharp-eyed bastard that he is, didn't spot them, but he was obviously looking for the watchers."

"What are the lads looking at the address for?" Johnston asked.

"Prostitution, in the main. But they do have some very strange people going in and out. On the q.t., I am also told that one of the women is of interest to Special Branch!"

"Emil, why is it that Ridge is always the name that crops up. Why, not any other members of the team?"

Kimber smiled. "Ridge is a natural. He has his fingers in lots of pies. He is never one to sit in the office. He is always out on the street. Why he was at that house in particular, I have no idea. Perhaps it was simply that he was getting his leg over, who knows. It is worth bearing it in mind if we need a lever at some stage in the future. It is still a discipline offence, shagging tarts whilst on duty!"

"Yes," Johnston said, "you are so right. Emil, it's now down to you to get a grip of him. Sort it; right?"

"Yes boss!" Kimber replied, acknowledging that their meeting was over.

As he was leaving, Johnston suddenly said to him, "Emil, don't fuck this up, we can both benefit from seeing this job through to a successful end with or without Ridge!"

Chapter Ten

The next day Kimber kept watch and waited for Johnston to leave the building before sliding open the hatch between his office and Ridge's office and summoning him round to his office for a talk. As Ridge entered Kimber's office and shut the door, Kimber looked up from his desk.

"What the fuck do you think you are playing at Ridge? Yesterday I had to sit in the guvnor's office and pretend that I knew exactly what you were doing in London yesterday. The fact is I didn't even know you were in London talking to an informant, much less that it was this man Ford. The fact of the matter is that I know fuck all about what you are doing. What is all this crap about a drugs job and precisely who are you seeing in connection with it? I want names and details now!"

Ridge looked squarely at his supervisor. In spite of his aggressive outburst, Kimber had come to a stop, not knowing how to press home the advantage. His bullying tactics had reached their zenith and it was clear to Ridge that he ought at least to try to calm him, he might need his goodwill at some stage.

"I have picked up with an informant, a trusted informant who I have previously worked with. He is currently working his arse off to provide me with a nice little job with which to end my career in this police force. I've told the guvnor about it and he has told you about it, hence your more than usual interest in matters appertaining to police work."

Kimber, very red in the face, rose to the taunt from Ridge.

"Each and every day I want from you a detailed intelligence summary of your progress together with any anticipated course of action you see being required in the immediate future. Is that understood?"

"If that's what you want Sarge, that's exactly what you will get. I aim to please!"

Somewhat taken aback by this apparent capitulation on Ridge's part, Kimber sat back in his chair and thought how to strengthen his position. After all, he was a detective sergeant and this stroppy person in front of him was just a constable.

"I also want to know the name of this informant you are involved with and the time and date of your next meeting! I am also telling you that the guvnor has been told by the DCI that he is to be the joint handler of this informant from now on. Is that understood?"

Ridge sighed as if he was talking to a naughty child who could not grasp matters of importance.

"I did explain to the guvnor and I am now going to explain to you very slowly so that you also understand just how many beans make five. I am the officer dealing with this informant. The informant has made it extremely clear to me in the past that he will not deal with someone else as well. He feels that any conversations involving two officers leaves him at a disadvantage. With two people involved, things said can get misunderstood to his detriment. As he has a very colourful past and comes from a very violent crime family, I must say that from a very personal point of view, I do not want any misunderstandings between us to take place. Apart from that, I have seen too many good jobs compromised in the past by too many people jumping in at the eleventh hour and effectively doing their best to influence events when they do not possess an in-depth knowledge of matters they are trying to affect!"

Kimber arched his shoulders at this clear defiance of his authority, just as it seemed that he was on top.

"I see no reason at all why the guvnor should not meet this informant; and there is no reason why I should not have a casual meet with him from time to time. You are just being bloody minded!"

"Very well," Ridge said, rapidly losing his sense of humour. "The informant's name is Charles Ford. A name you are already familiar with. His details are on the system, look him up and see the warning signals covering him and his family. Whilst this job is running I do not want any behind my back approaches made to any member of this family because of the risk that I will then be exposed to. If I find he has been approached, and I will, then I will immediately walk away from the job and ask for an interview with the chief constable."

"Mark my words," Kimber said, "you will not get away with this insufferable arrogance!"

Ridge walked out slamming the door behind him.

Back in his office Ridge made himself a coffee and sat at his desk looking out of the window at the minarets. The light was bright as it bleached the colour from the Royal Pavilion rooftops, too bright in fact to get a good photo. Late afternoon was the best time to see the pavilion at its best. Just as the setting sun was moving westwards over the building so the colours darkened and the whole scene became more colour-saturated, picking out the various blends of rustic colour from both the building and trees.

Ridge recalled what a wise old detective chief superintendent had said to him some years ago. It encapsulated precisely the circumstances arising now. He had stopped Ridge in the corridor one day and said to him, "Ridge you have been in the Intelligence Department some time, tell me, when you have collected and evaluated and then disseminated your intelligence information, what have you got left?" His penetrating stare bored into Ridge's brain waiting for him to reply.

Jason Michael

Finally, Ridge said, "Well sir..." he paused, carefully choosing his words, "...if it is dead information, then I have done all that is required of me, I've passed it on for others to deal with: but if it's live, active info then I will retain it and work on it, because I am then looking to get a result from it. But it has got to smell right for that to happen."

"Good answer," the old detective replied. "It is my experience that most detectives don't know when to let it go. Do not hang on to something that you cannot move on. Give it to the people who sit in their offices all day, every day. Let them try to do something with that type of info. You will know," he said, pointing first to his stomach and then to his head. "You will feel it in your gut and then your head. The trick then is to give the info legs to keep the momentum running. Be careful how and when you do that, because there are always people in this business waiting for you to make a mistake." With that the old man continued his walk down the corridor.

Thinking of his conversation with Kimber, Ridge's hands were shaking slightly as he evaluated the likely outcome. At this stage of the game he did not want either of his supervisors attempting to involve themselves in the game. The end was so close. Neither man had what you might call people skills and would therefore be a hazard to him personally and to any chance of success that the job might have. It really was amazing the way some supervisory officers tried to bask in reflected glory in order to improve their own prospects.

Ridge had long known that intelligence gathering was a bit like being involved in the unacceptable face of policing; if you were involved in that process, then it meant problems all the way along the line. With any one single piece of information put into the system, others scrutinised it and came to a conclusion, based on that information alone. Sometimes that was enough, often it wasn't. Behind the information there was always a story. It was often that story that either supported and even enhanced the information or gave lie to it.

Ridge smiled to himself as he thought of a job sometime earlier in his service that had found its way on to his desk because his supervisors did not want to involve themselves in its investigation for fear of causing that well known brown substance to hit the fan and cause fallout they could not control. They had assessed the information at face value and concluded that it was serious enough for someone to investigate, but not them. It was best passed on to someone else to resolve and take the flak that was surely there, just waiting for someone to open the can.

The information had come into the office via a report from HQ and later, by telephone, from a Customs official at one of the ports up on the east coast.

The report had then bounced through the Customs Service, the Police Service for that area and the Met Police down to Sussex because of one word: Brighton.

The information referred to an overheard conversation in a pub which was: A thousand Russian dogs were going to be smuggled in to this country by people living in Brighton. Part of an address was included in the report.

Because it had been submitted by a Customs man the report was assessed as substantial and likely to be accurate. It had been viewed by a number of supervisors who each had considered that someone else ought to investigate what they thought was a serious matter with all sorts of animal regulations offences attached to it. Ridge was the last person in the office that the report could be passed to unless you considered linking in the office cleaners!

He had quickly identified the address and the two most likely people involved in such an operation. The factors that caused him doubt, apart from the sheer logistics, was that both the identified subjects were little more that drunks living in a doss-house. Hardly, Ridge thought, on the face of it, successful smugglers.

By pure chance a couple of days later one of the two men was arrested for fighting in his local pub, and was kept in custody overnight. Ridge, luckily had picked up the name and address from the daily intelligence sheet circulated around the offices first thing in the morning, every morning. The intelligence sheet was a godsend to people like Ridge. It covered details of all persons arrested, and for what offences, in the previous twenty-four hours. Reading that summary over his first morning coffee often opened the opportunity for him to interview someone at a time when they were still in custody and he could bring some pressure to bear on the person concerned.

Under interview the arrested man was still suffering a little from the after-effects of too much alcohol the night before. He spewed out his story with just a little coaxing. The thousand Russian dogs had quickly changed to a thousand Russian dolls! Of the type that fitted one inside the other.

The first time that this venture had been tried a number of issues had come to light. The first was the reliability of the Volkswagen they had used as transport. The vehicle had broken down twice on the journey to Poland causing the two girlfriends some stress getting it fixed. The other issue that caused concern was that the two men who had hired the boat for the final leg of the journey had to reduce the size of the boat to something not much larger than a rowing boat with a motor on it, owing to the costs involved. Five miles from the coast of France the motor had conked out and they were forced to row the rest of the way. They literally had to beach the boat the other side of Fe Camp harbour and remain their overnight. Both men were reluctant to have the boat engine repaired for fear of arousing suspicion about their activities and also the cost factor involved. Neither man had sufficient funds to cover the cost of repairs!

Eventually, finding their two women waiting for them outside the harbour with the dolls, by this time packed within four large suitcases, they quickly drove to where the boat was tied up, and loaded the suitcases aboard. With no option but to row the boat back to Brighton Marina, the men were eventually waved off the seashore by their women who drove on to Calais for their return journey on the ferry.

Unfortunately for both of the intrepid smugglers, the journey home exhausted both of them and was not helped when the weather deteriorated when they were within sight of the coast of Sussex. The last few miles proved almost disastrous for them as they were blown along the coast in a heavy wind and pouring rain, missing the marina altogether. Fortunately for them they were blown ashore close to the Palace Pier under cover of darkness suffering from exposure from the weather, seasickness and blisters on their hands. Both the men were so exhausted that they left the boat where it was and struggled back to their room and collapsed in a state of exhaustion.

When the two men returned to the boat the next day they were surprised to find that the Russian dolls in the four suitcases were no longer where they had been left. The entire stock had been stolen overnight.

Although somewhere along the line these two were likely to be committing offences, it was difficult to see what they could be prosecuted for retrospectively. It was generally thought that punishment for their crime might be best if it was just left as a lesson to be learned!

★ ★ ★ ★

Ridge thought it a good idea if he spent a couple of days in the office and cleared some of the paperwork leaving him free if he needed time to spend chasing about after Ford. He knew that whether it was one or two week's time, sooner or later he would need to commit himself to dealing with the drugs job. He already felt the early pangs of excitement. This is what it is all about. The final game had begun!

Chapter Eleven

Ridge walked into his office with his freshly made morning coffee and stood looking out of the window at the morning view. It had rained hard during the night refreshing all the greenery surrounding the Pavilion. The sky, dark grey and still full of rain yet to drop, created an intense, moody backdrop. There was just a glimmer of reflection from some of the large rain puddles on the pavement running the length of the building. Quite an impressive image at the start of the day, thought Ridge. He set to work and cleared the paperwork that had accumulated over the last few days.

Ridge waited for the rest of the team in the office to arrive, do their morning checks and then go out and about on their enquiries. Most of the team took only a few minutes as it was not one of those offices where members of staff were encouraged to spend the day behind computer screens.

When the office was cleared, and there was no one left to overhear his conversation, he dialled a direct line number into the offices of the Organised Fraud Office of the Department of Work and Pensions (Fraud Investigation Serivce). Josie Browning answered. She was a senior fraud investigator. Although he recognised her voice, Ridge adopted a formal approach because he never assumed that calls were not recorded. Better safe than sorry.

"May I speak with Miss Browning?" he asked.

Josie Browning recognised Ridge's voice and, aware that he was using this particular approach for the usual reasons, adopted a similar approach. "Browning speaking!"

Ridge smiled. "Miss Browning, there are matters that I am currently dealing with that may fall within your particular area of operations. May I suggest a meeting at a time when we can discuss those matters?"

Josie knew what he meant. "Of course you may," she said, throwing caution to one side and not in the least inhibited by the secretary sitting a few feet away from her and listening to every word. "Do you realise it's weeks since you have been to see me: what are you playing at?"

Ridge tried to retain his composure and not laugh at her response.

"My pace of work during the last few weeks has been such that I have been restricted to dealing with domestic matters; however, this evening is a good time!"

Josie thought quickly, glancing at her desk diary.

"Okay," she said. "My place at seven."

Ridge grinned. "The time and place are most suitable for what I have in mind." He put the telephone down and began whistling.

★ ★ ★ ★

At seven on the button, Ridge appeared in the entranceway of a block of flats in Kemp Town. As usual with Ridge he had taken precautions when walking to the building. He had left his car several streets away and walked the remaining distance on foot, changing directions a number of times. He rang the buzzer to Flat Three and after a few moments a woman's voice said, "Can I help you?"

"Miss Johnson, please," Ridge replied.

"No, I am afraid not, I don't know anybody of that name. What flat did you want?"

"Number thirteen," Ridge lied. "Have I pressed the wrong buzzer?"

"Never mind I'll let you in as you are there."

The main door buzzed and Ridge pushed it open and walked to the lift doors. Even if he had been seen going into the building, Ridge knew he could not be placed at Josie Browning's flat. If for some reason it later became necessary to make enquiries then the most that anyone could say was that someone had made enquiries at that time for flat number thirteen. It would not lead back to Ridge. Simple precautions like that were necessary if only to protect the person he was going to spend the evening with. The lift opened on the fifth floor almost opposite her flat. Ridge knocked on the door and waited.

Josie opened the door dressed in a very white terry towelling dressing gown. She had obviously just got out of the bath because her short elfin hairstyle was still very damp and she was still sweating profusely. Ridge could see small rivulets of perspiration running down between her breasts. She looked pretty good to him!

She let him in, closed the door behind him and pressed him back against the door frame. She kissed Ridge and then stood back and looked at him. Josie then kissed him again.

Ridge picked her up and carried her into the bedroom and laid her on the large, spotlessly clean duvet. He bent over and kissed her gently on the lips before moving his hand downwards and parting her dressing gown, exposing her nakedness. With slow positive moves he moved on downwards, using his tongue to good effect. He felt her body begin to move, slowly at first, but building momentum quite quickly.

Josie waited for Ridge to slow down before trying to remove his clothing. Their lovemaking increased in pace as they sweated into each other's body. Ultimately, they both reached the point of no return and joined together in the rush to total surrender, before lying back in each other's arms breathing heavily.

Sharing the bath, Josie lay back and studied Ridge. "You obviously missed me!"

"Just, a little bit," Ridge replied. "I need a favour."

"What, apart from screwing me again?" She grinned.

"It is a favour that only you can grant. If I could avoid asking you and go elsewhere, I would."

"I bloody well thought you had some ulterior motive for coming here and taking full advantage of an innocent girl!" she said. "What can I do for you?"

Ridge knew that he could trust Josie. She had shown herself trustworthy on more than one occasion in the past.

"I want to monitor a large importation of cocaine coming into this country within the next few weeks. I can't apply for telephone taps because, firstly, that would involve too many other people in knowing what's going on and give too many of those the chance to refuse. I believe that would put a spanner in the works. Secondly, that would only give us the telephone numbers not the conversations. I just sort of wondered if your CSM 7700 would be available for my exclusive use!"

"You don't want much do you? Do you realise what would happen if I were to be caught using that item in unauthorised circumstances?"

Ridge had noticed her automatically including herself in the use of the equipment. He looked at her.

"As it is an illegal piece of equipment, I can't see how you can get permission anyway!" He tried not to smile.

"Who will be aware that the piece is being used?" Josie asked, ignoring his comment.

"Nobody will know of its use. I may not need it," he replied. "But it would be nice to have it available for use if it was needed."

Josie stood up and got out the bath. "Well," she said, "it just depends how good you are during the remainder of the evening." With that she draped a large pink towel around herself and flounced back into the bedroom.

Chapter Twelve

Ridge was sweating profusely as he stood his ground and waited for the next man, the ninth in the line, to attack him.

So far so good; none of his opponents so far had caused him too much of a problem, but it was not over yet. Some of the strongest fighters in the club were yet to play their part and Ridge knew that they would give no quarter. Ridge loved this part of the training schedule; every Tuesday evening. If ten other members turned up, you fought against the ten: if twenty members turned up, you fought the lot! It was a good way to test not only coordination in applying a variety of techniques, but also it was a test of stamina, quickly sorting out those who trained on a regular basis and those who did not.

The man rushed at him and tried an overarm strike. Ridge countered with a high block with his left arm and struck an open-palmed blow to his sternum. The contestant stopped dead in his tracks and began trying to get his breath. Ridge, seizing the moment, rushed in close and struck a rear hand blow to the face and swiftly turned for a successful *ippon seoi nage*. On the floor and badly winded, the man could not continue and so indicated his inability to the referee. As Ridge lined himself up ready for the next attacker, he heard his mobile telephone going off in the dressing room. He refocused on his opponent who was just stepping forward to bow. The referee hearing the phone knew it was Ridge's by the distinctive ringtone. He stopped the contest immediately and gave Ridge permission to leave the *tatami*.

The text on his phone was concise: Must see you tonight. Usual place ten-thirty.

It was eight-thirty. Ridge showered and changed in record time, afterwards hurrying to his car. He made a fast drive to the edge of town and then onto the motorway and then to North London. Previous meetings over the years with Ford had developed into a routine of different meeting places to protect both of them from being observed meeting in the same place on more than one occasion. Neither man had ever taken the meetings for granted, aware that even being seen together on a single occasion could set alarm bells ringing and provoke drastic action by someone who thought they were being betrayed.

The place Ridge was going to had previously been agreed as a standby so there was no need to identify the premises in any message.

He drove into the pub car park a short walking distance from Ford's stylish house. Parking the car, Ridge slowly locked it, taking in the variety of other cars present in the car park. He guessed that Ford had walked the short distance from home and was probably already inside waiting for him.

Entering the pub, Ridge walked through the premises looking at the customers in both bars. Satisfied, he walked back into the larger of the two bars and stopped beside Ford who had already ordered him his usual half pint of lager. It was sitting on top of the bar still gassing. Ford knew that Ridge paid particular attention to times and would not be either early or late. On time was the case with him. That was businesslike.

"Thanks for coming at short notice." Ford sipped from his pint tankard. "Much of my time is now spent with both my brothers, going over the plan, so the opportunities to sneak away are a bit limited."

"That's okay," Ridge said. "What's happening at the farm?"

Ford looked at him clearly startled. "Farm, what do you know about the farm?"

"That was just a manner of expression, that's all. Why, is there something you ought to be telling me?" He looked at Ford a little bit concerned that such a simple verbal expression had alarmed him.

Charles Ford tried not to show his discomfort at this little gem tripping out of Ridge's mouth. Does he know or not? he wondered.

"No," he lied. "It's just that I used to own a farm and I thought that you were referring to that. That's all. I just wanted to ensure that the money matters we spoke about are in hand because your lot have always been slow payers. Paul is expected back in the UK tomorrow. I think that once he is back things will start to move quickly. He will not leave the stuff on its own in Portugal for long. He will want to shift it before somebody else does."

Watching his friend talking, Ridge saw that there was a thin bead of perspiration now showing in a line across the top of Ford's forehead. It was slight, but it was there. Ridge had not noticed it when he had first entered the pub, but it was definitely there now. It must have been his comment earlier about the farm that changed Ford's body temperature, but why?

Ford was in his stride. He had recovered his confidence and was back to being the charming host.

"The main reason I called was because there is talk of the route being planned up through Portugal and France using the autoroutes for most of the journey. My bro's intend stopping somewhere as yet unknown in France and doing the last leg to Calais in one hit. They are thinking of going for a Saturday sailing as Customs cut their staff over weekends. So Paul thinks there's less chance of being stopped by the filth."

"Do we know the lorry firm yet?" Ridge asked, closely monitoring Ford's eyes for any telltale signs that he was being deceived.

"Not yet." His eyelids fluttered open and closed momentarily, giving Ridge the clue he was looking for. "But I will know that when Paul gets back home."

"What about the driver, does he know what he is carrying?"

"I don't know for sure at this stage, but I will find out," Ford said. "But assume he does not: he is just a driver sent out to drive the lorry back, the lorry could be carrying anything. He will not be aware of the overall planning. The less he knows the better."

"What about firearms?" Ridge asked. "Please tell me the driver will not be armed?"

"No he won't be armed." Ford's eyes moved away from Ridge's face, giving Ridge another clue.

"I will know more when I see Paul. Keep alert for a quick run back, and make sure that Customs stop the lorry at the port. Don't let it get through the port, and also don't forget to have my money ready to hand over to me the moment the job is done."

They exchanged a few more pleasantries and shook hands before parting company. The meeting had lasted thirty-three minutes.

★ ★ ★ ★

Ridge always enjoyed the return journey from such meetings. Driving home with the CD ROM playing his sort of music allowed him time to relax and ponder the events of the evening. Another link in the chain completed, a bit more knowledge to consider. Slowly, slowly, catchee monkey!

He had reached the M25 turn off when he considered Ford's reaction about the farm. What farm? Where was it? Clearly a farm was involved somewhere, possibly to store the lorry. Ford had showed alarm when he had mentioned it. All things considered, Ford was playing his own game and his sweating forehead showed he was nervous about something. Ridge had not forgotten Ford's sweaty handshake on their first meet. Bring it on, he thought, we will see who wins and who loses this one!

Ridge arrived back at home and put the car in the garage making as little noise as possible. The house was in darkness as he crept upstairs and into the bedroom. He started removing his clothes when Marie opened her eyes. "You might as well switch the light on for all the noise you are making."

"Sorry," he said, "I thought I was being quiet!"

"What sort of evening have you had?"

"I got called when I was at the club and had to rush up to London to see my man."

Marie looked at the clock again and squinted, eventually focusing her eyes on the time.

"I thought it was late. Tamara phoned earlier on this evening. Apparently all the kids at school have been given a letter to take home. Some of the mums are up in arms about a couple of men who have been seen watching the school recently. They were seen watching some of the kids on the playing fields. Tamara wondered if you would have a word with the plods that cover the area and get them to have a look at the appropriate times!"

Ridge thought for a moment. "It's probably a couple of the dads watching the kids play football. But I will have a word in the morning."

Ridge fell into bed and a deep sleep within minutes.

Marie lay awake, much to her annoyance, for nearly three quarters of an hour before dropping into a restless sleep.

Chapter Thirteen

In the office next day, Ridge sat at his desk and completed the intelligence summary concerning his meeting with Ford. It was a fairly accurate summary as summaries went, detailing some of the conversation with Ford. Ridge was content to give most of the detail but omitted enough facts from it so that others reading the summary could not gain sufficient information from it to forge away in a direction of their own choosing. He then took the document next door and dropped it into Kimber's in-tray.

Kimber was in his office looking into space as if seeking some kind of spiritual intervention. He ignored Ridge although he did notice the document fall into his in-tray. The moment Ridge had left his office he picked up the information sheet and quickly scanned it.

Ridge walked back into his office and was just about to sit down when the small sliding window in the intervening wall was slid open with some force and banged loudly when it reached the stop point. Kimber glared at him from the other side. "My office, now!" he said.

Ridge picked up his coffee mug and walked back into Kimber's office, sat down in the visitor's chair and sipped at his, now warm, coffee. Kimber waved the intelligence summary in the air.

"I don't recall giving you the authority to go to London and see the informant yesterday?"

Ridge, poker-faced, looked at his detective sergeant. "I was out socially last night and got an urgent telephone text. I had to make the decision then, whether to go or not, so I decided to go!"

"As a constable you do not have the authority to decide something of that importance. You are required to inform your supervisor and await a decision!" said Kimber, little flecks of white spittle appearing at the corners of his mouth. He was clearly angry.

Ridge put down his coffee mug on the plastic surface of Kimber's desk, hoping that the mug would leave a stain. He knew that Kimber was paranoid about coffee mug stains on his desk.

"I have been making decisions like that ever since I have been involved in this type of work. I have always had that flexibility, why not now?"

Kimber, almost at a loss for words, sprayed spittle as he spluttered, "I will bring this to the attention of the detective inspector and see what he thinks about it."

Kimber picked up the summary and rushed out of his office and down the corridor towards his inspector's office.

Ridge picked up his coffee mug and walked out, noting the stain his mug had left on Kimber's desk. He had just settled back down in his chair when he heard his name called out and guessed it was a summons to Johnston's office. He walked down the corridor to his boss's office where he knocked on the door and waited.

The raised voices died down and Ridge received the command, "Come!"

He entered the office and saw that both Kimber and Johnston were hunched over his typed summary. Johnston, just like Kimber, raised the summary and waved it in the air as if it was a government document of vital importance.

"What's the meaning of this?" he asked.

"I'm sorry," Ridge said, "I do not understand: what's the problem?"

"The problem is you went off in the middle of the night to see an informant who only the other day you said was dangerous and should not be approached by us. Yet you go off without as much as a word to us! Had you called in then, at the very least, you could have been accompanied, thereby reducing the risk!"

Kimber had a smarmy, I-told-you-so look on his face. He was enjoying every moment of this conversation.

Ridge addressed his remarks to Johnston.

"I was texted by the informant late in the evening when I was out and the office was closed. I had to make a decision to go or not, so I elected to go and write a detailed summary for your information as soon as possible which is what you now have in front of you. Yes, you were right Guv, I did say that Ford was dangerous and should not be approached by you and Sergeant Kimber. That was my advice because neither of you know him and he certainly does not know you. To me, that sounds like a recipe for disaster. I did not consider myself at risk because, after all, I have known and worked with the man for years!"

Johnston felt himself flush at Ridge's apparent dismissive attitude towards complying with his instructions.

"Ridge, I am the detective inspector of this unit and I am the one who will assess the danger levels that you and other officers within this unit may be exposed to when dealing with informants. Is that understood?"

Ridge took a deep breath.

"I understood what you said without too much difficulty, but as the officer on the ground dealing with such people, I think that I am the one best suited to making that sort of decision. After all, sir, how can you possibly make such a decision if the people you are making the decision about are unknown to you?"

Johnston looked at Kimber as if he did not quite know how to respond to Ridge's analysis.

"I am a trained decision-maker that is why I hold the rank that I do!" Although Johnston knew that Ridge had a valid argument he was not prepared to acknowledge it in front of Ridge or Kimber. "Also," he said, "had I been involved in this from the very beginning, then I could at least have covered your back."

Ridge had difficulty in not laughing out loud.

"I presume that you are talking about physical violence being offered, about me being attacked by Ford in other words?"

"Yes of course," Johnston replied. "At last you are realising the significance of my words!"

"In that case, I do not see your rationale," Ridge said. "For instance, if you or him (Ridge indicated Kimber, by pointing a dismissive finger at him) was present and violence was offered by Ford, I am not sure what either of you think that you could do. Both of you would be well out of your comfort zone coping with something like that for a start. Neither of you are trained in self-defence or are in the best possible physical condition to engage in violence, because that is what it would come down to, meeting violence with violence. And apart from that, I would feel embarrassed having to look out for you two as well as myself!"

"Ridge!" Johnston said, his face bright red, "I am not going to enter into any form of argument about this. My word is final, but once again I am warning you about your behaviour. You are coming very close to being suspended again and, furthermore, it could end up costing you your job!"

Ridge said, "All I have tried to do so far is get hold of a good job and work to bring it to a successful conclusion. I think that a good result would bring credit on this unit and the Force. All I have had from you two is grief! I also think the chance of achieving any success with any sort of intelligence job in this unit is limited, when not only do I have to compete with those outside, but also those within."

"You will obey orders," Johnston said. "That's final."

"Right," said Ridge, "if that is your position, this is mine. As of this moment, I intend to fully withdraw from handling Ford or any other member of his family as an informant. I would appreciate it if you and Sergeant Kimber take over complete control of Ford and, further, the importation of cocaine in to this country as best you can. I am sure that if a detective sergeant and a detective inspector are managing the job it can only lead to success!"

With that Ridge turned and walked out of the office.

Kimber looked at the crestfallen face of his superior.

"Fuck me boss, this is the last thing we want. If Ridge doesn't want to deal with the job, who is going to take it on?"

"Emil, shut up and let me think for a moment," Johnston said, quickly considering his choices.

After a few moments, he turned to Kimber.

"The way round this Emil, is for you to take charge and deal with it. I will act as joint handler. We do not need Ridge to bring this job off!"

Kimber turned pale at the suggestion from his supervisor.

"I don't think I could deal with it boss, after all, I have a lot of office work to contend with and other supervisory matters that keep popping up on a daily basis!"

Johnston looked angry and at the same time gloomy at this attempted get-out response from his subordinate. He placed his fingertips together.

"Emil, you are right, you cannot deal with it. You would probably fuck it up from start to finish. No, the way forward is for you to have Ridge in your office, eat a bit of humble pie and convince him that all we are trying to do is support him in this venture. Are you on my wavelength yet Emil?"

Kimber didn't like this one little bit. "I thought the idea was to have Ridge in your office and bollock him rigid about the way he has left us out of this job. We are never going to get the credit for this job if Ridge stays where he is. He is always going be the OIC."

"Emil, we cannot possibly get rid of Ridge if he isn't dealing with the job. He must be the officer in charge of the job for our plan to succeed. You do see that, don't you?"

Johnston felt his patience slipping. Kimber couldn't detect a dead fish on a fishmonger's slab if it was looking up at him with its eyes shut! Why must he, the detective inspector with his career ahead of him, always end up dealing with the either stroppy or dopey members of staff?

Kimber was not a happy person and it showed. "As I see it boss, I think Ridge will do his best to keep things as they are and at the end of the day present us with a fait accompli: what do we do then?"

Johnston was close to despair. "Emil, we chop his fucking legs off before it gets to that stage, that's what we do. Have you got that?"

Seeing his boss's temper starting to show, Kimber simply nodded in his direction.

"Good, at last. Now go and get Ridge back on board before he fucks off out of the office!"

Kimber walked out of the office and round to Ridge's office. He was fuming. He walked up to Ridge sitting at his desk. Ridge looked at his watch pretending that he was not aware of Kimber's presence. That didn't take too long, he thought.

Kimber hated what he was about to do.

"John, I think we all got a little excited back in the boss's office. We are right behind you in supporting the good work that you do. However, we both feel that we want a closer involvement, because three heads are often better than one! I'm sure you will agree with that?"

Ridge said, "No, I don't actually!"

Kimber sighed. "John, let's put our disagreements behind us and move forward. We all want the same thing. I'll tell you what, let's carry on as before and try for a better working relationship between all three of us, how about it?"

"Okay," Ridge said, knowing that if he wanted to continue with the job he would have to compromise some of his views.

"John, that's good. I will tell the boss that we are all together on this and await the next stage. Is that okay?"

"Fine, all I want to do is get on with the job without these distractions."

Kimber was furious. "That's what we all want, John." He patted Ridge on the shoulder and left the office thinking to himself, one of these days, Ridge, I will most definitely fuck you well and truly where it hurts!

Chapter Fourteen

The large silver bird lined itself up on the radar beam at Heathrow Airport and began its gentle descent towards the main runway. Down on the ground it taxied purposefully off the main track towards the buildings where it came to a stop and began the disembarkation process. The flight in from Portugal had been smooth and uneventful.

The passengers, mainly holidaymakers, poured off the plane in their sombreros and carrying their half-size donkeys and other assorted large toys and made for the border control point.

The Special Branch Officer, standing close to the Border Control Immigration Officer, had his scanning technique in full swing. He was looking down the queue of people waiting their turn to re-enter the United Kingdom.

With nearly five years' experience of working the control desks he found no difficulty in spotting Ford, about a dozen places back in the queue. It was not anything to do with Ford's appearance that caused the SB officer to notice him. Generally speaking, apart from a slightly aggressive posture, he blended in very well with people around him. What gave him away, instantly, was the fact that Ford was also scanning ahead and looking at him and the Border Control Officer with some intent. It was obvious to the SB man that Ford was not a punter returning from holiday. For a start, the man was obviously on his own and was not carrying any of the usual trashy souvenirs that most seemed to possess. No, the man scanning the desk in front of him knew what the desk represented and appeared just a little anxious. He glanced at the control desks either side of the queue he was in to see which one of the desks was moving forward the fastest, but stayed in the queue he was in and shuffled forward with the rest of the passengers.

Ford reached the front of the queue and was called forward by the Border Control Officer. At the desk, Ford threw his passport on the desk in such a way that it did not go unnoticed. The Control Officer, a man with something like twenty years service, recognised the signs. He slowly picked up the passport and began to slowly look through the document page by page. He turned the pages slowly so as to give his friend the SB man, who was now standing immediately behind him, the time to scan each of the pages. When he had finished going through the passport he closed it and held it forward and upwards, but not quite passing it back to the owner. The Special Branch Officer swiftly took the passport from him and beckoned Ford through the desk area and into the United Kingdom.

"Have a nice holiday, Mr Ford?" he asked, without opening the passport.

"Yes!" Ford replied, sensing the start of his problems.

"What do you do for a living, Mr Ford?" the officer asked, opening the passport and looking at the array of visas covering Pakistan, Thailand, Turkey, Colombia and Portugal. The answer to his question was there, plain for him to see. He knew exactly what Ford did for a living.

Ford, by now, was becoming irritated by the questions. He was on the hook and he knew it. "I'm a general dealer," he growled.

The SB man was quite deliberately taking his time. He had scored for the first time today! He could sense that he had struck a nerve with Ford and he was now going to fill his boots.

"Step this way Mr Ford, I want to ask you a couple more questions and then examine your luggage."

He took hold of Ford just above the elbow as an indication that he was detaining him and moved him in the direction of a small office nearby.

"Sit down Mr Ford," he said. "I just want to examine your passport."

Ford sat down, worried now because perhaps a little unwisely he was travelling in his own name and using his original passport.

When he was finished with the passport, the SB man pressed a buzzer on the desk and waited for his colleague to enter the room. He gave the passport to him and the man left the office without a word said.

"Where the fuck is he going with my passport?" Ford asked in a loud and aggressive way.

"The officer is just going to perform a couple of checks Mr Ford. You will have it back in a moment," the SB man replied, smiling at Ford. "Now, let's have a look at your luggage."

He placed the small suitcase on the table and went through it slowly and methodically and carefully so that his hands did not come into contact with anything that may have been left in the suitcase ready to catch an unwary searcher by surprise.

There was nothing in the suitcase, not even a bit of dope for personal use, although that did not surprise the officer. He thought Ford was well above that level in the food chain. He knew the risks attached to coming through an airport.

The man returned with Ford's passport. He handed it back to his colleague and again left the room without a word. The SB man got up and handed the passport to Ford.

"Have a nice day Mr Ford," he said, still smiling.

Ford knew that his details would be recorded and that all sorts of checks would be made. He could not do anything about that now.

"You have a nice day, arsehole."

With that he picked up his small suitcase and left the office and headed for the exit about thirty minutes behind everybody else.

When he had gone the SB man went into the adjoining office and looked at the printout covering Ford's antecedent history. It showed Ford's rise in both quality and quantity of criminal offences over the years. His last conviction said it all. Ten years for importation of cocaine. It was all there like a CV. The last five years were free of any form of conviction. It appeared that Ford had turned over a new leaf and gone straight. The officer knew that the absence of any conviction in the last five years in all probability indicated Ford's involvement in drugs, big time. It was obviously paying him sufficient to keep him away from robbing post offices!

The officer picked up the telephone and dialled an internal number and spoke to the officer on the other end for a few moments. He then returned to the Control Desk and looked out at the incoming passengers with their sombreros and half-size donkeys.

★ ★ ★ ★

Ford had almost reached the exit when a uniformed customs officer appeared from a door marked 'Staff Only' and stopped him.

"Where have you come from sir?"

Ford looked at him and knew.

"I have just had this fucking nonsense with SB. My bag has been searched. Now fuck off and leave me alone."

The Customs officer, at six foot three in his socks and weighing in at nearly eighteen stone, was not in the least put out by Ford's response. He had seen it all before. They try it on, if they get away with it, great, it was a result.

"We can do this my way or your way, sir. I personally do not mind either way, you choose!"

Ford guessed he would lose in any physical confrontation with this man.

"Okay, fuck it!" He paused just for a moment then threw his suitcase onto a nearby table.

"Search my fucking suitcase if you have nothing better to do with your time!" He stepped back and glared at the officer.

The officer, who had his reasons, said, "Pick up your bag and follow me into the office where we can have some privacy."

Ford snatched up his suitcase and entered the office where his suitcase was again opened and slowly searched. When that had been completed, the officer pressed the buzzer and was instantly joined by two burly uniformed Customs officers.

"Mr Ford," the first Customs officer looked Ford in the eyes, "I require you to take off your clothes and submit to a full body search. If you refuse, the search will still take place with the assistance of these two officers. How do you wish to play it?"

Ford stared at them. He knew all three would knock seven bells out of him given half a chance. Why make life difficult. He slowly removed his clothes until he stood naked. All his clothes were turned upside down and shaken until all the contents had dropped onto the floor.

"I suppose one of you at least wants to stick his fingers up my arse?" Ford said, bending over.

The lead officer pulled a face. "I don't' think so, thank you Mr Ford, I am shortly due to go for lunch!"

Ford was allowed to dress, inwardly relieved that they had not searched him intimately. Had they done so they would surely have found his private stash of coke!

Dressed and on his way at last, Ford walked as quickly as he could, and by the time he had reached the exit his normal swagger had returned. He found the car park and saw the Range Rover waiting for him. He greeted Charles and Peter as he threw his suitcase in the boot. He failed to mention his stop and search by the authorities. Ford knew that if he did the other two brothers would take fright and call the job off. After months of planning plus his torture at the hands of the Colombians he had to get this load through without a hitch. He could not afford any mistakes. Peter drove out through the car park exit unaware that the Nikon cameras had captured images of all three people and the vehicle they were in.

Chapter Fifteen

When the Serious Organised Crime Agency was formed in 2005 its major objective was to combat those who were involved in the planning and operation of organised crime crossing borders of individual Police Forces up and down the country.

The importation of drugs was a main plank of its investigating services. To this end, intelligence gathering by the Police Forces took on a new and more demanding professional approach.

Intelligence gathering units at airports, sea ports and on the ground at Force level were galvanised into forwarding basic intelligence through to the organisation, centralising everything. Profiles were drawn up on most of the major players involved in serious crime. Specially selected task forces, amalgamated from different Forces each with a common interest in dealing with such people crossing their borders, were tasked with bringing them down.

Dedicated teams of officers from SOCA then began the labour-intensive task of sifting through the mammoth amount of information produced by the new system.

It was as a direct result of the new intelligence gathering that at nine o'clock the next morning, an e-mail from the Special Branch office at Heathrow Airport fell into the computer inbox of Detective Sergeant Jon Snow, a Kent Police Officer attached to the newly formed organisation.

Snow opened the e-mail and studied its contents, including the photographs. He went through all the information carefully, paying particular attention to Ford's associates. Going back onto the national computer system, Snow then did a number of other checks that added a little more to the information. He studied the whole lot again and pencilled in a few notes of his own. He had identified Ford's two brothers, Charles and Peter Ford. The Ranger Rover was shown as being owned by Peter Ford.

Fifteen minutes later Snow, complete with a bundle of papers now neatly placed within a folder, walked into the office of his detective inspector. Snow was now ready for the morning briefing. Six other detective sergeants formed the morning briefing team, each with a specific area of interest. They all had files similar to one that Snow was holding.

The DI opened the briefing in his usual way with just a quick bit of gossip about someone on the unit but not present. His comments caused a laugh from almost everyone present. Then the first officer to start the briefing began his lecture.

When it came to Snow's turn for centre stage, he started by outlining the antecedent history of the Ford brothers before moving onto the incident at the airport. Snow was a good storyteller who, as he reached his conclusion, observed that most of the listeners were still following his comments about the Fords with interest.

He closed his file and sat looking thoughtful. "On the surface of this little drama, what have we got? Well, we have one member of a quite notorious family with proven drug experience arriving back in the UK from Portugal. He and his limited belongings are searched but nothing is found. When his passport is checked it is found to contain entry and exit stamps from Pakistan, Thailand, Turkey and, last but not least, Colombia earlier this year. Ford is picked up at the airport by two of his brothers who have taken time off from their public spirited work of ripping off some member of the unsuspecting public. They then drive off into the sunset. I may be wrong but I think we are looking at the early stages of an importation of drugs from Colombia. We do not know where Ford stayed whilst in Portugal, but what we do know is that Oporto in Portugal is one of the tried and tested routes into Europe, if you were inclined to import drugs from, say, Colombia! These three shitheads are at work, I can smell it all over this information. I recommend that we mark this file as 'Live' and set the wheels in motion to ascertain just what this little trio are up to." Snow paused and looked at his DI for support.

Detective Inspector Peter Jameson looked around at those present. They were all experienced dicks and he always believed in giving support where he could. It wasn't often that any of them were wrong and SOCA had had a good run of successful jobs to their credit as a result of the work put in by these boys. Jameson was also aware that Snow did have that uncanny ability to smell a job even on scant information.

"I am going to give the green light to Jon on this one." Then, turning to Snow, he said, "What's the next step, Jon?"

Snow pursed his lips, trying hard not to show his glee.

"There was a marker on Charles Ford's record, so I am expecting a telephone call from the copper in Sussex who put the marker on. Now, why someone down south should put a marker on the file is a question I want to resolve soon. I suspect that it is because the man, Charles Ford is an informant. It must be that, because neither of the other two have a marker against their names from the same officer. This Sussex officer could undoubtedly move the job on leaps and bounds."

Jameson considered what had been said. "Get it moving Jon and report back?"

The meeting broke up and all the officers went back to their respective desks.

Pleased as Punch that he had got his own way, Snow returned to his office a put through a call to Ridge. He couldn't wait for Ridge to contact him.

The call was rerouted to Kimber's office as Ridge was out of his office. "Detective Sergeant Kimber of The Force Intelligence Unit," he intoned in his best telephone voice.

Snow identified himself and gave a brief account of the Heathrow drama to Kimber who, listening to it, saw his opportunity to step into the action without causing another rift with Ridge. After all, he reasoned, if Ridge wasn't in the office then someone else had to seize the reins, so to speak!

Kimber arranged a conference with Snow, himself and Detective Inspector Johnston at SOCA for later in the week. Once Snow agreed to the meeting and was off the telephone, Kimber wasted no time in hurrying round to Johnston's office and knocking on the door. Once invited in he sat down and quickly informed his DI of his actions. Johnston sat back and considered Kimber's sly way of stepping forward with this job and at the same time leaving Ridge out of the loop.

"Emil," he said, "I am pleased that you listened to my advice and are now moving forward with the job." He reached down into his bottom desk drawer and pulled out two glasses and an unopened bottle of *Famous Grouse* whisky. Glancing at the contents he unscrewed the cap from the bottle and poured two shots of whisky, passing one to Kimber.

"I think it high time that Ridge was made to realise that this drugs job is a unit operation based on teamwork and not the secretive actions of one arrogant bastard in the unit that I am in charge of."

He took a swig from his glass and smiled at Kimber.

Emil Kimber sat close to his boss watching with interest the ritual with the whisky. As he sipped from his glass he thought that, at last, his detective inspector was beginning to appreciate some of his qualities.

Chapter Sixteen

Ridge made his way into the office for a nine a.m. start. His first task of the morning, any office morning come to that, was to wash his coffee mug and make himself a decent coffee. It was almost unthinkable to begin a day without the burst of caffeine to set him alight.

Just as he was completing his task, Emil Kimber put his head around the door.

"John, when you have made yourself a drink, will you pop into my office for a chat?"

Ridge looked at him, surprised by his civil, almost friendly approach. "Okay Sarge, be with you in a few moments."

Entering Kimber's office Ridge saw that Kimber was seated in one of two chairs by the window. He knew that Kimber used the careful positioning of the chairs to invoke a confidential, and at the same time informal, atmosphere when talking to people as opposed to talking to people across a desk.

Ridge picked up the chair that he intended sitting in and moved a few feet away from Kimber and sat down. There was no way that he wanted a folksy chat with Kimber. He preferred the space between people. That way you tended to get a better visual of them and were better able to asses a body reaction that they made, knowingly or otherwise.

Ridge sipped his coffee. Not bad he thought.

Kimber stood up and moved his chair a little closer to Ridge. He was determined to have things the way he wanted them.

"John, the DI and I are going to a meeting with SOCA later this week to discuss your man. In the meantime, it has been decided that an intelligence watch, if I may put it like that, will be kept on the progress of his information to you."

He paused watching for Ridge's reaction. Seeing nothing that caused him concern he carried on.

"It is important for me to know exactly what you are doing with this man. I need to know everything about him so that I can keep the guvnor in the loop. Also, it may be the case that at some stage in the near future I ought to meet him!"

Ridge placed his coffee mug on Kimber's desk. He noticed Kimber glance at the desk as he put the mug on the polished desk top surface rather than the cardboard coffee floater.

"I always submit an intelligence sheet following a meeting with the informant. That contains the latest information about him and the job in question. As for meeting him, in your bloody dreams! I have said many times before, one officer interviewing an informant is the way to do it. Once you get to the stage of interviewing, anyone for that matter, with two officers, then you can and often do get two different accounts of the same information. That is not the way to get a result in my view!"

"John, the DI has stressed that I must be on top of this job in order that I can keep him informed. Don't make this any more difficult than it already is."

"This job is now up and running and as the officer dealing with it I am not prepared to introduce you to the informant, particularly when I know that he will not speak to you. Why throw this spanner into the works now? This informant is a clever bastard and will soon try to play us off one against the other. All you will do for sure is to weaken my position with him." Ridge picked his mug up off the desk and noticed that it had left a stain. Now his sergeant would have to get the furniture polish out. He stood up, but paused before moving.

"Look, I am not trying to be difficult, but there is no way that I can go along with your suggestion."

Ridge left the office whilst Kimber sat with his mouth open not knowing what to say.

Kimber remained seated for a few moments, then he opened a drawer and took out a yellow duster and a can of spray wax furniture polish and began rubbing away the coffee stain.

Ten minutes later and pleased with having completely removed the coffee stain before it had a chance to permanently stain the top surface of his desk he got up and walked along the corridor to his inspector's office and knocked on the door. After the customary wait he heard the command to enter and went in.

His DI looked up. "What is it now Emil?"

Kimber stood and relayed the essence of his conversation with Ridge. He stopped and waited for his boss to say something.

Johnson sat back and placed his fingertips together. "Emil, I am getting fucking tired of Ridge deciding what he will or will not do. I consider it is your job to supervise him and get from him all that you need to do your job properly. I am the detective inspector and I should not be worried by your inability to control Ridge, although I am! As I see it, what Ridge wants or does not want should have no bearing on my ability to run this unit. Is that clear?"

"I understand what you are saying boss, but I am in a Catch-22 situation. Ridge will not be told, so what can I do?"

Johnson looked at Kimber who was clearly sulking. "Are you up to the job Emil or not? I can get you replaced you know!"

Kimber looked at Johnson. "I am trying my best, boss."

"Emil, get out and sort him out, do you understand?" Johnson sat back in his chair and sighed. "Where is Ridge now?"

"He is in his office," Kimber said.

"Get him in here!"

Kimber scurried out, returning a few minutes later with Ridge in tow.

"I understand that you have a problem with Sergeant Kimber meeting your informant?"

"I don't have a problem with something that is not going to happen," replied Ridge.

"Well, let me tell you something Ridge. I don't want to look a fucking dope at the forthcoming conference with SOCA because of your fucking secrecy. Take it from me, that situation is not going to happen. Things are going to change in and out of this office. I want to know what is going to happen before it happens and the best way to achieve that is to have a second officer dealing with this informant. The days of you wandering in and out of this office and no one knowing where you are, are over, do you understand?"

"I think," Ridge said, carefully choosing his words, "that it might be the best thing in the world if I just withdraw from this job and stop seeing the informant. Then the way is clear for Detective Sergeant Kimber to take over and start dealing with his informant on his own or alternatively assisted by you. I too have had enough of this nonsense. If you cannot trust me to do the job, I'll get on with something else."

Johnson was beginning to go bright red at the challenge to his authority. "Ridge, you will do as you are told, now get out of my office!"

When Ridge had left the office, Johnson turned to Kimber. "He is holding all the aces for now, but it won't last. I intend for you to meet with Ridge's informant whatever he says. It would certainly enhance both our careers if we could be seen as the prime movers in any successful drugs importation job!"

Not one to miss the opportunity, Kimber said, "The next time that Ridge puts his pudding up for treacle, I am going to jump on him from a great height and teach him a lesson he will never forget!"

Chapter Seventeen

Sasha sat at Ridge's desk and played with the computer. Whenever she came to Ridge's house she always made for the computer. She seemed to know that in using computer technology she was just as good as anyone else. She did not need her hearing to work the keys and understand programs. At school she had quickly picked up the advantages of computer skills and saw the pleasure on the face of her teachers when she succeeded in mastering the basics.

Ridge sat with her and guided her through various parts of the *Windows* system. He had noticed before, and indeed it was common knowledge, that where someone was deficient in one of the senses, then quite often they compensated for it unknowingly sometimes and became stronger in other ways.

Sasha's lip-reading skills were an example of that, thought Ridge. Watching her lip-read you could see her little eyes narrow as she focused in on the lips and made sense of what was being said. Her skills were so sharp that she sometimes gave the impression that she could hear. It was only the regular hearing tests undertaken at Addenbrooke's Hospital that conclusively established that Sasha could not hear and was totally reliant on picking up clues from people's lip patterns. They were both looking through a section of a replay of a TV programme when the telephone rang. It was Ford.

"Must see you tonight," he said.

"Okay, let's say seven-thirty in the usual place?"

Ford agreed and put the telephone down.

Ridge sat for a moment watching the computer screen with Sasha, then picked up the telephone and called Kimber's home number.

It rang but was not answered. There wasn't even an answerphone in place. Ridge then tried Johnson's home number without success. Getting just a little desperate, he called Police Headquarters and asked for them to try both telephone numbers in an hour's time and explain that he had been contacted by an informant whom he intended to visit immediately. Replacing the telephone Ridge smiled to himself.

★ ★ ★ ★

Driving towards London, Ridge pondered his position which seemed to be getting more tedious as the days passed. Whilst he did not want to keep baiting his supervisors, he had just tried to comply with their instructions to no avail. In the real world if you were sniffing about then you had to be available twenty-four-seven to deal with matters, a nine-to-five approach would not work.

There was no way that he could introduce either of his supervisors to Ford. He knew that Ford would quickly spot their naivety and start looking for ways to exploit both men. That's when it would become dangerous. Informants were predators within society, constantly looking for an easy touch. Ridge had always believed in the single officer approach with informants, although it was becoming fashionable to have more than one person involved in talking to a source.

Ridge believed that an informant had to be aware that they were dealing with one man who, on the one hand, would deliver on promises made in return for information and at the same time would wreak havoc on them if they took the piss. There had to be a certain amount of trust between the source of information and the officer and that was best served by minimising the number of officers dealing with the source, and those that were involved pulling together with a single purpose determined to make things work. When people like Ford gave information to the police they were quite often risking their lives. It was a difficult balance sometimes. Ridge knew that Ford trusted him and he was not about to jeopardise that trust.

Ridge parked his car some distance away from the pub and did a quick circuit checking for vehicles that looked out of place. Often you could tell police surveillance vehicles, simply because there were always two men sitting in the front of the vehicle. It was always a dead giveaway.

Finding nothing that caused him concern Ridge walked into the pub. He saw Ford sitting at the end of the bar watching customers come and go. Purchasing two halves of lager Ridge walked up to Ford, placed them on the small table and shook hands with Ford. There it was again. Ford had a sweaty palm. Ridge felt the droplets of sweat in the small of his back. He knew this primeval warning, for that is what it was, was in effect trying to tell him that something was not right. But what was it? Why should Ford be sweating? What a strange thing to do, he thought. Anyone watching would think they were simply good friends meeting for a drink, instead of two people on the opposite sides of the fence meeting to effect a common aim. Yet it opened their meeting in a very social way with neither man seeking an advantage over the other.

Ridge looked at Ford and grinned.

"Come on Charles, what was so bloody urgent that you needed to see me tonight?"

Ford stopped drinking from his glass and placed it slowly on the table.

"It looks as if things are on the move at last. The vehicle is on its way up from Oporto in Portugal as we speak. It is travelling slowly so as not to be stopped for any reason. It should make the top end of France by this weekend."

"Where is the lorry stopping over the weekend?" Ridge asked.

"All being well, it should make Béthune which is where it is going to stop, on the autoroute to Calais. The stopover will be on a small farm near a village called La Basse. The farmer is tried and tested. I have used the small airport next door many times to land the helicopter on. He has large barns on the farm, so the lorry can just be driven in and kept there over the weekend. No one will be any the wiser."

"What are the arrangements to get it back across the water?"

Ford looked at Ridge. "The beauty of the location is that it is a short run to the port at Calais once we are sure everything is okay."

"Why shouldn't everything be okay?" Ridge asked.

"It will be I'm sure," Ford said, and for a fleeting nanosecond seemed a little embarrassed.

Ridge gave no hint that he had noticed the change. "What about the vehicle? Have you got the index number? We will need that for the search at the port."

Ford reached into his pocket and brought out a crumpled piece of paper bearing a number written in blue biro. He passed it to Ridge.

"Good," he said. "How will we know the time and day that the lorry crosses the water? I want as much time and information as possible to set up the Customs search party at Dover?"

"Once I know I will let you know," Ford said.

By now Ridge could smell a trap formulating but could not isolate anything positive.

"Charles, this all seems so easy. Is there a catch? What are you not telling me?"

Ford was sweating slightly and Ridge could see the fine sweat line on his forehead.

"I have told you everything I know." He was getting just a little fidgety. "I will ring you on the Sunday evening to let you know the ferry times."

"Okay," Ridge said. "Let's leave it like that for the moment. I'm going to make a start back to Brighton. Keep in touch and don't give me any frights," he said, grinning at Ford. He stood up offered his hand to Ford and noticed that Ford's hand was still sweating.

Ridge left the pub and walked slowly back to his car. The bastard is up to something, he thought, but what?

Ridge knew that in talking to an informant you never ever got the equivalent of a brain transplant from them. They always had their secrets, like most people. They told you what they wanted you to know and you had to guess the rest. It was a bit like playing poker. He knew he had two choices, let it run and await the outcome whatever double-dealing was going on, or stop the whole thing from taking place. That way he could possibly avoid it blowing up in his face thus avoiding all sorts of complications back at the office. What to do, what to do, he thought.

119

He grinned to himself. This is what it is all about; intelligence work is not like normal police work. It is all about the ifs, buts and the maybes. Trying to sort the wheat from the chaff was not going to be easy and it was now being made much more enjoyable in the knowledge that Ford was trying to work a flanker on him at some stage of the game.

Chapter Eighteen

Ridge walked into the office next morning and began opening his inbox. He heard Emil Kimber walk down the corridor and left turn into his office and close the door shut. Kimber had a lazy, slouching, almost shuffling and very distinctive foot pattern for a comparatively young man.

Ridge gave him a few minutes and then knocked on his door and entered. Because Kimber was only a detective sergeant, it was acceptable that the swift knock on the door followed by immediate entry to the office was the state of play. It was only at the rank of detective inspector and above that one was required to wait until the command 'Enter' was used.

"I tried to get hold of the pair of you last night," he said. "Both your lines rang without answer. Not an answerphone between you. Are you two an item or what?" Ridge grinned at Kimber who seemed to take offence at his words.

"Ridge, your humour is not appreciated first thing in the morning or, for that matter, at any time through the normal working day. Now what are you talking about, what did you want us for?"

"Nothing really, just a small matter of a bit of police work, that's all! Both of you want to snatch my informant away from me, but neither of you are ever available to put in the groundwork that is required to keep the informant up and running. He rang last evening and wanted me to pop up to see him. I tried to contact the pair of you as I have already said, without success."

Kimber sat upright at his desk and stopped smoothing down his creased rugby shirt. The same rugby shirt he had been wearing for the last three days.

"You are not telling me that, after all the discussion that we have had recently, you went to London and saw your informant unsupervised?"

"As it happens, yes I did. I had no option. That's what I am employed to do. I tried desperately to contact you both, but I had no luck again! I had to make the decision myself!"

Kimber stared at Ridge. "The guvnor will go fucking mad when I tell him what you have done." He realised that he had been outmanoeuvred by Ridge. "You will never learn will you? You want to do everything by yourself. You don't want to be part of a fucking team!"

"You sit there Sarge, I will tell the guvnor myself. I don't need a wanker like you to cause further problems."

With that Ridge walked out of the office and went directly to his inspector's office. He knocked on the door and, not waiting for the command, walked straight in. He relayed the complete story to Johnson and waited for a response. Johnson sucked his teeth and put down his copy of the *Daily Telegraph*. He could see that Ridge was spitting with fury over his conversation with Kimber. He decided not to enrage him further.

"What did he have to say to you, John?"

Ridge looked at him, noticing the use of his Christian name. "Guvnor, you are the first person to ask that question. That dozy twat sitting in his office was more interested in causing me problems than taking an intelligent interest in events as you have done sir!"

Ridge then went into precise detail of his conversation with Ford, embellishing his comments where he thought necessary but omitting any mention of his own suspicions about Ford. When he paused for breath, Johnson saw his opportunity to jump in.

"I think we ought to be trying to verify Ford's information. Our colleagues across the water may be able to assist us in locating where the overnight stop is taking place and perhaps putting a watch on it?"

Ridge was horrified at this suggestion and it showed on his face.

"Guvnor, with the greatest possible respect, we do not want the Frogs sticking their noses in, they will only fuck things up. If you recall the last job of mine that I gave to the French, one of theirs got shot. I suggest we keep a watching brief for just a little longer. As things are now starting to move, I think they will move pretty swiftly from now on. The last thing we want to do is spook any of them!"

Johnson sucked in his teeth and placed his fingertips together.

"I concur with your comments this time Ridge, but I want no further fucking nonsense from you. Brief Sergeant Kimber on the latest if you haven't already. Then I want daily reports from you. Understood?"

Ridge smiled. "Certainly sir, to hear is to obey!"

As he left the office, Kimber passed him and walked into his inspector's office. Not waiting for an invite he chose a chair and sat down. Johnson saw that Kimber was in an ugly mood. Reaching down he opened his drinks cabinet drawer and pulled out the by now half-full bottle of whisky and two glasses. He poured two small shots of the amber liquid and passed one across the desk to Kimber, who by this time had lost his scowl.

"Where do we go from here, Guv?" Kimber asked, putting the glass to his lips and taking a small sip of whisky.

"Emil, we keep our powder dry for the present. But, believe me, my patience with Ridge is growing thinner by the fucking day. If you keep close to him I think we will have him over, within a week. I want to take over the control of his informant as soon as possible, or rather, you do!"

Kimber almost choked on his whisky. "As you are the detective inspector, I thought you might want to take charge of the informant and lead from the front on this one, given the problems we have had with him in the past?"

"No, Emil, I will be in overall charge, but I cannot do everything! Once we have taken away Ridge's informant, you will do the day-to-day running of the snout; got that?"

Kimber nearly wet himself. The cunning bastard, he thought, he wants me to risk my career on this job dealing with Ford, but if anything goes wrong he will keep clear so he will not be blamed for anything.

Johnson looked at Kimber, knowing what he was thinking.

"Don't worry Emil, I will support you at all times, just get me a result without Ridge being involved. Also, when we go to the conference with Customs I am going to hold back some of the information. We don't want them to go off at a tangent, do we?"

Kimber sat up straight as if by doing so he meant business.

"Right Guv, that sounds like a good idea. It means that we have something in the bag to trot out when we see fit."

He finished his whisky and took his leave, returning to his office where he began making notes of his conversation with his inspector and Ridge. If it all blew up in their faces he did not want to be the one taking the can, no sir, he did not.

Kimber dialled John Snow. "I have some current info on that job I am dealing with, if you have a moment I can explain how the job is progressing?"

Snow sighed down the telephone. "I have just had your DI on the phone telling me how his information on the same job is progressing. Don't you two ever talk to each other?"

Stung by Snow's comment, Kimber replied, "Well, actually it's both our information, we work closely together in this unit." He paused because Snow's laughter came down the telephone.

"I'm sure you do," he said, still laughing. "I understood from someone else that the info is sourced by your man John Ridge. Are you two trying a takeover?"

Kimber let fly. "Ridge is a member of this unit and will do as he is told. I am his supervisor and take ultimate responsibility for his workload. I supervise him on a daily basis and know exactly how much our job is moving forward. I demand to know if you have been meeting Ridge and putting ideas into his head."

"Bollocks!" Snow said, slamming the telephone down.

Chapter Nineteen

On his way home from the office, Ridge stopped at a telephone box and got Josie to call him straight back.

"How do you fancy an overnight stop in France, leaving tonight?"

"That sounds great," Josie responded. "I'll put a few things in a carrier bag and that's it. Where are we going?"

"I know a great little hotel not far inland from Calais. I thought we could meet at your place later this evening and go from there in my car. How does that grab you?"

"Leave yourself plenty of time and I'll have something waiting for you before we go," she laughed.

Ridge smiled at that thought. "I want to catch the nine o'clock ferry from Dover, so if I pop around about six p.m. we can decide a master plan then, okay?"

"Whatever you do, do not be late," Josie said. "I want to fuck you before we leave my place!"

"With that type of invitation, I will most certainly not be late," laughed Ridge. He replaced the telephone in its cradle and went home.

As he stepped into the kitchen and closed the door behind him, Marie greeted him with a kiss on the cheek. "Had a good day?" she asked.

"I have had a pig of a day," Ridge lied. "What is more, I have to go up to London tonight for a squad conference tomorrow and Saturday, and possibly a Sunday in the offing. Heaven knows it's the last thing I want to do, but needs must I am afraid."

"What's that all about?" Marie asked, looking away from her husband but listening intently to his words.

"It's the drugs job I told you about. It's finally beginning to move forward and Customs want a full briefing so that they can plan for when the stuff comes into the country. They really want this job."

Marie was wise enough not to push things and seek further information from her husband. She knew he liked keeping things to himself, that was part of his job and she understood that. There were times, however, when she had just a little niggle at the back of her mind. She was aware that John would deny that he was superstitious when it came to talking about a job that was up and running, but he was just that. He was reluctant to talk about the job in hand in case it became an instrument of bad luck.

Ridge came back into the kitchen with two glasses of red wine, one of which he handed to Marie. "First today," he said. "Let's hope it's not the last!"

"If you are driving tonight, that's the only glass of wine you're getting tonight," she admonished. "I'll finish the bottle later." They sat down at the kitchen table and talked over the day's events as they ate. She could see that he was fidgety and kept glancing at the clock. "Why don't you have a shower and I will pack you a bag with two days' change of clothes?"

"Good idea," he said, pleased to make a move in that direction. He hated lying to his wife. Normally it was the last thing that he would do, but the job was the job. Sometimes in the course of his job it was necessary to fuck other women: that was the way of the world, a bonus if you like, but it was a bonus he kept separate from his home life.

When he was ready, Ridge picked up his bag and kissed Marie on the cheek and said, "See you soon." He walked towards his car thinking of what lay ahead in the next few days.

Marie watched him go, knowing deep down that something was not quite as it should be. She just hoped and prayed that he would stay safe.

Twenty minutes later Ridge drew up outside Josie's flat. He let himself in with the key previously supplied by Josie. She was quite obviously waiting for him, because she appeared from the bedroom wearing the skimpiest of black silk underwear and smelling of some exotic perfume.

Ridge seized hold of her breasts and nuzzled into her neck. His hand moved down and released the straining bra clasp. Josie slipped her arms out of the bra and threw it across the room. Ridge picked her up and carried her into the bedroom and placed her gently on the bed. He reached down and quickly removed her black lace panties and buried his tongue deep down into her. Josie was delighted at this turn of events and was wriggling slowly but provocatively in sync with Ridge's movements as she struggled to remove his clothing. The pace built, with the two of them sweating with the effort. Finally they climaxed together and lay back almost exhausted on the bed. Then they showered together and dressed.

Leaving the flat secured they went to Ridge's car and set out on the journey to Dover Port. Josie slept most of the way leaving Ridge to consider the plan of attack once in France. He glanced at Josie. If anything, when she was asleep she looked even more beautiful than when she was awake. The tension seemed to leave her face relaxed and the facial structure less angular.

At Calais Port they sat in a corner booth of *Caffè Nero* and sipped their coffee while Ridge went over his plan. To any casual observer, they seemed like two consenting adults intent on a good weekend.

Once clear of the port and safely settled into driving on the right-hand side of the road, Ridge headed out towards the autoroute and the signs for

Béthune. The roads were dry and the evening warm as they headed towards their destination. With a woman like Josie beside him in France for the weekend, he had high hopes that a repeat performance was on the cards. He looked again at her and felt himself start to get an erection. God, he thought, I am not even trying and yet I could easily stop the car and do it again!

Within an hour of leaving Calais Josie spotted the signs for Béthune. Once on the outskirts of the town Ridge drove on for nearly two miles until Josie indicated a *Campanile Lodge Hotel* up ahead. They booked for the two nights that they intended staying and left the additional night to chance. The hotel was not full, so they could simply extend their nights if it became necessary. Once in the room, Josie went to the window and looked out and checked the car park and the cars parked near their car.

Ridge got a set of maps for the area out of his bag and laid them out on the bed. Josie came back to the centre of the room and stripped off.

"I'm going for a shower, please do not keep me waiting."

Ridge grinned. "I'll soap your back so as to save time!"

Although it was getting late, Ridge wanted to locate the farm where, with any luck, the lorry containing the cocaine would be waiting for the right moment to make for the port and the UK with its illicit load. As

Ridge talked, Josie's eyes widened, as for the first time the ramifications of the Ridge's plan became clear.

Police officers, spies, special investigators all spent ninety-nine per cent of their lives talking about the value of intelligence and one per cent dealing with it. That one per cent was the reality check. It became a whole new ball game when the intelligence moved on to active intelligence. The human factor became involved to make it work and to make it work required careful planning and a little bit of good luck.

They drove to La Basse, a small village not far from Béthune. The satnav was a godsend and took them to the small airport close by.

It was a small airport in a woodland setting, one of those places that was easy to drive past if you weren't careful. Alongside the airport was a farm with a number of buildings. It was a bright night with a half-moon that gave enough light for Ridge's needs.

He saw the windsock limp on its pole. Ridge could see the pole had a bend in it which meant that the whole thing leaned over at a forty-degree angle. Next to this airport was the farm where the drugs lorry would be garaged waiting for the right ferry. The next bit could wait until the morning.

They returned to the hotel and retired to bed.

★ ★ ★ ★

The next morning Ridge and Josie had breakfast in the restaurant. The porter on duty at the end of the room noticed that the two of them were very touchy-feely with each other.

After breakfast, Ridge loaded the equipment into the car and with Josie set off towards Le Basse. They followed the same route as they had the previous night and within minutes saw the bendy windsock. Ridge stopped the car and leaving Josie in the car made for a small hill from which he thought he should be able to look down over the farm. Arriving at the top of the hill, Ridge found he had a perfect view of the farm. There were a number of large buildings, maybe five in all, each of which could hide the lorry without a problem. Again he saw no signs of life.

He scanned the area with his binoculars and focussed on the airport next to the farm looking for any signs. Just two small aircraft near the runway and no sign of life. Both the airport and the farm were off the beaten track. It was unlikely that anybody would simply drive past either place and see anything wrong. There was a small road passing by both properties which split into an even smaller access road leading into either property.

Both the farm and the airport were surrounded by trees blocking any rear exit. One way in, and the same way out! The trees extended along the outside of the farm to a point where they almost joined the last of the buildings. Linking the barns on the farm was a narrow unmade roadway that began at the farmhouse. The place looked a little on the shabby side with paint on the main house showing signs of peeling. It was not surprising that the place had been chosen as a hideaway. Ridge took photographs of both the airport and the farm; they would be invaluable at any future conference.

Returning to his car Ridge told Josie what he had found. He showed her the images on his digital camera. Josie listened spellbound to Ridge's account, aware that she was now participating with Ridge in a real crime investigation. She was slightly awed by Ridge's apparent cunning. It excited her to be part of it, however small a part. Josie recalled assisting Ridge once before on a job and noticed that Ridge became intensely focused on succeeding.

On that occasion all was going well, until there was a dispute with his supervisors. Ridge lost the job in hand and appeared to be blamed for its loss. He lost his position on the unit and was returned to uniform duties. He had never spoken to her about the problem, but she knew that he had been very upset at that outcome.

Ridge watched her face for a moment. "What are you smiling about?" he asked.

"I was thinking of the way you nearly raped me last night. You were so good!"

"I thought you were the one doing the raping. I couldn't even shout for help!"

Josie coloured slightly. "I thought I couldn't hear you complaining!"

Ridge smiled. "Tonight is a working night for both of us, but before we go out tonight I want to file your teeth down. They were a bit on the sharp side last night."

Josie laughed. "What about tonight. What do you want me to do?"

"I want you to listen on that telephone transcriber you have for any English phone calls to the farm or even the airport. Literally anything English within the area. Record any numbers and wait for me to return! I am going to have a look at the farm buildings. Hopefully one of the buildings will have a lorry inside."

"I knew I would get the difficult part. You do know the equipment will not indicate particular premises, just the vicinity and of course the strength of the signal will indicate it's close to us."

"This is deepest France; anything in the immediate area has got to be suspect. I will check it all out once we arrive back home."

Josie got out and dragged a large suitcase to the front of the boot. She opened the lid and Ridge saw one of the most sophisticated telephone eavesdropping devices on the open market. Josie plugged in the cigar lighter type plug and the machine came to life. She turned a switch marked 'mixture'. Until the screen showed that scanning was taking place. When the needle settled she turned up the volume. The machine was now calibrated to pick up any conversations from within its range or telephones being used within its four mile radius. They sat in the car, enjoying the sunshine and listening to the local French telephone conversations being picked up by the machine.

Ridge knew it was a long shot but sometimes a long shot paid dividends. Even if, because of the distance, the conversation was not strong enough to pick up they still had the telephone number and that could be researched once they returned home. All they needed was a little bit of luck.

They had a mid-afternoon snack of French cheese and fresh baguettes, downed with warm *Coca-Cola* they had bought on their way to the site. Patience was all they needed: they were not required to go without food as they waited out the daylight hours.

Chapter Twenty

A t 8pm it was dark enough.

Leaving Josie to monitor the telephone wire taps, Ridge made his way along the road until he came to within sight of the farm. He could see lights on in the ground floor of the farmhouse and lights in one of the barns. He scouted the entire circumference of the farm and eventually found himself once again at the front of the farm.

Ridge bent down and picked up a handful of grass and threw it into the air. He checked the wind direction as best he could in the dark. Couldn't be too careful in the circumstances, most farms had a dog or geese or a cat, all of which could sound the alarm to those in the house. It made sense to be down wind, just in case. Ridge slowly covered the ground towards the farmhouse. He kept low until he reached the main downstairs window. The curtains were drawn but there was a gap sufficient for Ridge to count six adults seated at a table eating a meal. Five male persons and one female were there. Ridge reasoned that if this number were sitting down to a meal in the farmhouse, it was unlikely that anybody else was out walking about. One of the males seemed to be leading forth to all the others, but Ridge could not hear the conversation.

He decided to check the barn with the lights on. Slowly and quietly he moved on past the farmhouse keeping a wide berth as he approached the front of the barn. One of the doors was open shedding a light trail, which made entry difficult as he would be seen by anybody looking out of the farmhouse windows. Creeping around the side of the building, Ridge made his way to the back. He found a small door that was locked by a simple *Yale* lock. Using a small pencil torch he examined the lock. Ridge knew he could easily force the door with body pressure, but decided not to do that because that method would leave a trace of his visit. He slipped his *MasterCard* in the small space and gave it a gentle push. The door opened and he was inside in a flash. The barn was huge. The light at the front of the building was a bulb hanging off the end of a long flex. It just illuminated the door entrance, not the entire barn. Ridge could smell the petrol fumes and warmth of the English-registered lorry parked immediately in front of him. As his eyes adjusted to the dark areas of the barn, he could just make out a French tractor in front of that vehicle, effectively applying a block to getting the lorry out of the barn.

Ridge spent the next few minutes walking around the barn. He was reluctant to try the doors of the lorry in case the cabin lights gave him away.

He could hear what he thought was the lorry refrigeration unit and walked close to check it out. He wondered what else the lorry was carrying. The darkness made it difficult to explore the lorry to any great extent. There were no markings on it, which was strange, Ridge thought. Most companies travelling the continental autoroutes saw the value of advertising their company vehicles. The vehicle had English plates, so it appeared that it had been sent out from the UK, done the run from Portugal, collected the gear and was on the return leg of its journey.

It had to be the vehicle he was seeking. He quietly recorded the registration number and was in the act of standing up straight when he sensed something in the barn with him. He heard the deep throated growl and turned just in time to see the largest Rottweiler he had ever seen bearing down on him. As it closed on him the dog reared up on its hind legs and sought a chest high bite. Instinctively Ridge put out his right arm to prevent the dog from going for his throat and the dog seized on Ridge's forearm and clamped down. He could feel the pressure as the dog's jaws tightened and began crushing his forearm. The animal was almost as tall as him, and was going to require instant action before either causing him a severe injury or, worse, alerting those in the farmhouse to his visit.

It was obvious to Ridge that the dog was not going to let go of him. Turning in towards the snarling animal, Ridge put his free arm around the dog's neck and grasped it tightly towards him. Then, pivoting on his right foot, Ridge turned into the fastest *Harai Goshi* he had ever performed. His left leg turned up and then backwards, sweeping both of the dog's hind legs off the ground. Ridge then sacrificed his own body weight bringing the animal crashing on to the concrete floor underneath with him. The first part of the dog to hit the floor was its large head. It bore the brunt of its own weight and that of Ridge as its head connected with the concrete floor causing it to yelp and then go quiet. Ridge forced open its jaws and removed his arm. He rolled away from the silent animal and stayed very still on the ground for a few moments trying to normalise his breathing pattern and work out whether the dog's noises had alerted those in the farmhouse. When he was sure he remained safe, Ridge turned his attention to his injured arm.

The Rottweiler's jaws had penetrated the skin and had caused large puncture wounds down his arm causing some bleeding. He wrapped his arm back into the sleeve of his jacket, trying to keep his blood off the floor. Then grabbing the unconscious dog by its hind legs Ridge dragged it to the rear of the barn where hopefully it would remain unseen until it regained it wits. Locking the back door behind him, Ridge left the barn and made his way back to Josie and the car.

Chapter Twenty-One

The farmer stood outside the back door, drawing slowly on his cigarette. He was not allowed inside the house when the need took him to smoke. Most of the time it didn't bother him having to stand outside the building to smoke, but there was no way that he was going to stop smoking. He felt it was one of his few pleasures in life, apart from helping to smuggle cocaine into the UK.

He stood there smoking and looking across to the barns. He was going to make a lot of euros out of this little scam. More than he made last year or the year before that.

He cupped his hand over the lighted end of his cigarette so that the glow was not seen and watched as the shadowy figure left the nearest barn and walked back along the roadway until he was lost from sight.

The farmer stubbed out his cigarette and walked

over to the barn and called his dog. The dog normally responded to his name but on this occasion did not.

The farmer, thinking something was amiss, turned away from the front of the barn and began a search of the grounds before going back into the barn. He had almost reached the rear of the barn when the dog appeared from behind the lorry. It wagged its tail, pleased at the sight of his master although it appeared to be a little unsteady on its feet.

The owner seemed not to notice the dog's unsteadiness and thought that it had just been lying down. He wondered how it had not caused a ruckus when Ridge had entered the barn. He switched the light off and went back to the farmhouse.

★ ★ ★ ★

Josie sat in the car and watched Ridge returning from the farm. He seemed to be holding his right arm. She saw the blood dripping from the wounds as he opened the door.

"Take your jacket off and let me have a look at your arm. Have I got time to fix it before we move?"

"Two minutes, that's all then we must leave. I don't want anyone from the farm creeping up on us." He looked at Josie cleaning the wounds. Already he was starting to feel the bruising effects of the bites and noticed that his arm was beginning to swell. "I've just met the biggest fucking Rottweiler that I have ever seen," he said, trying not to show how much pain he was in.

Josie smiled. "I guess he didn't like you either?"

"No, he didn't," Ridge said. "I am just hoping that he wakes up in the morning and doesn't say a word." He jumped a little as Josie's efforts at first aid were finished. Ridge then swallowed a couple of paracetamol to ease the throbbing in his arm.

"Any luck with the device?" he asked, as he drove away from the parking place.

"Not sure. There was one English call to the farmhouse, but it wasn't picked up. I have the telephone caller's number so we can look at that once we arrive home." Josie looked at Ridge who was clearly in pain but doing his best not to show it. She did not probe Ridge about his findings at the farmhouse. He would tell her if he wanted her to know. Josie felt excited being with Ridge. If anyone could make this job work it was him. He had a charisma about him once he was on the move. Josie had never felt this way about any of her colleagues or his for that matter. Once she got him back to the hotel she would fuck him to sleep. Josie smiled and reached a hand down onto Ridge's thigh. She could feel he was hard.

Ridge concentrated on driving determined not to show any anticipation, but guessing exactly what Josie was about to do. She carefully unzipped his jeans and gently separated him from his clothing before going down on him and beginning a rhythmical backwards and forwards movement. She felt him start to squirm and adjusted the pace of her movement.

Ridge was perspiring now and finding it very difficult to focus on his driving. His excitement grew, making it clear to Josie that he could not continue driving for much longer. She produced a large handkerchief from a pocket and covered him as she suddenly racked up the volume of her hand movement causing Ridge to shudder as he arched his back towards the steering wheel in an uncontrolled spasm.

He lost control of his driving as the car swerved across the road and missed a tree by inches. Ridge jammed his foot down, braking hard, skidding slightly and coming to a stop almost against another tree on the other side of the road.

He glanced across at Josie who held a hand across her face and was trying hard not to snigger.

Keeping a straight face Ridge said, "Do you think these tremors I keep getting are a sign of things to come?

★ ★ ★ ★

The next morning, following a light breakfast, they drove to the port arriving with time to spare. Josie remained in the car while Ridge booked in at the desk. Ridge found he was able to book a cabin for the return journey. He saw the young female clerk look at him as if wondering why he would want to book a cabin for a journey lasting not much more than an hour and a half. He held up his injured arm. "My dog bit me last night and the jabs that I required afterwards have made me drowsy. A good sleep will put it right."

She looked sympathetically at him and seemed to accept his lies at face value. She handed over the tickets. "Have a nice return journey."

"I'm sure I will," Ridge said. Returning to the car, he showed the cabin tickets to Josie. "We have got a whole hour's sleep on the way back!"

"You must be joking!" she laughed.

Chapter Twenty-Two

Parking the car in the driveway, he walked into the house and was greeted by Marie with a kiss. She noticed that he had reapplied his aftershave and wondered why. After all it was not exactly first thing in the morning. She stepped back and looked at him. "For someone who has been at a conference, you look bloody awful. Who dragged you through the hedge? What's happened to you?"

"I have had a very difficult weekend, that's all. I have really missed you, what have you been up to?"

"Why are you holding your arm like that? Show me."

Helping him off with his jacket Marie saw the blood stains on the inside of the sleeve. "Have you been to the hospital with your injury?"

"No, not yet, but a nurse has seen and dressed it, so there is not much to worry about," he replied, beginning to realise that he was on dangerous ground. "You may not believe this, but I got to the conference on time and was just having a natter, when I got paged and then had to rush over to France on a job and then met a bloody big dog who thought I was a bone."

Marie went to him and removed the bandage from his arm. Looking at his injuries she felt a little relieved and at the same time slightly ashamed of the thoughts that she had just entertained. She did not want to know the inside of a duck's bottom: his job was his job! She knew that, all she really wanted was a little confirmation that he had behaved himself instead of a gut feeling that he had not! But, she thought, at least his story ties in with his injury. It was clearly a dog bite or bites, no doubt about that.

"Why don't you get someone else to do the sneaky bits? Let someone else get bitten!" she asked, watching him. "When you retire next year I want you in one piece!"

Ridge placed both hands on Marie's waist and gently kissed her. "Don't worry," he chided, "this is going to be the final game. Once this job is over, I am coasting through the next few months until that happy retirement day arrives!"

She finished dressing his arm. "Did you remember to have a word with the local plod who covers Sasha's school, about those two men seen hanging about?"

"Yes I did, why?"

"They have been seen by people at the school again. One of the men remained sitting in a car, the other watching the playground. Some of the young mums are getting a bit agitated about it, especially after those recent stories in the paper about kids going missing."

"I will have another word with the plod in the morning," he promised.

★ ★ ★ ★

They retired to bed earlier than their usual time because Ridge was looking tired and feeling very drowsy. They had been in bed for less than ten minutes when Marie threw back the bedclothes. "Damn it," she said, "I forgot to put the washing machine on." With that she leapt out of the bed, slipped into a dressing gown and went downstairs to resolve the problem. On top of the pile of clothes in the basket was her husband's dirty weekend wear. As she loaded the machine Marie caught the unmistakeable smell of a woman's perfume and, even worse, the strong smell of sex emanating from Ridge's casual trousers. Her eyes filled with tears at the glaring evidence of her husband's indiscretions. She remained in the kitchen for some time trying to come to terms with her thoughts. Eventually she made her way back to the bedroom and quietly slipped in beside her now fast asleep husband. Her last thought before closing her eyes was to wonder who he had spent the weekend with.

Breakfast the following morning was a quiet affair. Marie had barely slept the night before. Over the years she had had her suspicions, but that's all. To be confronted like this, out of the blue, was unbearable. It was as much as she could do to make conversation with her husband. She decided that she did not want to confront him and force the issue, in case that provoked a situation where he, or even she, felt they had no option but to become defensive and then destructive.

The last thing she wanted was to lose him. She loved him dearly even in spite of this revelation. But she was so bloody angry. How dare he jeopardise their marriage with a casual fling with some tart! Wait and see, she thought. Give him a few days. Wait and see if it was a once only or likely to continue.

Ridge, nursing his sore arm, which was thankfully much improved since his fretful night's sleep, noticed Marie was quiet and hardly talking.

"You seem quiet this morning," he said. "Is there anything wrong?"

"I didn't sleep very well last night, that's all," she replied.

"No, I didn't either; I must get ready for work." With that he left the room.

Marie smiled to herself and prepared to attack the washing-up. Later she would take his clothing to the cleaners. Her eyes welled up with tears at the thought.

Chapter Twenty-Three

Peter Ford sat and listened to his French friend shouting down the telephone, doing his best to explain in broken English about the man seen running from his farm the previous night. Eventually, Ford stopped him and asked if he knew the man he had seen. He got what he thought was a no in reply, although it sounded a bit like someone just about to spit! Ford asked for a description of the man and waited for a reply.

"Dee-scription!" he screamed down the telephone. "Eet was, you English call, fuckin' dark!"

Hearing this response, Ford knew the Frenchman had his limitations. "Okay," he said. "Do we know if he was French?"

"Peter," the Frenchman said, making it sound like Pee-ter, "all I saw was a man running away, nothing else. Everything is okay on the farm. I don't know why my stupid dog did not bite him."

Ford considered the problem for a moment.

"Andre, I want you to check the barns and make sure that nothing has been tampered with. When you have done that, do it again just to make sure. I won't do anything until I know for sure that we are still secure, okay?"

Andre ran off a torrent of French and English, most of which Ford failed to understand. Then he put the telephone down with such force that it vibrated loudly through Ford's eardrum. Ford replaced his handset and sat and thought about the development and how it would affect the plan. He had used the farm and its outbuildings for a number of years without anyone being any the wiser. Maybe it was nothing more than a local druggie having a look at the place to see what he could scavenge. His friend Andre could always be relied on to deal with any intruders and that dog of his was a nasty bastard to get past: but someone had.

Paul entered the room, tottering slightly as if he was just a little drunk, although Peter knew it wasn't drink affecting him. "For Christ's sake why don't you leave that stuff alone, at least until we have done this job?" he said, with more than a little anger in his voice.

Paul stood up straight. "Bollocks. I've just had a line, that's all. Who were you talking too on the blower?"

"It was Andre, our French farm owner. It seems he had a prowler around his farm last night. Nothing has been touched, but he is going to double check and let me know. Nothing moves until we know for sure."

Paul sniffed, running the back of his hand across his nose. "That's all we need, some fucking nosy Frenchman poking his nose in where it is not wanted. I bet that dopey fucking Frenchman has been gobbing off in the local whorehouse and someone has overheard him. Take my word for it, that Andre is dick mad and far too talkative! What are we going to do?"

Peter watched Paul as he slumped against the door. "We are not doing anything until I am sure it's okay to move the stuff. We are not getting careless on the last leg of the journey."

"What about over here? Is there anyone here who knows what we are doing and wants a bit of the action?" Paul asked.

Peter looked at his brother. What a fucking waste of space he is turning out to be. "Only the police or Customs, you fucking dingbat!"

Paul stabilised his posture against the doorframe. "Are we going to tell Charles about this? You know what he is like. He will start panicking and want to call the whole thing off."

Peter thought about it. "No, we are not going to tell Charles just yet. Let's wait until Andre comes back to me on the phone. We will have a better idea then!"

Paul sniffed again and made a show of focusing his eyes on his brother. "Let's send little brother Charles to France tomorrow to check out if everything is okay, because if not, we will have to adjust the times of the return journey, which will be a fucking nuisance to say the least."

Peter watched as Paul seemed to slide along the wall about three feet until the large, slightly old-fashioned sideboard stopped him from going any further. "Paul let's you and me go to the farm and make sure that everything is ready at this end. At the very least we can make sure that everything is as it should be ready for when the gear arrives."

Paul, by this time, had righted himself. He put his arm around Peter's shoulder and began singing, "Here we go, here we go!"

Chapter Twenty-Four

At six-thirty the next morning Charles Ford left his house and made for the motorway towards the Port of Folkestone. He wanted to use a different route out to France than he intended using on the way back. That way he avoided his Range Rover being clocked twice at the same Port and, perhaps more importantly, he would avoid being seen by the same Customs officer on the outward journey and the return journey. You could not be too careful with Customs; some of them were right sneaky gits! Travel out from Folkestone to Boulogne, and back via Dieppe to Newhaven, that way leaving Dover clear ready for the lorry's return journey. Even if he was checked, no one was going to link him with an importation through Dover in the coming days.

Arriving at the port, Charles went to the reception desk and bought a single ticket to Boulogne. As he waited, he eyed up the attractive young woman dealing with his request. Not bad, he thought, I could easily pass away the time with her!

The receptionist scanned Ford's documents and hesitated. She saw Sarah Mundey watching her and raised her eyes in the direction of Ford. She returned to Ford with the ticket and was just about to pass the ticket to Ford when Sarah Mundey walked over to her and took the ticket from her outstretched hand. She scanned the details and glanced at Ford.

He smiled. "Fancy a coffee?"

Sarah Mundey blushed slightly and declined Ford's offer. "May I see your vehicle insurance documents, please?"

While Ford fished out his vehicle documents, it gave her time to appraise Ford. Flash bastard, she thought, but he is quite attractive. When she had Ford's documents she went to a photocopier in another room and quickly made a copy and added it to the other copies laid out on her desk.

Returning the documents to Ford she smiled at him. "Have a nice day."

Ford grinned at her and turned away.

Mundey walked through and into the general office. Picking up the photocopies of Ford's documents she walked across the room and to the desk occupied by the Port Special Branch Officer. "Can you whiz these docs through your system for me, Adam? He is on the next sailing."

Adam gazed up at her. "For you, anything is possible." He smiled at her and looked at the documents and then back at her. "What's wrong with him?" he asked, admiring Sarah Mundey's breasts.

"Not sure. He just seemed a little smarmy to me, that's all!"

Taking his eyes off her roundly sculptured body, the officer punched the details on the passport into the computer.

There was a brief second's hesitation on the screen before the screen format changed completely and Ford's criminal record was displayed. A red warning signal began flashing in the corner of the screen. Adam Brown, a Kent Special Branch Officer with nearly fifteen years' police service behind him, sat back in his chair and whistled.

"Sarah, my darling, you have just won the lottery! What on earth made you pick on him?"

"He tried to pick me up by offering to buy me coffee."

Adam Brown stared at her. He was thinking, the bastard; fancy wanting to do a thing like that with a nice girl like you! He grinned, wishing he had made the offer.

She looked at Brown and saw what he was thinking. She struck a pose. "You lot are all the same. You think you are God's gift to bloody women and are totally irresistible. What do I do now with that info?"

"Nothing, I will do it for you. First things first, I am going to inform SOCA that their target has been spotted. According to their report this man, Ford is his name, is not to be stopped. He is to be allowed to proceed to wherever and as many details as possible obtained without alarming him. Perhaps, my dear Sarah, you had better try and have that coffee with him after all?"

"Why not," she quipped. "Let's see how bloody good he really is!" With that she quickly made her way to the restaurant and saw Ford about to be served with coffee. Sarah stopped directly in front of him and smiled. "Can a lady change her mind?"

Ford smiled at her. "Of course you can, what do you want?"

Sarah settled for an espresso and waited with him while he paid for both drinks. They selected a table away from the mainstream of seats and sat down. Ford noticed that as Sarah sat down her uniform skirt rode up high displaying an ample portion of shapely thigh. They sipped their coffees in silence, each looking directly at the other. In the end Ford broke the silence. "Do you believe in love at first sight?"

"All the time," she responded, laughing. "Is that your best chat up line?"

Ford liked her easy style. "It's my only chat up line." He laughed with her. They continued with the small talk, light easy conversation, until the public address system blared into the restaurant advising all drivers to return to their cars to prepare for loading.

Ford stared at Sarah. "What are you doing the other side of the water?"

"I'm staying with a girl friend for a couple of days," and she smiled.

"I've got a bit of business in France," Ford said, smiling at her. "It's not far from the port. Once I have done that, I will have the night free! Why don't we team up?"

Sarah thought about the offer. She had manoeuvred matters now to the point where, over the next couple of days, she hoped she would be able to get firsthand intelligence from Ford without him realising what she was doing. Later she would submit the info to SOCA officers and see what they thought of it.

She nodded her head. "Okay, I can stay with my friend at some other time."

"Fine, we can meet up when we disembark."

Sarah nodded, gave Ford a peck on the cheek and moved away from him. Ford could smell Sarah's perfume. He began to feel excited about this small unexpected diversion.

★ ★ ★ ★

Disembarking from the hovercraft, Ford pulled to one side away from the mainstream traffic and waited, hoping that Sarah would put in an appearance. As the thought was going through his mind he saw her running along the foot passengers' walkway towards him. She was carrying a small overnight bag.

Sarah had not mentioned her change of plans to Adam Brown or even her supervisor. At this stage, the less they knew the better.

Ford opened the door and Sarah jumped inside the vehicle. She threw her overnight bag over her shoulder into the rear of the Range Rover. Placing her hand between Ford's legs she could feel him hard.

"Let's go," she teased.

Ford leaned over and kissed her gently on the cheek. Tonight he was going to fuck Sarah in a way that she probably hadn't been fucked before.

Driving east on the N42, Ford soon left the town and port traffic behind him. They stopped for a light lunch of fresh crab salad and white wine at a roadside restaurant. Ford noticed that Sarah's breasts were struggling to get out of the top of her bra and blouse which had somehow managed to unbutton itself a further two buttonholes since Sarah had got into the car.

Aware of what was transfixing Ford's eyes and what he was probably thinking about, Sarah continued to enjoy the meal. If she could stay with Ford while he was in France, not only would she have a good couple of days she would also find out just who he was going to see and why. Passing on quality information about a target like Ford would soon bring her to the notice of the drug team at Customs HQ. This could be a very useful introduction to the movers and shakers on both sides of the water and it would do her career no harm at all. So Ford wanted to fuck her. So what! She was hardly a virgin.

Once the meal was over, they continued their journey through Béthune until they were a few minutes from La Basse. Ford drove around until he saw a large shopping centre. Pulling in to the kerbside Ford stopped the car. He reached into his jacket pocket and pulled out the equivalent of two hundred pounds in euros. He pressed the money into Sarah's hand. "I can't take you with me. I have a meeting lined up and I must attend that meeting on my own. Take the money, go into the shopping centre and buy yourself something small to wear tonight. I will return here and pick you up at seven p.m. Okay?"

"That's fine." She watched him drive off feeling slightly peeved at the way he had suddenly dumped her in the middle of nowhere. Sarah also did not like the inference behind his words. It was unmistakeable. She realised that she had just been bought for two hundred pounds and was expected to behave like a prostitute later on that night. She began to have her first sense of misgivings about Mr Ford.

Chapter Twenty-Five

The Rottweiler watched as the Range Rover came up the drive. Its top lip stretched and curled upwards as it identified a stranger on its home ground.

Ford saw it lying near the front door to the farmhouse. Fucking thing, if it starts its nonsense I will kill it, he thought, although he wasn't very happy at the thought of trying to do that. It was a really big animal. He saw that the long rope lead was tied to a large metal ring embedded into the flint wall about a yard up off ground level. The end of the lead connected to a large link metal check collar around the dog's neck.

Ford decided that if the dog was to lurch forward towards him one of two things was likely to happen. Either the metal collar would throttle the dog or, most likely, the metal ring would pull straight out of the wall. He stopped the car, far enough away from the dog in order that he could get out of the car, but close enough to get back in the vehicle should it become necessary.

He saw Andre open the barn doors and walk in his direction. When Andre saw it was Charles Ford, he extended his hand and smiled. Of the three brothers he liked Charles best; the other two brothers were a little too slippery for his liking.

"Charles, it is good to see you again." Andre's relatively good English died at this point and his fractured English took over. "It eez about the man I saw near zee barn is it not?"

Ford shook his hand displaying some warmth in the shake. He liked Andre. "It is good to see you again you old bastard," he said, grinning from ear to ear. "My brothers are a bit concerned about what happened, can you tell me about it?"

Andre winked at him and indicated that they should go into the farmhouse and have a welcome drink. He indicated this by the time honoured method of raising a cupped hand up and down as if drinking from a glass. They both walked past the dog, which showed no interest in Ford, although Ford kept one eye on the animal as he walked past it. They entered the lounge where the usual French niceties were begun. Andre poured two very generous measures of local brandy and toasted Ford. "Welcome to my farm." His speech then lapsed into broken English, "Owee, is it you say, round zee teef round zee gums, 'ere it cums?" He swallowed his measure of brandy in one gulp.

"Salut!" Ford said and swallowed his measure in one go too.

Andre then told Ford about the incident with the intruder.

Ford could feel the effects of the brandy taking place. When he had initially consumed the measure, as it slipped down his throat, he thought it was going to take the lining off his throat. It was now swirling around his stomach gurgling as it went.

From Andre's vivid account of what had taken place, it seemed to Ford that the man seen by Andre was most likely, Ridge. He cursed, as he realised that Ridge was ahead of the game and now knew where the lorry with the cocaine was. The last thing he wanted was Ridge jumping ahead of himself and placing the whole operation at risk.

To Andre he said, "It doesn't sound like anybody I know. Perhaps it was a local just having a sniff around?"

"Maybe, I think you are right. If it was a stranger, my dog would have 'ad 'im for sure!"

Ford looked at his friend. "You checked all the buildings and nothing is missing?"

"Yes, that is, 'ow you say, ready to go!"

"What about the other lorries? Where are they?"

"They are okay. I put them round the back of the hanger at the airport. You said to keep them on their own?" Andre raised an eyebrow at Ford.

Ford smiled and glanced at his watch. "That's good, Andre. One more thing, I want some gear for tonight, have you got any cocaine lying about the place?"

"For you my English friend, I always have something special!" With that he reached under the large cushion in the dog's basket and withdrew a clear plastic envelope containing a white powder. He gave it to Ford who thanked him. Andre grinned. "Zere is enough in there to liven up zee 'orse."

Ford was now confident that the night ahead was going to be something special, although his Sarah was not yet aware of that. He stuffed the envelope into his pocket. There was no need to check the barn. If Andre said that it was okay then that was good enough for him. Besides, with that great big fucking dog sitting outside, there was no chance anyone was going to get past it. Although Ridge had. He wondered how Ridge had managed that: maybe he would ask him next time they met.

As Ford left the farm, Andre walked back to the barns and again began to check the lorry for any sign of interference. With the lorry containing sixty kilos of cocaine on this trip alone, Andre did not want anything coming back to bite him. He also knew that if this shipment went through without problems there would be more to follow. Flooding the UK market in the way that the Ford brothers anticipated doing would have an enormous effect on the market. It would depress it for a start, wiping out the hundreds, if not thousands, of small and large dealers. Within weeks the Ford brothers would have complete control of the demand/supply and price factors. They would control everything. However, this came with the proviso that their first shipment, this shipment, was delivered on time. The surprise factor was important. They would be required to swamp the whole market in one go, that was key to their planned and anticipated success. With such success behind them, they would then become the largest drug suppliers within the UK.

★ ★ ★ ★

Having taken his leave of Andre, Ford left the farm and made his way back to the place where he had left Sarah Mundey. He parked the car and texted Sarah who joined him fifteen minutes later.

Chapter Twenty-Six

Ford booked into the hotel. Sarah noticed that he did not seem short of money, wanting the best of everything the hotel had to offer. They were escorted to their room where Ford tipped the elderly member of staff generously for carrying what little luggage they had to the room.

Ford closed the door and stripped off his clothes, thinking about his visit to the farm and Andre's freely supplied brandy. He could still feel the effects of the alcohol in his system, although he had sobered up considerably since leaving the farm.

Sarah watched him. She could see that he was distracted and wondered what he was thinking about. It obviously wasn't about her; she could see that much with a sideways glance!

Ford seemed to snap out of it. "I'm just going to have a bath."

With that he walked into the bathroom and closed the door.

Sarah could hear Ford in the bathroom running the water. She quickly looked through his bag and wallet. In his wallet she found a piece of paper with a French telephone number on it which she assumed was the telephone number he had used for his business appointment. She memorised the complete number with just a second's glance and replaced the paper back in the wallet, noting the white plastic bag with the white powder in it. Job done!

Looking around her, Sarah realised that she was now at a loose end. She needed to loosen up a bit and start to enjoy her time with Charles Ford. Quickly removing her clothing she walked into the bathroom and joined Ford in the bath. The room was now warm with steam rising from the hot water in the bath. She quickly fitted her legs either side of Ford's legs and slipped back into a relaxed position, looked at him and waited. Sarah knew that she was playing a very dangerous game with Ford, but she was determined to enjoy her time with him.

Although fairly new to her job with Her Majesty's Customs and Excise Port Investigation Unit and untried in dealing with informants, Sarah wondered just how difficult it could be. She felt excited at the opportunities that this little clandestine meeting with Ford would offer her. Clearly, the best way to get Ford's confidence, or any man's confidence for that matter, was to go to bed with him!

Prepared to fuck his brains out if necessary, Sarah could not wait for the moment when she would walk back into her office and regale her colleagues with sufficient information enabling them to arrest however many people were involved and to recover a large amount of drugs or whatever! Of course she would play hard to get over the inevitable question of who she got the information from and how she got it. No, no, no. That was going to stay her little secret! Her career path would be assured. She would be on her way up.

She saw that Ford was staring at her. "What about a drink?" she murmured. "I'm thirsty."

Ford sat up and reached forward so that he could stroke her breasts. His fingers tweaked her nipples. Sarah felt excited as he caressed each of her breasts with gentle circular movements. Ford then stood up in a very ungainly manner displaying his excitement. "Just a moment; don't run away!"

Without drying himself or even putting a towel around his waist, Ford walked through into the main bedroom and poured two glasses of champagne from a bottle he had ordered when he had booked in and which had been delivered and placed in the room fridge before he and Sarah had stepped into the room. Walking over to the bed he checked his wallet, taking from it his credit card and a transparent plastic packet containing a white powder.

He returned to the bathroom with a glass in each hand. Sarah was lying back in the bath looking up in a very expectant way. She took a glass from him and sipped the contents. The bubbles tickled her mouth as she sunk the remainder of the glass.

Ford smiled. "Just a moment, I will get you a refill; you were thirsty!" He took the glass from her and left the bathroom to refill it from the bottle in the bedroom. Ford came back a few moments later with Sarah's glass filled to the brim in one hand. In the other hand he was carrying the plastic bag containing the white powder. Between his fingers were his credit card and two straws.

He passed the glass to Sarah and then sat down on the toilet seat and pulled the chrome waste bin towards him. The lid was flat and about ten inches across. He cleaned the top with a piece of toilet tissue before emptying half of the contents of the bag onto the top surface. Ford then began dividing the powder into two separate lines with his credit card.

Sarah had watched Ford closely and now knew what was expected of her. She didn't want any part of it. She wasn't averse to a bit of sex, rough or otherwise, but there was no way she was going to snort coke with Ford. No way!

She rapidly consumed her second glass of champagne and decided that she would appear drunk, or at least too drunk to snort cocaine. She coughed and spluttered as some of the champagne went down the wrong way. Her eyes watered, as she tried to play her part. On an empty stomach the drink was taking effect. She was now on the verge of panicking.

Charles Ford swallowed his champagne and, putting the glass on the floor, he picked up one of the straws and placed one end against the line and sniffed. A third of the cocaine disappeared up Ford's nose. He paused and sat back against the toilet cistern allowing the drug to wash through his central nervous system. He was sweating profusely and in an almost dreamlike state within seconds.

Sarah watched him balling his fists as the cocaine did its work. She saw his eyes recede back into his eyelids before rapidly opening and closing.

All of a sudden, he opened both eyes and focused on her. "Now it's your turn!"

Ford stood up and turned towards Sarah. She did the only thing she could think of: she raised herself onto her knees and took hold of his erect penis and placed it inside her mouth. She had to gain time. Sarah moved forward and backwards, her tongue pleasuring his body.

Ford felt wonderful. Every nerve in his body seemed excited. He loved what she was doing to him; she was really very good at it. She had so much more to offer!

He stepped into the bath and moved closer to her. Sarah kept her movement going hoping to keep him occupied. With both hands she began massaging his buttocks at the same time. Leaning in towards Sarah, Ford was pushing her head back and his penis deeper. Sarah was by now becoming uncomfortable with her position. Her body was arching backwards and her knees bent under her in a painful way. She did the only thing she could think of simply to get some relief: she bit into him!

Ford screamed at the pain and removed his penis from Sarah's mouth. Looking down, Ford saw that he was already showing signs of bruising from both sides of the bite.

"Fucking bitch!" he shouted and hit her directly in the face. With one hand he grabbed her hair and jerked her head back. Sarah was now semiconscious following the blow and was bleeding from the mouth. Ford dragged her the length of the bath, banging her head on the side of the bath and then pulled her out of the bath and onto the floor. He placed one foot on her neck to keep her still and gently examined where he had been bitten. The pain from the bite was receding although the marks were still prominent. He calmed down when he realised that the injury was not as severe as he had initially thought.

"Sarah, I have tried to be nice to you, and you treat me like that. There is still time for us to get to know each other and enjoy ourselves. Let's try again, but no biting this time." Now that he had calmed down, he was beginning to feel like sex again, but he was not going near her mouth. She had had her chance. Perhaps now they ought to try things in a different way.

Taking his foot off Sarah's neck he grabbed her hair and pulled her up on to her feet and dragged her through into the bedroom where he pushed her onto the bed. Sarah just lay still, terrified of moving in case Ford hit her again.

God, he felt good again, there was nothing quite like a drop of coke for getting a hard on! Ford knew he could party on for some time before he descended from the wonderful feeling now enveloping his body. Sarah was going to enjoy it just as much as he was: it was really just a case of getting her started.

Ford went back into the bathroom and carefully picked up the chrome waste bin and carried it back into the bedroom close to the bed. He sat down on the bed next to Sarah and began tidying up the remaining line of cocaine.

Sarah moaned and turned over so that she was facing Ford. She felt as if her nose was broken and a number of teeth were loose as a result of the treatment from Ford. There was blood over her face and in her hair. Her head ached from where Ford had dragged her backwards along the length of the bath and smashed her head against the tiled wall at either end. She could see what Ford was doing and guessed what he intended doing to her. She realised that she was in no state to resist him.

When he had finished preparing the line of cocaine, Ford looked at Sarah. "I'm sorry I had to hurt you Sarah but you shouldn't have bitten me. You hurt me, but never mind we can get over that problem. Just lay back and enjoy the ride!"

With one hand he again grabbed her hair and held her head down as he moistened a finger on his other hand and dipped into the cocaine. Ford then rubbed the white powder into Sarah's mouth and around her gums to increase the speed of absorption into her body. Almost immediately Sarah felt something strange happening to her, the room was moving. She assumed that she was hallucinating as she glanced around her. Ford was watching her with close interest as she tried hard not to panic. Suddenly she was past the panic point and began to smile at Ford. He saw her reaction change and let her go.

Sarah reached out to him and began to embrace him. Ford moved closer to her and began caressing her breasts. This time she was going to do as she was told. He kissed her and moved his hand down between her legs, parting them so that he had room to enter her.

Sarah was so relaxed by now that she welcomed him into her. She lay back and drew him closer until their sweating bodies began making slurping noises as the perspiration levels increased. Ford was close to reaching the zenith of his powers in normal circumstances, but knew with the amount of cocaine now circulating in his body he could keep going, and he was going to. Sarah had to realise the error of her ways. He gripped her left breast hard and began to squeeze as he increased his pace. He kept one hand free and ready just in case the bitch tried anything.

Beneath him, Sarah felt his hand begin to squeeze her breast and hurt her. She noticed that he had also speeded up and was now effectively ramming into her, she had become nothing more than a battering ram for him. She was now becoming so miserable that she wished he would simply put her out of her misery.

When Ford had finished with Sarah, he rolled over and away from her.

The coke on the waste bin had all been used and he felt he could really do with some more to keep him going, so he emptied the last of the contents of the plastic bag onto the waste bin and formed a further two lines. He looked at Sarah lying on the bed moaning.

"Turn over, I haven't finished yet."

She turned over and lay quite still, hoping that Ford had been sexually satisfied. He crawled across the bed towards her and straddled her. He began massaging her neck and back with strong movements that hurt her. Sarah was deliberately trying not to respond to his cruelty. The walls seemed to be moving; she was sweating and at the same time cold with the fear of what was going to happen. She just hoped it would stop soon and she could go home.

As Ford traversed down her back, she knew where he was going, what he was going to do to her. He moved further back and placed his hands into the top front of Sarah's thighs at the point where they joined her upper body. He dug in and eased her up on to her knees so that her buttocks stretched out and towards him.

He felt her resistance to his actions. The bitch was trying to stop him. The next thing she would want to do is bite his cock again. Would she never learn! Ford hit Sarah in the small of her back causing her to cry out in pain. The blow also caused her to relax her resistance to his determination to position her to his satisfaction. He was still sweating profusely and feeling good as he made his move forward and began ramming into her.

Sarah screamed in agony and passed out.

★ ★ ★ ★

At seven the next morning, Ford showered and dressed ready for the day. He packed his overnight bag and glanced at Sarah still lying on the bloodstained bed. She was either asleep or still unconscious. Ford didn't know which, not that he was bothered. The bitch had got what she deserved. He locked the door to the room on the way out, placing a 'Do Not Disturb' notice on the door handle as he left. At the desk he asked that his wife not be disturbed until at least eleven a.m. as she was enjoying a sleep in, following an active night. He smiled at his choice of words. The receptionist agreed, making a written note on her blotter. She received the generous tip from Ford with a smile.

Ford then made his way to Dieppe for the first available boat back home.

★ ★ ★ ★

At eleven-thirty, the sixteen-year-old cleaning maid on a temporary work contract, pushed the trolley along the passageway and stopped outside the room. A small radio was on top of her trolley and playing a popular tune that she was more or less humming along to. This was the last room to clean before its new occupant booked in at two p.m. She wanted to finish her work schedule as soon as possible in order to create a good impression. She was hoping to become a permanent member of staff in the near future.

She removed the Do Not Disturb notice on the door handle, unlocked the door and opened it enough for her to put her head through and call out. Getting no response to her shout she opened the door wider and backed the trolley into the room. As she closed the door and turned around she saw Sarah Mundey. Her screams alerted the hotel staff who came to see what the fuss was about. The manager took in the bloodstained figure lying unconscious on the bed. He went white at what he saw before him. Then his training kicked in and he took immediate charge of those around him. He cleared the room and then went around the bed and placed two fingers on Sarah's neck. He was surprised to find a faint but consistent pulse.

Ford sat back in the chair and looked out of the ship's window. The weather was good and it was a calm crossing. He sipped his *Costa* coffee and thought how lucky he was. He had sorted out the problem at Andre's farm and now knew who the intruder was. He also had a good overnight with the tart he had chatted up at the port on the way out. It was a shame that she tried to bite his cock off, but that was life. He had made her pay for that, the bitch! He was coming down now from the cocaine-fuelled last evening, but he had enjoyed himself, no doubt about that. Life was so fucking good!

Down below on the vehicle deck a random check of vehicle registration plates included Ford's Range Rover. The list was completed and taken to the Purser's office where all the numbers taken were checked via a telephone link with the Police National Computer.

Customs Investigators at Newhaven Port were in place when the ship berthed and disgorged all the passengers including those with vehicles. They were waiting for the only vehicle to have shown a positive result following the PNC check. Ford's vehicle was photographed coming off the ship and also as he left the port. He appeared relaxed and unaware as he made his way back to London.

Chapter Twenty-Seven

Detective Sergeant Jon Snow looked out of the window at SOCA HQ at the cherry tree planted about ten feet from the edge of the building. The blossom had long since gone, and now even the leaves were starting to curl at the edges heralding a change in the season ahead. He was thinking about the computer information from Newhaven Port officers that had arrived for him this morning. Snow opened a filing cabinet and withdrew a large file which he placed on his desk. Much of the detail within the file he knew by heart. He had spent enough time reading it to have committed much of it to memory, so he went to the last piece of information that related to Ford's departure from Folkestone Port. So, the bastard has now returned home, he thought. Snow looked again at the information.

Ford had left Folkestone Port on his own on the way out, and had returned alone via Newhaven. Why come back that way. Why not do a simple out and back in via the same port? he wondered. It was a deliberate action, for some reason as of yet unknown. And where was Sarah Mundey? What was his connection with her?

After having checked him going out, Sarah had left the papers on her desk. She had last been seen leaving the ship in Boulogne in something of a hurry and jumping into a Range Rover that appeared to be waiting for her. There was no doubt in Snow's mind that it was Ford's Range Rover that Sarah had jumped into, although nobody could say that for certain. It was too much of a coincidence, there had to be a connection. But what on earth was she doing?

She was fairly new to the job but the Intel she had sent to Snow had included Ford's previous convictions so she knew what sort of bastard he was. Why had she not sought advice before embarking on this trip with Ford? Did she simply go with Ford for a leg over weekend or was there something more to it? Time would tell, he thought.

Snow picked up the telephone and called Newhaven Port and spoke to a colleague. He requested a check be made of the ship's manifest, just in case Sarah was on board for the journey back to UK, but did not want to be seen with Ford. He hung on until told that there was no trace of Sarah on the ship. One of the team of Customs photographers knew Sarah and was able say that she certainly did not leave the port in Ford's Range Rover. Ford was on his own as he left the port.

Snow sat and thought about matters and decided that there was no point circulating details of the Ford brothers and the missing Sarah Mundey. All it would do was to bring the Ford brothers once again to the attention of all intelligence agencies and might cause work-hungry ferrets to start sniffing around and work their own system to find out why the Fords were of ever-increasing interest to Customs investigators. It was a strange old world, thought Snow, because not always were they all on the same side. Some were very competitive, some were very parochial and some were just plain jealous of another agency's expertise and success. Rivalry was a good thing most of the time, but sometimes it had the power to be destructive.

Frustrated at not being able to find a connection that would link all the outstanding questions now running through his brain, Snow telephoned Emil Kimber. He caught Kimber on the hop.

Kimber was at his desk studying the latest list of promotions. His name was not on the list, and that was something he simply could not understand. Many who were on the list were little more than uniform carriers and unworthy of the next rank!

Kimber's desk was overflowing with paperwork and gave the impression to any visitor (as it was supposed to) that he was a very busy person. Kimber picked up the telephone and silently groaned when he realised who it was on the other end of the line.

"What can I do for you Jon?" he asked.

"Just listen, Emil, that is all." Snow related the story so far about Ford's visit into France and the missing Customs investigator, Sarah Mundey. "Has there been any update from Ridge concerning the Fords?"

Kimber sighed. "Not so far as I am aware. Between you and me, I think Ridge has shot his bolt on this one. I am thinking of taking over the reins, just to give the investigation a little impetus!"

Snow quickly responded, advising Kimber against changing informant handlers midway into an investigation. It was critical to keep continuity when the informant was up and running. Snow felt the job would be at risk if Kimber went down that road and, apart from that, he personally felt that Kimber was not a good enough police detective to succeed. You needed a ferret, someone who could sniff out the facts and manipulate the informant to his advantage. Ridge could do that. Kimber couldn't.

Kimber listened and was hurt at Snow's comments. "Okay," he said, "I'll leave a memo for Ridge advising him of your comments."

He was about to replace the telephone, when Snow jumped in. "Emil, it is no good just leaving a memo for the man who might know something or might be able to move things on. You must get hold of him now and see if he can help us. On top of everything, we have an officer missing on duty: we need to take that very seriously if she is connected with Ford in anyway."

Kimber didn't like being told that his memos were not the answer. He didn't much like Snow anyway and as for the missing female, well, that was their problem, not his.

Snow picked up the vibes coming down the telephone line. "Emil, the situation demands that Ridge should be appraised as to what has occurred and requested to make urgent enquires to see if he can add anything. I am sure he will be pleased to help move this on anyway, do you agree?"

"I hear what you say Jon and I will pursue that angle as soon as I can. In the meantime is there anything else I can help you with?"

Snow realised that, in police jargon, he was now being told to fuck off. He expressed his thanks and hung up.

Once Snow was clearly disconnected from him, Kimber still held onto the telephone and began shouting obscenities down the line while he punched an imaginary person. He continued with this verbal abuse for several minutes, completely unaware that his detective inspector was watching him through the hole-in-the-wall window that separated Ridge's office from his sergeant's office.

"Is everything all right, Emil?" he asked, trying not to smile and not really interested in what Kimber had to say anyway.

Kimber, wearing a startled look on his face a bit like a child caught out doing something he shouldn't, gathered his composure. "Everything is fine boss. Just some annoying fucker who thinks he is cleverer than me, would you believe!"

"No, Emil, I wouldn't believe that at all!" With that Johnston walked off before he got further involved with Kimber.

Watching him go, Kimber smirked. He decided he was going to keep things to himself and not keep passing on progress reports. That way he could better control events to his advantage.

★ ★ ★ ★

Peter Jameson, a senior police investigator of about twenty years, looked up from his desk and out through the glass window and into the general office. He could see Jon Snow's desk and Snow sitting in the chair. It seemed to Jameson that Snow was engaged in one of those telephone conversations that all investigators are used to where the person on the other end is not altogether helpful. He saw Snow replace the handset in its cradle.

Snow was engrossed in thought when his supervisor walked past and noticed his look of intense concentration. "Okay there Jon?" he asked. "You look as if you are carrying the world's problems."

Snow looked up. "Yes, fine Guv. I have just telephoned that wanker Kimber in Sussex: talk about bullshit. He is so far up his own arse that he can't see whether it's day or night!"

Jameson smiled. Peter Jameson, a senior detective with SOCA and about twenty years police experience, looked up from his desk and out through the glass window and into the general office. He could see Jon Snow's desk and Snow sitting in the chair. It seemed to Jameson that Snow was engaged in one of those telephone conversations that all investigators are used where the person on the other end of the line is not altogether helpful. He watched as Snow replaced the handset in its cradle. Snow was engrossed in thought when his supervisor walked over to him. "Okay there Jon?" he asked. "You look as if you are carrying the world's problems on your shoulders."Snow looked up. " Yes, fine Guv. I have just telephoned that wanker Kimber in Sussex; talk about bullshit! He is so far up his own arse that he can't see whether its day or night. Jameson smiled. "Jon, with Sarah Mundey missing, this job now takes on a more serious aspect, and we must all be seen to be assisting our friends in the Customs. If anyone on our team is dragging their feet in assisting Customs, let me know. I want Sarah Mundey back in one piece, anything else is a bonus.

"I've got it, boss! So far so good, I will speak to Ridge in Sussex ASAP. I think he may want to assist us once he knows the score."

Just to give Snow that little bit of extra power and support, Jameson said, "Jon, I think you ought to go down to Folkestone tomorrow and glean what you can and then sort out that lot in Sussex just in case they are dragging their feet. If you need me to ring anybody, just ask. I have a few friends in that Force?"

Snow smiled at this attempt to empower him. "Thank you, boss. I will get on to it!"

Chapter Twenty-Eight

Ridge walked into his empty office and made a start on clearing the e-mails that had come in since his last check. It was almost impossible to keep up with the flow of daily information that lay in wait for him. The vast majority of info coming from either people or e-mails was likely to end up being not that useful to him as a field officer, but nevertheless was still useful to know of because of the larger picture. He knew from the mass of info, somewhere there might be a little gem waiting for him to spot and lead him to his next job. He smiled as he realised that he didn't want too many little gems. There now wasn't the time to play with them and to bring them to fruition.

What Ridge did not know was that one little gem was not there for him to view. Emil Kimber had whipped into the office early that morning and opened up Ridge's incoming messages and forwarded an e-mail from Snow the SOCA Investigator to Ridge, to his own inbox and then removed any trace of it as an incoming e-mail.

As Ridge scanned his list of messages, he printed some and made short notes on the paper before placing them in his in-tray.

He became aware of Kimber at the office window watching him. He looked up at Kimber, who then walked from his office next door to Ridge. He bent over the desk and said in a conspiratorial voice, "Have you heard from your informant recently?"

"Which one?" queried Ridge, trying not to smile.

"Ford, of course," Kimber said, sensing he was being teased.

Ridge slowly sat up in his chair and put down his pen. "The last time you and I spoke, I rather felt that you and the detective inspector were going to deal with Ford, without recourse to myself. As far as I am concerned that still stands."

Kimber knew his bluff was being called. He tried to salvage what he could. "Well," he spluttered, "that most certainly is the case. The leadership needed to control this man will emanate from the detective inspector and myself, but I don't think either of us would be adverse to you receiving a call from him on the odd occasion."

"Why are you asking? Has something happened that either of you can't deal with?" Ridge asked, sensing from Kimber's attitude that he knew something that he didn't.

Kimber was trapped and knew it. He pretended the question had not been asked and stood up straight, which was a sure-fire giveaway to Ridge.

"I want you to establish contact with your informant and ascertain whether he is up to anything at this time. It would be useful to know what he was doing over the last couple of days and if he is shacking up with anyone particular at this moment in time!"

Ridge looked at Kimber's face. He always thought that Kimber's face betrayed his brain. You could always see what he was thinking. The man could never be a poker player!

"I'll see what I can do," he said, somewhat graciously. "In the meantime, could you sign my expenses for the last time I saw him. For some reason they are still sitting on your desk!"

Kimber, who had delayed payment of expenses for everyone in the office in order to reduce the monthly office expenditure, realised that he was unlikely to get any cooperation from Ridge, or anyone else in the office for that matter, unless there was a little give and take, agreed by nodding his head. He then walked out the office.

Ridge watched him go and then shut the office window and door. He dialled Charles Ford's mobile number.

Ford answered the telephone and Ridge said, "Can you talk?" He always opened up his telephone calls to Ford without introductions of any sort, just in case.

You couldn't be too careful, the last thing he wanted was someone close enough to Ford to overhear what was being said between them.

"Yes it's okay," Ford replied.

"Where are you? The line sounds faint?"

"At home, I've just had a busy weekend, so I'm a bit tired even at this time in the morning. Why do you ask?"

"No reason," Ridge said.

"Have you been away this weekend?" Ford asked, trying to make it sound a casual, everyday type of question.

Ridge sensed that the way Ford phrased the question sounded as if he expected a particular answer. He saw no reason to hold back. In fact it might just speed things up a bit if Ford needed to update Ridge and hadn't, and suspected that Ridge knew he hadn't. He must push Ford a little each time they met or talked on the telephone.

"As it happens, yes, I did have a couple of days away. I managed to get a couple of bottles of duty-free as well. All in all, a nice little break."

Ford knew that they had started to play a game and that both of them knew something they were not telling the other, but hoping to coax whatever it was from the other one. He needed to keep Ridge onside if Ridge was to do precisely what was wanted.

"I need to see you soon. There have been developments," Ford said.

Ridge felt pleased. Ford was a tricky bastard. Ridge had found through his police service that dealing with informants was often a thought provoking business. Almost always you had to keep a step in front of them and be able to check their information, and at the same time keep watch for a competitive streak, where at some stage they would try their best to deceive you and lead you up the garden path over some small matter just to prove they were cleverer than you. He thought Ford was in that grey area now and wondered why was he doing it?

They agreed to meet the next day at two p.m. Ridge put down the telephone.

Ridge knew that by rights he ought to inform Emil Kimber of the arrangement, but he decided to keep it to himself for the time being. He was not a great believer in telling all those who thought they had a God-given right to know. After all, loose talk costs lives, as they used to say during the First World War!

Ridge opened the window in the wall to see if Kimber was in his office. He wasn't. Ridge closed the window and returned to his desk.

★ ★ ★ ★

The canteen lady was a young, good looking girl of about twenty-five years of age. She manoeuvred the trolley in through the doorway and paused. "John, do you want tea or coffee?"

Ridge looked at her breasts as she bent down and picked up the milk jug from the lower shelf. They were like two juicy melons waiting to be caressed.

"Coffee, please, Julie, no sugar or milk."

Julie filled up a mug with the coffee until the liquid was level with the top of the mug. She went to place the hot coffee on to the top of Ridge's desk, but wasn't really watching what she was doing so the mug was not level when it touched the wooden desk top. As a direct consequence of this inattention, a tsunami-like wave of steaming hot coffee overlapped the top of the mug and ran down its side, spilling on to Ridge's desk and soaking the nearest file.

"Sorry," Julie said, as she mopped up some of the spillage. She bent forward over the desk, and again Ridge felt forced to look at her breasts. "Watch your back," she said, conspiratorially, "I overheard Hansel and Gretel yesterday, talking about taking over a job you're dealing with."

Ridge smiled at her names for Kimber and Johnston. Again he studied her breasts and recalled the last time that they were a lot closer and he had examined them at first hand, so to speak. "Thanks for the advice Julie. I know what they are waiting to do. But, I'm ready for them this time!"

"Just thought I would warn you, that's all." She turned the trolley about and left the office.

Ridge looked at the coffee mug on his desk. The coffee had found its own level. On the surface, it was a mid-brown, muddy colour with what looked like an oil slick appearance to it. It reminded him of the sort of coffee that you got in those large tins for a fiver from the nearest *Asda* or *Morrisons*, some coffee but more than its fair share of coffee dust. Ridge lifted the mug carefully and tipped some of the contents down the flat metal grille on the windowsill before placing the mug on the nearest desk to the door.

Ridge never saw Kimber again that day. He left the office at five-thirty and went straight home.

Marie was in the kitchen preparing the evening meal. His daughter was also in the kitchen. As he stood in the kitchen trying to make conversation with Marie, Ridge sensed something was not quite right, but his mind was distracted by the sound of Sasha running into the kitchen from the lounge.

She ran straight to Ridge and threw herself at him. He caught her and swung her around in a circle. When he stopped she seized his hand and dragged him through in to the lounge. She was completely oblivious that a conversation had been taking place. In the lounge Sasha made Ridge sit down. She picked up her favourite book and perching on Ridge's knee began to read to him. The reading was not very coherent to anybody listening, but the kid was doing the best she could to get her tongue around words that were either completely new to her or words that she had known but had fallen into disuse when she became deaf. The pitch of her voice rose and fell over most words and sometimes she faltered over the construction of sentences. But she kept going right to the end of the story. When she had finished, Ridge spun her round so she was facing him and moved backwards from her in order that she could not only see he lips but his complete face as well. Translating facial expression supported her lip-reading skills. Speaking just a little slower than his normal pace Ridge told Sasha how much he had enjoyed the story. She focused on his face and lips and took in most of what he had said. She smiled in the shy way that she had, and immediately picked out another story for her granddad. When she wanted to read, Sasha did so with great enthusiasm. Her listeners, whoever they were, just required a little patience.

Ridge was amazed at Sasha's progress. It was hard work most of the time but Sasha had a good team behind her at Addenbrooke's Hospital in Cambridge and at home. All the family members did their bit and she was well supported at her school in the village of Ovingdean. All in all, Ridge thought, Sasha was a very lucky girl. Things could have been so much worse. He shuddered at the thought.

After tea with the family Ridge took his daughter and Sasha home. On his return, he changed into his running gear and went for a run.

Chapter Twenty-Nine

Ford was waiting for him in the coffee shop. He was sipping from a large latte and seemed his usual smiling, self-confident self. He was sitting with his back to the wall so that he could watch the traffic in and out of the shop. The waitress arrived and showed Ridge a table near the back of the shop which suited him fine. He was able to watch the entrance way. She took his order and left. Their eyes met and a slight nod came from Ford who then got up from his seat and, carrying his latte, joined Ridge just as his Americano was delivered. Ridge surveyed his coffee, found it to his liking and turned his attention to Ford. The whole procedure of their meeting had taken a few minutes longer than it would normally have done, but they were both careful and well aware that they could be under surveillance by people from either side.

Ford offered his hand in the usual way. His grip was firm, but there was a slight sweatiness to his palm.

"What's happening Charles, are events occurring with our friends across the water?"

"We have now selected a day to move the gear in France." Ford looked directly at Ridge as he spoke. "It will be the Saturday after next. I thought I would let you know in time for your lot to get organised."

Ridge stared back at Ford who was now scanning the shop area. "Have you been across the water?" he asked, noticing a slight shiny sweat line on Ford's forehead.

"I've just got back. I had a couple of days over there with a friend to get things ready for the move and to check out a problem that occurred earlier in the week."

Ridge laughed to cover his next comment. "Do you mean your brothers?"

"No." Ford sipped his coffee. "A small hitch where the lorry is that's all."

"What are the ferry timings and the port in question?" Ridge asked, not wanting to expand Ford's line of conversation. The less Ford knew of his activities the better.

"It's Dover, of course on a Saturday as I said. We picked a busy day, so we anticipate that the lorry normally would just be waved through. I haven't got the sailing times yet, but I can phone those through as soon as I know them."

"What about the driver, is he armed?"

"No. He will not carry. There is no need, it's a drive-through."

"What about the driver, does he know what he is carrying or has he just been bought for the day's drive?" Ridge asked, noticing that the level of perspiration on Ford's forehead was increasing.

Ford was again scanning the coffee lounge. He smiled at Ridge. "He is being paid a couple of grand extra to drive the gear through so, yes, he does know what he is carrying."

"Where's the home location?"

Ford seemed to pause as if unsure of what to say. "I don't know that yet either, but I will soon," he lied.

Ridge showed a touch of irritation. "Charles, are you fucking me about over this. There seems a lot you don't know about this job? Why don't you know the location? Better still, you must know the location. Why aren't you telling me? How the fuck can I set anything up when I don't know the times of the start and finish. Come on Charles, don't fuck me about!"

Ford looked hurt at the accusations from Ridge. "The moment I know, you will too," he protested. "I can only give you what I have got. The times that I haven't got are agreed at the present time, but are subject to change at a moment's notice. You would complain if I told you one thing and then next day it was changed. Be patient. Once I am sure, you will have everything, trust me!"

"Okay," Ridge said, "I accept what you say. But what about the vehicle registration number, that is a constant factor throughout, you must have that?"

Ford reached into his breast pocket and withdrew a piece of paper with some numbers written on it. He passed the paper across the table to Ridge. "There you go!" he exclaimed. "What else?"

Ridge looked at the piece of paper. "Okay," he said, "I can at least research this number. It won't come back to you will it?"

"Not a chance," smiled Ford. "By the way, just so you know, the lorry is an artic. The gear will be in the back of the vehicle; inside the refrigeration unit. The lorry has a refridge unit with a false compartment riveted in place. There are over five hundred rivets in the compartment to make it look good. Once the gear was put in place and the compartment riveted to seal it, the compartment was then sprayed with a specially aged paint that blends well with the colour of the surrounding paint. It's quite well done and is unlikely to be spotted unless a major search is undertaken and the paint scraped off the rivets."

Ridge was thinking about the vehicle. It seemed too easy. "I assume that you are going to travel through the port on a Saturday because of reduced Customs teams on duty?"

"It's amazing isn't it?" Ford said. "Customs still assume that weekend travel is for the mass weekend traveller and that most smugglers would use either

Monday or Tuesday, thinking they were quiet days, when the reverse is true. Smugglers want to mix with the ordinary punters. They want to get lost in a crowd. Although I am not sure of the times yet, you can bet on a morning crossing. It's a short distance from the farm to the port. The driver would want to do the port in one hit. It's too risky stopping on the road overnight."

Ridge was listening to his friend expanding on the detail. It was as if he was warming up and had more to talk about. In principle it seemed straightforward enough.

Ford sipped the latte and watched Ridge for any reaction. "Once at the port, the lorry will go through as normal, but get called from the mainstream into the bay for a quick check. If you have a dick with a growler doing the check, then the growler should, by rights, not pick up a scent. But the dick can make it appear that the dog has and then demand a full check. Is that the way you see things taking place John?"

"Yes, something like that. The lorry will be in line as it approaches the check bay so it will be simple enough to stop the lorry. The driver will not suspect anything other than a normal stop-check situation."

Ford sat up and glanced around. Satisfied he leaned over. "Whatever happens John, this vehicle must be stopped and checked, and must not leave the port, is that understood?"

Ridge thought over what Ford had just said. He was beginning to smell a rat. Something was not quite right, but what was not right? Why was Ford insistent that the lorry not be allowed to leave the port?

Once he had the ferry times it was cut and dried. They could not go wrong. The Customs dog handlers would play their part as they had done a thousand times before; yes, it was all going to be easy, maybe too easy.

"It sounds good enough to me," Ridge lied. "I have spoken to my bosses and they have agreed that once the lorry and driver have been detained and the cocaine found on board, you will be paid the cash sum of twenty thousand pounds and no questions asked. Okay?"

Ford grinned. "That sounds good to me John. That way we both get what we want."

Ridge felt his telephone buzz him. He looked at the screen. "Charles, I must run, I need to meet my glorious leaders in town. As soon as you have that info let me have it, I will need to start telling people what to do before much longer. Let's make it work between us!"

He stood up and offered his hand to Ford and shook hands with him. Ridge noticed that Ford's hand was still sweating. They parted company, each going in a different direction, both using nearby shop windows to check for surveillance. It was only when Ford was seated on the Tube on the Northern Line that he realised that he had forgotten to ask Ridge if he was the man at the farm in France. He cursed himself.

Chapter Thirty

The French emergency medical services were very efficient. Within minutes of the hotel manager calling them they were on the scene. The two medics got to work and examined Sarah Mundey. It was clear to them that she had been subjected to a severe beating and had been sexually used. The traces of a white powder on her mouth were also clear evidence of some drug participation, voluntary or otherwise. The lead medic checked Sarah's pupils with a small torch and got little reaction to the bright light. She was not responding to any questions he quietly put to her. Sarah's body arched from time to time in a jerky uncontrollable way. The medics did what they could at the scene before taking Sarah to the local hospital.

The French police who turned up at the hotel were uniformed officers. They studied the scene for a few moments and realised that the situation was beyond their skills. They called in and requested assistance.

Twenty minutes later two detectives arrived and began a thorough search of Sarah's belongings. Sarah's handbag was searched and her warrant card tucked away behind the lining was found. Suddenly, the incident took on a new perspective. One of the detectives picked up his telephone and spoke to his detective inspector, Raoul Bernand. Bernand listened for a few moments before dropping everything. He arrived at the hotel within minutes and took charge. Bernand had with him a forensic team who immediately set to work to examine every square inch of the room. The injured woman could wait. She was in safe hands at the hospital. Bernand telephoned his police station and ordered an armed guard be placed outside Sarah's hospital room and await her recovering consciousness. No person, other than medical staff, were allowed access to her.

Once satisfied that the investigation of the room was underway, Bernand returned to his office and collected his thoughts. He picked up the telephone and made the telephone call to Sarah's office and asked to be put in touch with the senior officer on duty. The senior Customs officer at the Port of Folkestone, James Brownlow, listened as one of his French-speaking subordinates, Robin Green, translated the conversation he was having with Bernand. Brownlow looked flushed and angry.

"What is Sarah's current state of health and when can she be repatriated back home?" he asked Green.

Green relayed Brownlow's question over the telephone in perfect French. He listened for a few moments and repeated part of it. He then turned to Brownlow. "Sarah is still unconscious in hospital but is expected to surface soon. No decision on moving her will be taken until the surgeon has a chance to satisfy himself that she is well enough to be moved."

Brownlow lit his pipe and sucked it. "Make arrangements for someone to go over to France tomorrow and take charge of that end. Someone who speaks the language would be useful."

Green spoke into the telephone and made the necessary arrangements and then replaced the telephone.

"The French see this as an English problem rather than a French one. But this Bernand chap has said he will give us whatever co-operation we want, we just have to ask."

Brownlow looked at Green. "Robin, you are now the senior investigating officer in charge of this case. Take over the boardroom and co-opt as many staff as you need. Clearly there will be an internal investigation over Sarah's involvement in this and how she came by her injuries, but that can wait. Our priority is simple. We find the person or persons who have caused her injuries. Sarah is one of us. No one is going to get away with this."

Robin Green had never seen his boss like this. He was clearly a good man to have on your side. He was quite certain that Brownlow would move heaven and earth to resolve this job to his personal satisfaction. Green left the room to set up the crime office from where they would all work.

Twenty minutes later Green was summoned back to Brownlow's office.

"Sit down Robin," Brownlow said. "I've just been on the phone to Adam Brown the Kent Police Special Branch man here at the port. I want him on your team as of now. He has told me that a man tried to talk to Sarah as he booked his ticket to travel to France. He was travelling on his own in a Range Rover. He has been identified because Sarah, bless her, was a tad suspicious." Brownlow peered at some notes on the desk pad. "The man's name is Charles Ford. Something about this fellow caused Sarah to ask Adam Brown to do a full check at New Scotland Yard. Apparently this man is something of a drug smuggler."

As Brownlow was speaking the desktop computer bleeped. Brownlow looked at the screen for a second or two and then pressed the printer button. A number of sheets of printed paper spread over the lip of the machine on to the desktop. Four of the sheets contained Ford's criminal record, the last two was a summary of events from Brown outlining Sarah's actions as far he was aware of them.

The two men studied the papers. Brownlow looked up at Green. "What is the girl like?"

Green considered the question. "She is new to the job, hasn't been with us for long, she is attractive and a bit of a babe magnet to put on the gate at the port. She is, I'm told, very keen to get on apparently. She is trying to get onto the drug squad."

Brownlow sucked on his pipe. "It looks as if she has the right skills that we need. She has made all the running on this man so far. It looks to me that she has gone a little overboard and got snapped up by the lions. First rule of the jungle Robin: the fucking lions can bite!"

"Yes, it does look as if she has not sought supervisory advice before slinking off duty and joining up with this man Ford for her own ends. That is a disciplinary matter for sure."

Brownlow saw where this was going. He put up his hand. "Robin, whether Sarah sought advice is neither here nor there. Any detective worth their salt would probably have done the same thing."

He picked up his pipe and began fiddling with it. "Robin, I look at it like this: Sarah Mundey is a member of our team here at the port. For whatever reason some fucking shitbag has seen fit to take her to a foreign country and then treat her in a most deplorable way. I am extremely pissed off that has happened to one of my team. I think it high time that this man Ford and anyone else with him are made aware that there are other members of Sarah's team who do not take kindly to this type of behaviour. Do I make myself clear?"

Robin Green swallowed hard amazed at the older man's controlled anger. "Clear as crystal boss. Now if I can have those sheets of paper I will get on with the setting-up process." He stood up, gathered the notes and left the room.

Brownlow picked up the telephone and spoke to Sarah Mundey's parents about their only child.

Chapter Thirty-One

The next morning, shortly after nine-fifteen, Jon Snow walked into the office at Folkestone Port. He went straight in to the Intelligence Office and spotted Robin Green.

"Just the man," Green said. "I was going to call you later on. We need your help."

Snow opened his briefcase and pulled out a large file. "That's good, because I need your help as well. Let's have a coffee and see where we go?"

Green made the coffee and they sat down at a nearby table. The window offered a good view out over the sea, of ships and boats of all sizes and makes pushing their way out past the harbour points to the open sea.

Green did as he normally did; he sipped his very hot coffee before saying a word. Satisfied that all was well with the coffee, he looked at Snow. "Jon, as of yesterday, we are running an incident room here at the port. One of our staff members, Sarah Mundey, is involved and is the principal subject of the investigation. She went missing from duty a few days ago with, we think, an Englishman.

"The next thing we know is that the French Police are ringing us from a small town called Béthune, I believe, saying that Sarah has been found. It seems that during her time in France she stayed at a small hotel in Béthune with the same Englishman. When Sarah was found in the bedroom of the hotel by the hotel cleaner she was unconscious and on her own. There was no trace of the Englishman.

Sarah is currently in a French hospital suffering from severe body injuries which include rape and sodomy. From the information that is available to us at the present time, we think the Englishman she was with is responsible for her present condition and we will pursue that line of enquiry until we know differently. Traces of cocaine were found on Sarah's mouth, so it is fair to assume that drugs were consumed by her during her time at the hotel. At the present time we have set up an incident room and are getting a team together. There is a forensic unit crossing over the water today together with a welfare unit officer to look after Sarah.

We obviously want Sarah home as soon as possible, but it won't be for a few days. I was looking to ask you to come on the team, Jon? With your contacts in town, you could save us a lot of wasted time and effort."

"Okay, that's fine. My boss will agree with anything like that. So as of tomorrow, I will be attached to your unit full-time."

Green sat back. "That's a relief Jon; Brownlow is spitting blood over this. He is on my back wanting a result yesterday. He is taking it very personally about this young girl Sarah Mundey. If that bastard Ford was in custody now, I'm sure that he would be in the cell block knocking seven bells out of him."

John Snow looked at Green with his mouth open. "What!" he exclaimed. "Did you say Ford?"

Green saw the reaction and smiled. "Yes, we think the offender is a man called Charles Ford, why?"

"That's the bastard I came here to see you about this morning."

Green showed Snow the printout from Adam Brown and then Ford's criminal convictions.

Snow could feel his blood racing. He compared his notes with the notes of Adam Brown. Finally he said, "Yes, it is the same Charles Ford. Robin, it's cards on the table time. Ford is of interest to us at SOCA, because he is part of a team: the others in the team are his two brothers, Paul and Peter Ford. All three are shortly going to import a very large quantity of cocaine into to this country via one of the ports. Some of the details are a bit vague at the present time, but it is ongoing. You say that Sarah is still in a Frog hospital?"

"Yes. She will be there for a few days yet."

Snow thought for a moment. "Robin, we need to get across the water and speak to her as soon as she is fit. Sarah may very well be holding the answers to a number of questions that we have. Clearly the matters are related, so what happens now? Can we, you and I, go over and sort this out tomorrow?"

Pleased as Punch that Snow was on his side and had already contributed to the investigation, Robin Green was quick to agree with any course of action suggested by him. Green went to advise Brownlow of the giant step forward they had just taken.

Brownlow looked up and sensed Green's excitement. "Get Snow in here," he said.

Green rushed out and found Snow making his arrangements for the next day. "Quick, the old man wants to see you."

They both returned to Brownlow's office and were offered a seat. Brownlow fiddled with his pipe, although he didn't light up. He looked directly at Snow. "I understand that you have been very helpful to my team investigating the Sarah Mundey saga?"

Jon Snow saw the trap opening up before him. "Yes sir, this job has shown up a common interest. I feel sure that if we get together on this, both our ends will be served in a very good way."

Brownlow tightened the noose a little closer. "Yes," he said and pointed his fingertips together. He pursed his lips. "You already have details and information concerning this man Ford, the main suspect in our job?" He paused and looked over the top of his glasses, waiting for an answer.

"Yes," Snow said guardedly, "that's right. We are working now on an importation of cocaine involving this man and others. We think the importation is due to take place soon." Snow paused, waiting for the sixty-four thousand dollar question.

Brownlow, still maintaining an air of almost innocence, then said what Snow was waiting, if not dreading, to hear.

"Who is your informant on this job?"

Snow went silent. Then he made his decision. Looking square on at Brownlow, Snow said, "With the greatest possible respect, sir, I am not at liberty to reveal that. The source on any job we deal with has to be registered, so the identity of this informant is known to my superiors, but I can't tell you who it is. However, what I can tell you is that I will work day and night with your team to help resolve this matter involving the Ford brothers." He paused.

Brownlow slowly smiled at Snow. "I thought you would say that. Help us get a good result on this job and I will buy the first round." The tension in the room fell away as they shook hands. "Welcome to the team Jon."

★ ★ ★ ★

The next day before leaving on the ferry, Snow telephoned his boss and gave him a full update. He also asked for a conference to be arranged for the next day at SOCA HQ involving Sussex and in particular John Ridge. That done, he left with Robin Green and travelled to Boulogne.

They were met on the quayside by local Customs officers and French police officers. Once the inevitable handshaking had taken place the police whisked them off to the hospital where Sarah Mundey was a patient. They were shown to her room where she lay in bed. Green and Snow sat down in chairs nearby and watched her stir. She seemed to sense someone in the room and opened both her eyes. Her eyes were black and swollen as was much of her face. It was obvious to Snow that talking to Sarah was not going to be as easy as he had thought it would be. Green saw the problem with talking to her as well. He leaned forward over the bed, his face close to Sarah's. "Sarah," he said quietly, "we need to ask you some questions. If you cannot answer, just nod yes or no."

Green sat back and gave her a minute or two to adjust her thinking pattern. He identified himself and Snow to Sarah and explained why they had travelled to France to talk with her. Green took time to assure Sarah that she was not in any trouble herself. She nodded as if relieved. Green looked at Snow, giving him the first question. Snow bent forward. "Sarah, the cocaine that was found in your system, was that taken voluntarily?"

She shook her head and began to cry as the memory of that moment came back to her.

213

Green held her hand. "Don't worry Sarah, I am going to sort this out for you."

She gripped his hand and squeezed twice. Sarah suddenly found the strength to raise her head just off the pillow. She licked her lips and in a quiet voice started to talk. "No, I didn't want the stuff, and then he started hitting me in the face. I was in the bath at the time. He banged my head against the wall as he dragged me out of the bath and onto the bed. He rubbed some coke into my mouth and then started hitting me again." Sarah paused unable to continue. Snow poured her a drink of water and brushed her lips with it. He then supported her head and gently helped her drink from the glass. "He forced me to take it. Then he raped me, I think twice without stopping." Again she paused as the memory returned. Sarah quietly sobbed for nearly ten minutes before she took another small drink and continued talking. "The bastard raped me and beat me because I wouldn't do what he wanted." Sarah cried again.

Green leaned forward close to her. "Sarah, it is all over now. We want you to get better and come home soon."

Snow intervened. "Just one last question Sarah. Did Ford take you anywhere special while you were together?"

Sarah, looking slightly brighter, considered the question. "No. He dumped me in a shopping centre near La Basse and went off by himself."

"How long was he away?"

"About a couple of hours I think." She paused and began sobbing.

Green and Snow agreed to call it a day not wanting to distress Sarah any more. They made their apologies to the nurse in charge and left. They both noticed that the armed guard was still in place outside Sarah's room.

The officers quickly briefed the French police who nodded sympathetically as the conversation came to an end. Once clear of the French police and other listening ears Snow turned to Green. "I know that Sarah is a member of your service, but I tell you now Robin, I am going to fuck Mr Ford one way or another. There was no need for him to treat the girl like that. For Christ's sake he beat her up, force-fed her cocaine and then, not satisfied with that, he fucked her a number of times. She will never get over it that's for sure. He will pay for that."

Robin Green looked at his friend. "Let's light the biggest bonfire of all time under Mr Ford," he said, unable to shake the memory of Sarah's badly injured body from his mind.

Chapter Thirty-Two

Charles Ford, back home following his trip to France, sat back in his armchair and took another large mouthful of duty-free whisky from the cut glass tumbler. He enjoyed a glass of whisky especially after snorting a line of coke. It sort of settled the senses, seemingly encouraging the blood to race around the body in a never-ending chase until it seemed to fade away of its own accord. It was a gentle return to normality as he processed the information that he was in possession of.

He knew deep down that it was Ridge who had been spotted at the farm in France. The one thing he could not understand was how he had got past that fucking enormous growler. The bloody dog was quite capable of ripping the throat out of any intruder if it wanted to. He must ask Ridge about that when this job was over. The big question that now concerned him was: should he tell his brothers?

Paul, he knew, would become enraged at the thought of a copper sniffing around one of his jobs. He was likely to consider the job at risk at this stage and might even want to postpone all activity until he thought it safe to continue. Paul's idea of 'safe to continue' was in all probability to get his shotgun out and deal with Ridge and anyone else for that matter in the only way he knew how, extreme violence.

Charles was only too well aware that Paul had taken that course with a man in Turkey whom he suspected was about to grass him up. As it happened, he was wrong, but that didn't seem to bother Paul.

Charles shuddered at the memory of that moment. He was with Paul talking to the man, when Paul suddenly opened up and shot the man at close range in the chest. Blood shot everywhere. Over them and, worse still, up the side of the vehicle they were about to move. The man was blown back against the side of the lorry, with three quarters of his chest missing, much of it stuck to the side of the lorry. They had to drag the body away and hide it in a skip. Then they hosed down the lorry before they were able to move it away from the scene.

On the other hand, Peter would want something done. Like Paul he would consider it risky not to do something about Ridge. Although Peter was a little more subtle than Paul, he still had the family tendency towards violence as the first option rather than the last.

On the last job coming from Cartagena, Peter heard that a Met undercover officer was seen sniffing around the house when he was doing his bit importing a number of Pakistanis into central London. Later the same week Peter became aware that he was being followed one night when he had the said six Pakistanis in the van. He did no more than stop the vehicle by the side of the nearest telephone box and call the police on the three nines. Using a falsetto voice he complained that he was being followed by what looked like a team of robber's intent on robbing him. The police bought the complete story and advised Peter to drive on until he came to the roundabout near Blackfriars Bridge, where they would be waiting. As Peter flew around the roundabout with the van still full of Pakistanis sliding from one side of the van to the other, he saw three marked police cars box in the surveillance car and force it to stop. Peter, by now laughing out loud, was soon lost in the side streets with his live cargo still intact.

Charles Ford knew that he had no choice other than to tell his brothers about Ridge. Fuck Ridge, he thought. He should keep his nose out and not cause me problems. Picking up the telephone he spoke to his brothers. He then finished his drink and got the Range Rover out of the garage and drove to Paul's farm in Essex.

It was a thirty minute drive and both brothers were waiting for him. Seeing his brothers sitting in the main room, both the worse for wear by the look of the empty whisky bottle near Peter, Charles began to wish he had thought matters out a bit more. If the job was likely to go tits up then this was the moment it could happen. Once these two had had a skinful Charles knew that anything could happen.

Peter stood up, went to a cabinet and poured Charles half a glass of whisky from a new bottle. "Tell us about this French business."

Charles relayed the story that he had obtained from Andre and then paused, waiting for either brother to make a comment.

Peter was the first. "Whilst we do not know for certain who it was sneaking about, clearly it wasn't the fucking tooth fairy. The whole job is now jeopardised from our point of view."

Paul took a gulp from his glass. "Someone must have heard something, any idea Charles, just who it could be? Did Andre have no idea?"

Charles guessed that he would now have to own up before it went on for ever. "I think from talking to Andre, we can rule out any of the local druggies. That leaves Ridge, the copper from Sussex, as the most likely person. He is a sneaky bastard, and I wouldn't put it past him at all."

Paul stared at Charles. "This means that he knows more than he should at this stage. We can't allow that to go on."

Peter smiled. "If it was him and he has identified the farm, we are in trouble." He burped loudly.

Charles smiled weakly. "I have seen him since I came back. He never said anything about France to me, but then he wouldn't would he? I think we still may need his participation if it comes to it, so I suggest we do nothing at this stage. Let the bastard think he is the clever one."

Paul looked at Charles and then Peter. "I think we should consider taking the bastard out before he causes further problems. I'll do it tomorrow!"

Peter stood up. "Listen to me, you two twats! We cannot rub him out just yet. We might need him, if it goes wrong at the port. We still need him."

Charles didn't like the way this conversation was going. "Hang on a second. The reason why we need Ridge is simple. If we have a problem at Dover with the four lorries, he will sort it. We have given him the first lorry, so that we can slip the other four full lorries through the port without Customs being any the wiser. By rights it should be a doddle, with Ridge not realising we have had him and the fucking Customs over at the same time until it is too late. If we change arrangements now, it could cost us millions, and the fucking Colombians will not be pleased!"

At the mention of the Colombians, Paul shuddered as he thought of the enormous bodyguard who was just waiting for him to put a foot wrong. "I agree with Charles. Let us keep calm and continue as if nothing has happened. Let's just play it out!"

Paul swallowed the contents of his glass, and looked at it as he could not imagine where the contents had gone. "The problem is, what if Ridge realises that we have other lorries on the next boat? He could set a trap for us. I don't trust him for one second. He is a cunning bastard and more than capable of doing it."

Peter spoke up. "Fuck it. Let's leave things to run. If Ridge crosses us Paul can deal with him. But also bear in mind, it might not be Ridge. It could just be someone who has heard a whisper or whatever. Charles said everything was okay at the farm, so we have lost nothing and there is still all to play for, that's my view."

"I agree with that," Charles said. "We need this job to go without a hitch to really set us up for all time. Let's go for it. Paul?"

"Okay," Paul said, a little reluctantly. "Charles, you give Ridge the ferry times on Friday so that he can organise his search team. I will brief the drivers so that when they turn up at the port on the Saturday no one will suspect anything is going on. This is going to be a piece of cake."

Charles was the first to leave and headed back to town. He was relieved that Paul hadn't got nasty about Ridge and chosen to kill him. Ridge was okay, a copper he knew, but still okay. With any luck, Ridge would never know he had been had over.

Peter and Paul watched Charles leave the farm. Peter was just getting into his Porsche when Paul came over to him. "Do we mention to Charles about the surprise we have in store for Ridge if he interferes early on?"

"No," Peter said, "we do not. We will bring that part into play later. For the time being just let it stay as it is without saying anything to him."

Chapter Thirty-Three

The conference opened sharp at ten o'clock, in the conference room at Spring Gardens. Tea and coffee were laid on for the delegates attending the meeting by invitation.

Seated around the table were John Ridge with his detective inspector, Roland Johnston, and detective sergeant, Emil Kimber. Next to Johnston sat Robin Green from Customs and Excise together with his boss, James Brownlow. Sitting on the right of Brownlow were two officers, Brent Talbot and Jess Atkins from a secret Customs Investigation Unit known as the Hunters. Detective Sergeant Jon Snow and his boss, Detective Inspector Peter Jameson, were seated directly across the table from Ridge.

Peter Jameson, head of ground teams at SOCA, opened the conference by welcoming the individuals present and calling on Brownlow to update everyone with a resumé of the known intelligence.

Brownlow stood up and looked around. He liked small conferences. Over the years he had found that with small numbers of people attending a conference there was a good chance of getting more done. It was often easier to nail responsibility down to particular people and thereby encourage action. Action was what was needed now, he thought.

"Gentlemen, as some you may know, last week a Customs and Excise officer by the name of Sarah Mundey met one of the targets of this operation, Charles Ford, on the ferry leaving Folkestone for Boulogne. For reasons of her own, Sarah became suspicious of him, and we think that is where and when she hatched her plan. Sarah was careful enough to check Ford out with the on-board SB man, who assisted in completing the checks for her.

"We know that when the ship docked in Boulogne, Sarah was picked up by Ford who was waiting to leave the terminal in his Range Rover. They appear to have spent the weekend together in a small hotel, near a town called Béthune." Brownlow looked down at his notes and again glanced at each of his audience before continuing as if he was speaking to them individually. "At Béthune, Ford dumped Sarah, not wishing to take her with him to some so-called business appointment. We are not sure where he went, but he later returned to the drop-off point, picked her up and together they went to a local hotel for the night.

"Sarah's plan was to entertain Ford and pillow talk him; however, she clearly came unstuck, because Mr

Ford had his own ideas as to how the evening and night were to progress. To cut a long story short, gentlemen, Ford at some stage viciously beat her up and force-fed Sarah a quantity of cocaine. He then raped her and sodomised her more than once during their night together." Brownlow paused letting his conversation sink in. "It appears that Ford had a light breakfast before paying the bill and returning to this country. Sarah was found by the French maid later that morning when she was still unconscious. The French police were involved and it was they who found Sarah's warrant card hidden in her bag. Sarah was taken to the local hospital and treated. I am pleased to say that she is recovering but will remain there in hospital for a few days more until she is well enough to be brought home. Our people are now with her attempting to make sense of it all. We have managed to get a brief account from Sarah of events, but it is limited because of her current condition.

"The good news is that Sarah has clearly identified Charles Ford as her travelling companion and attacker." Brownlow picked up his notes, paused and said to his still attentive audience, "I am hopeful that someone here today can move this operation forward, and that, folks, is about as far as I can go." He sat down.

Jameson rose to his feet. "I am sure that everybody here offers their sympathy to Sarah who has suffered at the hands of Charles Ford. Looking at the family's antecedent history, Charles Ford seems to be the most civilised member of the family which makes one wonder what the rest are like." He turned to Green. "Robin, can you bring us up to date with Sarah's last short interview with you?"

Jameson sat down as Robin Green stood up. He spoke surely and slowly.

"In all the years that I have been in this job, I have never seen anyone treated so badly. Sarah Mundey is lucky to still be alive. She is alive because Ford saw her as just a toy for the weekend. Her attempt to bed him and gain some Intel never got off the ground. Sarah made no bones about it, she saw the opportunity to get one over on Ford and enhance her career prospects at the same time. She got a lot more than she bargained for and it is likely to take her months to fully recover from this ordeal. There is, I think, a gap in the continuity of this story as we know it so far and we need to cover it.

"We do not know where Ford went to after he dropped Sarah off at the shopping centre. It is important that we find out this piece of info, because knowing where he went may well be critical to finding out what Ford's game plan is. I have spoken to my opposite number in France about suitable localities where Ford may have disappeared to, but so far no luck. Has anyone here today any bright ideas?"

Jameson looked around the table, his eyes raised as he settled on Talbot and Atkins. They shook their heads negatively whilst making notes. He looked at Robin Green. Green pursed his lips. "I have nothing, but I will pursue that angle once more with Sarah as soon as she is well enough."

Jameson looked at Johnston who indicated in a negative fashion that he could not assist. His eyes fell on Kimber who stood up. "I will further all local enquiries about this matter as soon as I return to base, thank you!"

Kimber sat down, not realising that just about everyone in the room was wondering what he was talking about.

Heaving a sigh, Jameson glanced at Ridge: "Anything to add, John?"

Ridge nodded and stood up. "I have known the Ford family for many years and Charles Ford in particular. As informants go, Charles Ford is a tried and tested source. He has proved his trustworthiness on a number of occasions. However, let me say, that does not mean the bastard goes to church on Sundays!

"Ford has recently reappeared in my life after a long absence and has offered to provide me with a large importation of cocaine due to manifest itself within the near future. It seems this job lot has been offered to me as a thank you for a favour I did him some time ago. At the present time, the indications are that this little present will appear within the immediate future, although I have not got a precise date. However, I am convinced something is amiss. I am not sure that I am being told everything or even nearly everything, so I am very cautious of him at this time. I saw him the other day and he did supply the registration number of the vehicle carrying the gear, so I can get that looked at in the meantime."

Ridge saw Brownlow look at him over the top of his glasses and raise his hand. Ridge paused. "Sir, you are looking at me as if I have said something important!"

"John, are you saying that you have spoken to Ford since his return from France?"

"Yes sir, I am," Ridge replied.

"Good man!" Brownlow said. "It's good to know that there is someone out there with his finger on Ford's pulse. It's the only way we are going bring this family to heel. Pardon me for interrupting you, do carry on."

Ridge, feeling confident that he could now speak openly, continued, "Ford only spoke of the girl as a weekend fuck. He never referred to her by name. When I spoke to him he had no idea of the effect his actions have had. He basically got what he wanted from her and then he discarded her. Really the man wants a bullet through his head as do his brothers, but the Home Office in this country frown on death squads!" There was an amused laughter around the room which caused some of the tension to fade. The only person in the room who did not laugh was Ridge's boss, Roland Johnston.

Johnston had sat there, content not to take an active part in the conference. In fact, for much of the time, he was mulling over in his mind the possibilities associated with getting rid of Ridge and assuming the mantle of handling officer with Ford. That would be quite a feather in his cap when the job came to fruition. Achieving something along those lines would enhance his promotional qualities no end. What was so bloody galling was that now, right now, right here in front of him was his bloody detective constable spouting forth all sorts of info and cracking jokes as well. It was just not on at that rank!

Ridge eyed those still waiting for him to continue. He looked directly at Jon Snow. "I know the address in France that Ford went to when he dropped off Sarah Mundey." Ridge let that little gem sink in while he passed the details across the table to Snow. "Actually, whilst I was in France on holiday last weekend, I managed to have a look at the place from the outside and inside on the off chance of gaining a bit of Intel!" Ridge paused again sounding a little bit embarrassed by what he had said. He cast a sideways glance at his two stony-faced supervisors before carrying on. "The farm is a little way from Béthune. It's a small hamlet, I suppose called La Basse. It's sited off the road out of sight, near a small aerodrome."

Brownlow interrupted. "You say you got inside John? What did you see?"

"It was one of those farms that, given its layout, appeared to be custom made for hiding drug vehicles that are waiting to reach the UK. There were a number of large barns on site mostly locked, but I managed to

229

find the one containing the lorry that we are interested in. I couldn't look inside for long because the farmer had this enormous Rottweiler wandering about the place. For some reason this enormous mutt took an immediate dislike to me!" Ridge held up his bandaged arm to show them. "I had to get out quick, because of the noise, but I don't think anyone was any the wiser that I was there."

Roland Johnston could contain himself no longer. Seeing the opportunity to exercise his supervisory authority he jumped up nearly knocking over his chair. "Ridge," he said in a strangulated voice, "are you telling this conference that you went into a foreign country last weekend and trespassed on private property, illegally entered a barn or two, maybe more, and became a burglar extraordinaire, without my knowledge or authority?" Johnston was almost foaming at the mouth, his face a deep red colour.

Peter Jameson smiled and said, "Come off it Roland, you cannot give your man authority to become a burglar! That's a criminal offence!"

Johnston sat down without replying. The rest of the room was convulsed in laughter.

Ridge waited for the laughter to die. "When I last saw Ford, he indicated that it was likely that the weekend after next was going to be D-Day for moving the lorry with the gear. It is going to leave La Basse and make for the port of Dover via Calais. I should get the ferry times within the next day or two. It will be a morning ferry. That's all I have at present."

Ridge sat down. He was aware of both Johnston and Kimber glaring at him.

Brownlow watched the reaction of Ridge's two senior officers. He got up and addressed the meeting.

"Gentlemen, I would like to thank John Ridge for coming along here today and giving us the benefit of his wisdom on this job. Having listened to him I know that we are a lot closer now than we were first thing this morning to not only achieving a result on the drugs side of things but, dare I say, a hell of lot closer to arresting Ford for the murderous attack on Sarah Mundey."

A round of applause rippled around the room.

The only two in the room with a different opinion were Johnston and Kimber. It did not go unnoticed that neither officer supported their junior officer.

Jon Snow jumped up and gathered everyone's attention. "When this job started a few weeks ago, it began as a small intelligence gathering operation. The matter has progressed well away from just that and we have evidence against one member of the family at least, of serious criminal offences. I would say that these three brothers are probably the most dangerous gang in Britain today. We have seen the way that one of these brothers has treated Sarah Mundey. If they became aware that we as an organisation were close to disrupting their game and putting them where they belong, they would most certainly become very dangerous indeed. So let's take care with these people and not place ourselves at risk."

A murmur of agreement went around the room in support. "From today, can I suggest we all wait on John Ridge for the final instruction? He will obtain the information on the ferry times and circulate it to all of us. I don't want anyone acting independently. When we move, it will be as a team."

The meeting broke for lunch, which for the detectives simply meant that they continued with the meeting on a very informal basis while they ate the meal. Both Johnston and Kimber ate their meal in silence. Neither man spoke to Ridge or indeed anyone else for that matter.

As they walked away from the conference Johnston turned to Ridge.

"Be in my office 9 o'clock sharp tomorrow morning." With that he walked away from both Ridge and Kimber. Kimber looked at Ridge and walked off towards the railway station.

Chapter Thirty-Four

Ridge was in the office early the next morning, quickly running through yesterday's e-mails. He heard Emil Kimber walk along the corridor, enter his office and slam the door. A few minutes later Kimber walked out of his office and headed in the direction of Johnston's office. Twenty minutes later Kimber, looking grim, walked into Ridge's office.

"Well," he said, "you have fucking well done it now Ridge. The boss wants to see you in his office now. I really can't wait for this!"

Ridge shut his computer down and walked along the corridor and into his inspector's office with Emil Kimber behind him. Johnston didn't invite him to be seated, so Ridge remained standing in front of the desk like a naughty schoolboy up in front of the head.

"Ridge, yesterday I sat in a conference with you and officers from other services and listened to you talking about a job which I should have known all about, but didn't. Can you explain why I, the detective inspector, knew nothing: nothing, not a single fucking thing?"

Ridge looked at him and tried to keep things calm. "Yes, I can explain it. Neither you nor sergeant Kimber are what I would refer to as normal supervisory officers. The pair of you are always trying to undermine my dealings with the job because you want to snatch the informant from me and use him yourselves. I know that, and other people know that. Recently, when things have happened with Ford, I have tried on a number of occasions to contact either or both of you, sometimes via headquarters and you have never been available."

"Ridge," Johnston said, now looking a little uncomfortable, "as a detective constable you do not run this office, I do. I have asked you to report your dealings with this man to your sergeant on a daily basis, yet you have refused to do that."

Ridge, very quietly, said. "What haven't I reported to Kimber that you think I should have?"

Johnston, by now very red in the face, looked taken aback. "I don't know, there must be something!"

Ridge smiled. "Well, please tell me?"

Johnston paused, and a smile lit up his face. "I know, what about this fucking French business? You went without permission to a foreign country and broke into someone's farm to find out about the drugs lorry."

Ridge sighed as if he was trying to be patient with Johnston. "I went away to France for a weekend holiday with a friend. I don't need your permission to do that. As for breaking into someone's farm, that is nonsense. While I was having a day out in the French countryside, I wandered on to a farmer's land and their dog bit me which made me realise that I had wandered off the beaten track. Anyone can make that sort of mistake. That's not breaking in; well it's not in my book. Perhaps, if you think it was a criminal offence, you can tell what was criminal about it?"

Ridge felt his nose growing longer, but he knew he had to call Johnston's bluff.

Kimber, standing behind Ridge, thought he ought to get his views known; after all he was the detective sergeant. He moved past Ridge and stood behind his inspector. "Ridge, I was not told about this escapade in France, why not?"

"I did not know that you wanted to know about my weekend off duty," Ridge smiled.

Kimber looked angry. "Ridge, I am fucking fed up with you taking the piss out of me. I am your sergeant and I should know about everything, but I don't, you just keep me in the dark!" Kimber had lost his smile and looked as if he was going to cry.

Ridge smiled, feeling that he had come out of the shadows and was now safe from harm.

"I tried to contact you the other night on the telephone. In fact I tried to contact the pair of you, because I needed advice. But, as you now know, even headquarters couldn't reach you. At least one of you is supposed to be available after hours, but you weren't. I cannot do much about that. As for keeping stuff from you, it was only because I was at the conference that some of the information I had became useful and fell into place. I did not know what some of the other officers knew because I think I was the one being kept in the dark by you two!"

Kimber bristled at the innuendo. "Ridge, I have told you before, the inspector and me make the decisions in this unit, not you. You are told what it is suitable for someone of your rank to know. That is the way we run this unit!"

Johnston sat and put his head in his hands. He wondered why he had to deal with people like Ridge and Kimber. He never had problems of this nature when he was on traffic duties. He knew that Ridge had turned this meeting around and had regained the initiative.

"Ridge," he said, almost wearily, "whatever your excuses are, they are not sufficient. As of now you are suspended from duty until further notice. Is that understood?"

Before Ridge was able to reply, Kimber jumped in on the act.

"I wholeheartedly support the inspector's decision, you are suspended!" He smirked broadly at his own words.

Johnston glared at Kimber and said, "Emil, for fuck's sake, please be quiet!"

Turning to Ridge, "Before you leave this building, I want a telephone introduction to your informant and all your paperwork on him, understood?"

Ridge reached into his pocket and produced one of his business cards with a telephone number written on it. He threw it onto Johnston's desk.

"There's his telephone number, call him now, while I am still here because I would like you to talk to him in my presence, just so that I know what is said. I just want everything clear between the four of us before I leave."

Johnston looked up at Ridge. The fucking bastard has turned it round again, he thought, I am now working under his instruction not the other way around. He picked up the card and squinted at the telephone number which he then dialled. He heard it connect and a voice answered. Johnston took a deep breath. "I am Detective Inspector Roland Johnston..." He heard the telephone being replaced and the line went dead. He glanced at Ridge. "Must be a fault on the line."

"Try him again boss," Kimber said.

Johnston glared at Kimber. "Emil, I am well aware what my options are." He dialled the number again and was connected. "I am..." he intoned, but again the telephone was replaced. Johnston looked up. "I'll call him later. Right now Ridge I want your warrant card."

Ridge handed over his warrant card and picked up his business card. "I'll have that back as it is my property." He turned and walked out of the office and walked back to his own office. He began sorting out some of the paperwork that Johnston had instructed him to hand over.

Kimber came in to his office. "Ridge, at some stage I believe formal disciplinary charges will be laid against you. In the meantime you are now out of this fucking unit is that clear? I have waited a long time for this. Now hand over the paperwork relating to this job." He stretched his hand out towards the file that Ridge was holding. "I know you deliberately fucked the inspector over with that dodgy telephone number, now tell me how to contact Ford, you must have another number?"

Ridge stood up passed over the file to Kimber and walked out of the office, slamming the door as he went.

Kimber returned to Johnston's office looking very pleased with himself. "At last we have got rid of him boss, I just hope that we can make something stick this time."

Johnston looked up and glared at Kimber. "Emil, you are quite right, this is a window of opportunity. I see you have the file relating to the job in hand. Knowing Ridge as I do I imagine that it is quite comprehensive? We have now achieved our objective and got Ridge out of the running over this job. What I would like you to do Emil is update yourself with the contents of the file and then bring this fucking informant, Ford, to heel. Make him realise that he is now working for us. Got it?"

Kimber was flabbergasted. "I thought you were going to deal with him?"

"No, no!" Johnston replied. "I can't do it all myself Emil, I am far too busy for that. You run him and put me down on the register as second handling officer. That way we both benefit!"

Kimber, accepting that Johnston had outwitted him, acknowledged Johnston's decision.

"Okay leave it with me, I'll sort it!" With that he turned and was about to leave the office when Johnston stopped him. "Emil, just don't fuck this up will you?"

Kimber ignored him and continued to walk out of the office. Fucking cheek, he thought, the bastard hasn't got the nous to deal with a job of this size, but I will show him that I can deal with it.

Kimber walked along the corridor and saw Ridge talking to a colleague from the office. He intervened and said to Ridge, "John, I am so sorry that matters have taken this direction, it wasn't what I wanted. Just for your information, the guvnor has instructed me to take over the reins and deal with your informant. Is there any way I can contact him other than by that dodgy telephone number you gave the boss?"

Ridge grinned. "That dodgy telephone number is the one that I have always used. As I have said so many times before, Ford will not speak to either of you. He knows just what a couple of wankers you two are! He speaks to me because he knows that he can trust me. He also knows that after the way you pursued me previously, he would never be able to trust you two!"

"I'll be the judge of that," Kimber replied. "And, furthermore, you are suspended from duty, so leave the building now!" He turned and walked into his office and began studying some obscure piece of paperwork on his desk, such as it was.

Ridge walked out of the station, seething with anger over the way he had just been shafted. He wandered into the town centre near The Lanes and went into his favourite coffee shop and sat at the back away from the doors and windows. He needed to think about things and work out his next step.

★ ★ ★ ★

Kimber, in his office, had finished reading the file. He saw that the telephone number on the front sheet was the same as the one Ridge had given to Johnston. This was a whole new ball game. He was now in charge of moving this job forward to a successful conclusion. All he had to do was to get Ford on his side and just carry on where Ridge had left off. From this moment on he, Detective Sergeant Emil Kimber, was going to become a force to be reckoned with.

Picking up the telephone he dialled the number in front of him. He heard the telephone connect but got no response from the other end. "Mr Ford, you don't know me, I am Detective Sergeant Emil..." the telephone line went dead. He put the telephone down and began punching the paper file in front of him. "Fuck, fuck and fuck, you bastard! I'll have you before long." Kimber then sat back in his chair, not quite sure of what to do next.

★ ★ ★ ★

Ridge sipped his Americano. It was nice coffee. He blamed himself entirely for his predicament. He should have taken more care with his supervisors.

He knew after the last time that both of them wanted him out of the unit and now he had played right into their hands. Effectively he was now out of a job for the foreseeable future. Ridge guessed that he could bypass Kimber and Johnston and carry on dealing with Ford. His problem would come when he wanted to set the job up and finalise the job at Dover. Johnston would block his every move. Fuck it, he thought, where do I go from here?

Ridge wondered how he was going to explain today's outcome to Marie. Did he simply walk in and say, "Sorry dear, I've just been suspended from duty. I will be at home from today onwards"?.

She, of course, would rightly say, "I told you so."

He recalled the last time he was suspended from duty. It had caused tremendous stress at home.

Marie didn't really understand the politics of it all; she just knew her husband, who loved his job, wasn't allowed to go to work. It was only later when she became aware of some of the backstabbing attacks made against her husband that she realised that being an operational intelligence officer could be fraught with internal jealousies and squabbles by senior officers who really ought to be above such matters. It seemed that it was often a case of, when you were in, you were in: when you were out, you were out, with a very thin dividing line between.

Sitting in the café sipping his Americano, Ridge thought a lot of the problems of today's policing techniques was that many officers saw the way forward via the promotion exam alone. There was no real requirement for anyone to have experience of anything in particular. One day you could be traffic officer and the next day you could, on promotion, become a detective. It was as simple as that. He would have to tell Marie as soon as possible. She would find out anyway.

He left the café and found a public telephone. Placing his head under the ridiculous plastic hood he dialled Josie and told her of his suspension. He felt angry and confused and sounded as much to Josie. She was at home so she invited Ridge around for a coffee.

Ridge gladly accepted the offer and walked the short distance to her flat. He played the buzzer and she let him in. Ridge used the lift to the correct floor. He saw that the front door was slightly open and Josie was waiting for him. She was dressed in a man's white shirt that was long enough to just cover her thighs. At the neck, three buttons were undone exposing her breasts in a decent but seductive way. She looked gorgeous.

Josie put her arms out and embraced Ridge, kissing him gently at first. She eased her tongue into his mouth and then deeper into his throat. Josie unzipped him and sank to her knees and continued her exploration of Ridge's body.

At the end of the corridor the elderly man from flat nine, just returning from taking his dog for a walk, saw it all. He felt an erection coming on, so stood still and watched. He hadn't seen live sex taking place for years; in fact the last time he saw live sex taking place was when he was a squaddie in Egypt more than fifty years ago. He relished every second of what he was now seeing take place before his eyes! He hurriedly let himself in anxious to make the bathroom in time. He had never ever seen his glamorous neighbour in such a position. He loved it!

Ridge heard the old man's key go in his door lock. He looked down the corridor saw the old man and smiled. He drew Josie into the flat and closed her door. Ridge pressed Josie up against the door and slowly undid the buttons on her shirt. As he thought, she was naked under the garment. She pulled him into her bedroom.

When they had finished, Josie wandered into the kitchen, returning a few minutes later with a tray of tea. Pouring two cups of tea she handed one to Ridge and placed her own on the bedside table. Jumping back into bed she looked at Ridge and said, "Tell me all!"

Ridge told her everything and waited for Josie to respond.

Josie knew that Ridge was exceptionally gifted when it came to his job. She had fairly frequent dealings with local police officers who in the main did not impress her. There was something about police officers like Ridge. They seemed to almost give out an aura of confidence. If they dealt with something, they dealt with it: not talk around it or pass it on. To lose someone like that, with those qualities, was just wrong. Josie knew both Kimber and Johnston and she was not surprised at their behaviour. She was just surprised that no one else could see their devious ways.

"John, you have allowed yourself to be captured by the very two people waiting for the right opportunity to fall their way. You need to ask yourself this, 'Can I beat them even at this late stage of the game or shall I look to another department to work out my last year?'."

Ridge looked at Josie, still looking lovely, her hair tousled as a result of her activity in bed and best of all still naked.

"I'm not sure," he said. "I'm half inclined to let it all go and throw a sickie for my remaining time in the job."

Josie had never seen Ridge so down. "This informant cost you dear the last time. Why deal with him at all? Of all the officers that I know you work the hardest, why not slacken off a bit?"

"Because," Ridge said, "this informant and the rest of his family are dangerous and because of that they represent a challenge to me as a police officer. Also, at this particular time, my informant is wanted for causing serious injury to a female Customs officer. I want to see him dealt with for that if nothing else."

Josie pulled him forward and reached down into the bed clearing a space before disappearing completely under the covers.

Afterwards they lay there enjoying being close to each other, feeling each other's body moving in time with breathing. Josie suddenly sat up in bed.

"John, have you told your wife yet?"

"Not yet, I'm going to tell her later."

"John! Get out of bed and go and tell her. She deserves that from you. Tell her before someone else does. Go now!"

She turned, bent her knees up and pushed him out of the bed onto the floor before he could do anything.

Ridge grinned. "Okay, I can take a hint." With that he made his way to the bathroom, showered and got dressed. He kissed Josie and left.

Chapter Thirty-Five

Aware that he would get scant sympathy from any investigating officer from what has always been known as Discipline and Complaints Department, regardless of its current abstract and forgettable name, Ridge consoled himself with the thought that there wasn't much evidence of a serious nature against him. But there was no getting away from the fact that he had condemned himself out of his own mouth at the conference.

Because no minutes were recorded at the conference, he could always claim that he was misunderstood by his supervisory officers. The problem with that was then the investigating officers would hotfoot it to the other people present at the conference and take statements from them.

The strength of the evidence against him was that he had failed to, or appeared to have failed to, inform his supervisors of his dealings with Ford. Much of that he knew he could counter with evidence that he had tried on a number of occasions to contact them and failed. Theoretically, he knew that he was facing dismissal from the unit and a return to uniform duties as the most likely scenario.

He put the car away in the large garage and went inside. Marie was sitting at the kitchen table. She got up and kissed him lightly on the cheek, smelling just the faintest trace of perfume on his clothing. Marie could not distinguish the name of the perfume, but it was there nonetheless. Drawing back from her husband, she looked him square in the face. "Where have you been today?" She bit her lip secretly dreading the answer.

"I've just been suspended from duty," he said and sat down looking distraught.

Marie's face fell. "Surely we are not going through that again, John. What is it over this time?"

Ridge got up and walked over to Marie. He put his arms around her, giving her another chance to smell the strange perfume. Again she drew back from him. "You have someone else's perfume on you. Whose is it?" Tears filled her eyes as she waited for a reply.

Ridge went cold. He normally took great care about his activities away from home. This time he had failed to do so. It was probably as a result of his present troubles that he became distracted and slipped up.

Thinking on his feet was something that John Ridge was good at. That ability was one of the standard techniques of his trade. "I had a shower at work this afternoon. It must be the soap you can smell." He paused, hoping this answer would suffice. The last thing he wanted was to cause his wife any sort of upset.

Not quite convinced but wanting to believe him, Marie looked at him and could see nothing in her husband's face that called him a liar. She desperately wanted to believe him, but she was hesitant about his excuse.

"Why did you need a shower at work?" she asked, trying not to stare at him.

"There was a bit of a fracas in the cells with a prisoner. I ended up sweating like a pig, so I took a shower."

Marie's mind eased. That excuse was at least consistent with his normal behaviour. He would take a shower at the drop of a hat. Marie knew that he had only to break out in sweat for him to want a shower. Was it possible she was looking for a problem when there really wasn't one?

Watching his wife, Ridge thought he had said enough to convince her. He wanted to take her in his arms and kiss her but, with Josie's smell still lingering, he kept his distance.

Ridge smiled at Marie. "Did you think there was someone else?"

Marie began to cry. "Yes, what was I supposed to think? I thought it was another woman's perfume, not cell block fragrance!" With that remark she alternated between tears and a strangled laughter.

Ridge picked up his slim chance and began to laugh with her. He could resist her no longer. He closed and placed his arms around her and began kissing her. The tension that had been there a few moments ago melted away from Marie. She responded to her husband's warmth and returned his kisses. They eventually made their way to the bedroom where Ridge expertly removed Marie's clothing before joining her in the bed. They lay there entwined with each other.

"I'm sorry John, sorry that I was suspicious of you!"

Ridge squeezed her closer to him. "Marie, I have never looked at another woman in my life. You have always been the only one for me. Let us just forget all about it." He began, caressing her body with his hands, feeling the excitement building within her.

Marie was nearly there. Her breathing had increased and she was responding with her hands. She could feel his strong erection taking hold and wanted him now. As they engaged she could still smell the perfume on him, stronger than ever. Marie suddenly pulled away from Ridge.

"I'm sorry John, I can't do it! I still do not believe you. It's not the first time that I have smelt a woman's perfume on you or traces of mascara on your shirt. I've never said anything about it in the past, but now I just cannot cope with it and the news you've brought home about your job. I can't go on like this, constantly wondering, doubting all the time; I don't know where I stand!"

Ridge was struggling and knew it. His whole world was crashing down around him and he seemed powerless to stop the direction it was taking. First, his job was in jeopardy and, if that wasn't bad enough, now his wife suspected him of all sorts. He was in danger of losing everything.

"Darling, I promise you that I am not seeing another woman."

Marie turned her tear-stained face towards him. "John, I want some time to think about things. I want you to go. Just go and leave me alone! Go and see your tart. Stay with her if that is what you want to do!"

Ridge felt stunned. In a daze he dressed and packed a bag. He stood and looked at Marie crying. "Do you really want me to go?"

"Get out!" she screamed.

Ridge picked up the holdall and left. They had, over the years, had their fare share of arguments, that was to be expected, but this: what the fuck was he going to do now?

Marie watched her husband drive out of the garage and turn onto the roadway. In a second he was lost from sight. She was hurt and so angry with him. Stupid man! Why couldn't he just go to work and come home like anybody else. He wanted for nothing.

Stupid man! She began crying again as the depth of her actions came home to her.

Chapter Thirty-Six

Detective Sergeant Emil Kimber sat quietly watching the other delegates shaking hands and chatting amongst themselves as they settled into the chairs arranged around the conference table. The same guests as before had arrived on time and looked as if they were ready to take part. In the typical scheme of things within investigative services each of the delegates was carrying a folder.

Kimber was dreading the start of this conference. He was on his own after his inspector had cried off coming to the conference. They'd had a falling out when he admitted to Johnston that he had telephoned Ford who had put the telephone down on him, clearly refusing to speak to him. Johnston had become abusive to Kimber and had ended up by telling him to get out of his office.

Kimber suspected that he had been left holding the baby because Johnston did not want to be placed in the position of having to explain Ridge's absence. What really worried Kimber was that at some stage the conversation would turn in the direction of Ford. Someone was bound to ask if progress had been made with Ford and what the outcome was. He did not fancy being embarrassed by any one of these wankers present at the conference.

Peter Jameson again opened the conference welcoming all the delegates and noticing that two delegates were missing from their seats.

He turned to Kimber. "Detective Sergeant Kimber, would you start. I notice that Detective Inspector Johnston and Detective Constable Ridge are not here, which I find somewhat surprising given the timescale and importance of the job in hand." He looked quizzically at Kimber, giving him the opportunity to explain the absence of his colleagues.

Taking a deep breath, Kimber stood and faced his audience.

"Gentlemen, I regret to say that there is no update from the informant at this stage. To be perfectly honest, we are having difficulty persuading him to talk to us. As soon as there is progress I will inform all those involved." Kimber, now red-faced and sweating, sat down.

The analyst, Jon Snow, stood up. He had sensed from previous conversations with both Kimber and Johnston that they were not the most supportive supervisors on God's earth. Turning in the direction of

Kimber, he said, "Can you tell the conference delegates why John Ridge is not here? After all, he is the officer dealing with Ford and the man driving this job forward." He sat down glaring at Kimber.

Kimber stood up. This wasn't going to be easy. That bastard Johnston is to blame for this.

"I regret to say that Detective Constable Ridge has been suspended from duty. As a result of his comments here a few days ago, Detective Inspector Johnston felt he had no option but to suspend him from duty. Fortunately, I am the second designated handler of the informant." Kimber was about to sit down when Snow again rose to his feet.

"I'm sorry," he said, "I don't understand. This is a conference involving a lot of investigating officers who, by the very nature of detective work, are expected to be open and up front at a conference. Sometimes things need to be said in confidence, that's how we move things on. Are you saying, because Ridge spoke freely he has now been suspended?"

Kimber was sweating freely now. "Yes, that is right. I did not personally agree with that decision but that is why Ridge is not here. I am in touch with the informant so we should not lose continuity of events."

Snow persisted. "But I thought you just said that Ford was not talking to you. You can't have it both ways. Is Ford, the informant, talking to you or not?"

Kimber wanted to die. "Well, no not actually. I tried to ring him, but he kept putting the telephone down on me."

There was laughter at this point from a number of very seasoned detectives sitting in the room.

Snow moved in for the kill. "It does seem to me that between you and Detective Inspector Johnston, you have not only suspended a good officer but, more importantly, you have jeopardised the job in hand. How on earth do we get the ball rolling again?"

James Brownlow, the senior Customs officer in the room, stood up and glared at Kimber. "It does rather seem as if Ridge has been suspended from duty over some petty infringement or jealousy. That seems to be a rather unfortunate state of affairs, given the closeness of the endgame of the drugs side of the operation. Also affected by this crazy decision of Detective Inspector Johnston is the ongoing investigation into those who caused serious injury to one of my staff. The man Ridge, as I see things, is a dedicated officer using the skills of his office in order to bring bastards like the Ford family to justice. He has my backing on this." Brownlow paused and then said very quietly to Kimber, "Who was the officer who suspended Ridge?"

Kimber knew he was in danger of being linked to Johnston because of Ridge's suspension. "Well sir, it was Detective Inspector Johnston who suspended Ridge. As I said earlier, it was nothing to do with me."

Brownlow ignored the get-out clause from Kimber who then sat down. Brownlow picked up his fountain pen and began making notes. Not a word was said for a full three minutes, then Brownlow stood up and addressed the conference. "Gentlemen, it seems pointless to sit here and simply seek to place blame for what has happened. If we reschedule this conference for a few days time, hopefully we will have John Ridge back in the saddle providing us with ongoing intelligence!"

Detective Inspector Peter Jameson stood up. "In view of this unfortunate state of affairs, I suggest we put this matter on hold until it resolves itself in the short term. Clearly, without John Ridge and his informant, Charles Ford, we cannot progress. In the meantime, I will write to the Force concerned expressing our views on the subject."

"Good man," James Brownlow muttered, loud enough for all to hear. With that comment the meeting concluded.

Chapter Thirty-Seven

John Ridge looked around the small room he had rented in a small East of Brighton guest-house. To say it was small and depressing was not an exaggeration. There was just room for the bed and a small wardrobe. A very compact toilet and shower capsule was against the wall opposite the window. However, it was clean and tidy.

He picked up his half-full glass of whisky and downed the lot. As the contents burned their way down his throat, he lay back on the bed and wondered how he was going to change events for the better. What worried him most of all was Marie. How was he going to set that right? It was now two days since his suspension from duty and him moving out.

Ridge had not heard from her. He knew he did not deserve to hear from her, but that didn't stop him wanting. He had treated her badly for years and had now been caught out. He was well and truly fucked and he knew it!

The whisky was having some effect on him and taking the edge off his concerns. He wanted to sleep and then wake up and find it was all a dream, but he knew that was not going to happen. He looked at his watch for about the twentieth time, but it was another twenty minutes before he finally dozed off. He was still asleep when Josie let herself in to his room. He had called her earlier in the morning and had waited all day for her to arrive. He needed someone to talk to.

The stench of alcohol was overpowering as she glanced around his little prison-type room. Josie woke him. "Get up; you are coming home with me!" With that she piled his few belongings into his bag and they left the premises. Josie got him to her flat and put a dazed, drunken Ridge to bed. He fell asleep immediately. She felt sorry for him and thought he was in danger of falling to pieces.

Ridge awoke some hours later feeling dreadful, most of that feeling attributed to the amount of whisky he had consumed on an empty stomach. Josie was their waiting for him. Seeing her, sitting, watching him, somehow installed a little warmth in him. Here was someone who cared about him. He knew that with someone like Josie to listen and talk to, he would soon start to show an improvement.

Josie made it quite clear that she was not going tolerate any drunk in her flat. The drinking had to stop. She insisted that Ridge start working on what she referred to as Plan B, as soon as possible. He was the only one who could change the direction of what she thought was the biggest fuck-up of all time.

Under Josie's firm handling Ridge made the effort. He stopped drinking and went running. He had always found running therapeutic and enjoyable and now it was a lifesaver. Returning to Josie's flat after pounding along the promenade, Ridge stripped off for a shower. As he threw his wet clothes into the basket by Josie's bed he noticed his telephone winking. He picked it up and saw that it was a message from Ford. Two simple words: 'Call me'.

Ridge suddenly realised that in the days following his suspension he had not given a thought to Ford. He had been so wrapped in his own personal problems that police work had gone out of the window, so to speak. He sat down for a moment and wondered what to do. Should he ignore the message or act on it and call Ford. Did he need to do business with this man again? After all, Ford in one respect was at the root of his problems

Ridge sat thinking for a few moments and then he smiled as he recalled a nonsensical expression frequently used by a colleague of his: As one door shuts, so another closes.

He knew exactly what he was going to do.

Ridge picked up the telephone and dialled Ford's number from memory. He quickly arranged an appointment for 7 o'clock that evening. Satisfied, he put the telephone back in its cradle.

Showering and then quickly dressing he left a short note for Josie. It said: Plan B in operation, going to see a friend, See you later. He guessed she would work out who he was going to see.

Catching the fast train from Brighton station, Ridge found he had plenty of time to check out the area where he had agreed to meet Ford. Satisfied that the area was free of police surveillance or of friends of Ford, he wandered up the escalator and around the entire upper-floor shop area before buying an Americano and sitting at a small table near the balcony. From there he could watch all that was happening below him.

A few minutes later he saw Ford approach the escalator, step on and be carried up to the floor level where he was sitting. Ford walked around glancing in the large glass windows of several shops. After a few minutes he seemed satisfied. He then walked into the coffee shop allowing Ridge to watch his back.

Leaving the shop, coffee in hand, Ford glanced at Ridge who nodded. Ford slowly walked over and sat down. They shook hands. Ford was sweating and his hand was shaking very lightly.

"It's starting to happen, John," he said, looking away from Ridge.

"Thank fuck for that, Charles. I was beginning to think that I was going to die of old age before you were likely to produce a result!" He smiled at Ford. There were small traces of a line of sweat on Ford's brow.

"John, I told you to hang in there. I knew it was going to come on top; it was just a case of when. It's looking good for the next full weekend!"

Do you mean in two days' time or the weekend following?"

"Yes, not this weekend, but the next."

Ridge thought about the day concerned. "What day is the lorry coming over the water?"

"On the Saturday morning, the eight-fifteen ferry, Calais to Dover. The lorry is having the gear sealed in the fridge unit as we speak. It will take a few days to do that and then the lorry will be ready to travel."

"Right," murmured Ridge, weighing up the permutations. "A lorry drives onto a ship. It is a straight line from Calais to Dover. The same lorry is stopped and checked inside Dover confines. The Customs growler sniffs around, finds the gear and the driver is arrested. For the life of me Charles, I cannot see anything that could go wrong, can you?"

Ford grinned. "Easy-peasy," he said.

Ridge looked at the man ultimately responsible for his torment. "Charles, this had better be correct. I am getting some grief from my lot and I don't want to add to it!"

"Trust me on this John. The gear is good, very good quality in fact. A lorry load of this gear to retire on: what more could you want? Also, let me tell you, this gear is well wanted in town. There are a lot of people who are going to be disappointed when it doesn't get through. Don't you lot fuck it up John. This lorry must be stopped in the port!"

Ridge smelt a rat, although he could not see from which direction the problem could possibly come. On the face of it, the job could not be easier, but he thought there was still something that he was not aware of.

"If we don't bust the lorry in the port itself, where is its ultimate destination? Where is the lorry going to Charles?"

Charles Ford looked very embarrassed.

"You stop it inside the port as agreed, otherwise the deal is off. Inside that lorry is about thirty-five million quid's worth of gear at street level values, possibly more. You get that when you stop it in the port. If you don't stop it in the port you lose the lot, it's as simple as that!"

"Okay, let's do it as planned," Ridge said, now feeling concerned at Ford's apparent determination to have the lorry stopped inside the port. Why does that bother him? What difference would it make to him if, for instance, it was stopped on the road away from the port? There was something not being said. There was something very wrong with the whole arrangement. But what?

"By the way, was that you at the farm?" Ford asked him.

"What farm?"

"Never mind," Ford said, now uncertain that it was Ridge. He could not tell anything from Ridge's poker face. If it wasn't him, who was it? Ford was now having a touch of the seconds. He stood up.

"I must rush." He looked at Ridge. "Don't let me down on this John and don't you forget the twenty grand you owe me once you have the gear in hand."

"Stay close to a telephone over the weekend, I have a feeling I may need to contact you," Ridge shouted as Ford walked to the down escalator. He watched Ford disappear from sight.

★ ★ ★ ★

The journey back to Brighton gave Ridge the opportunity to ponder the conversation with Ford. Clearly the bastard was holding something back, but what? They had always been friends, but they were on opposite sides of the fence and Ridge knew that as far as Ford was concerned it was him first, at all times.

With a few days left to tidy up the bits and pieces, Ridge now had the ticklish problem of how to pull things together. It would need a team of investigators all playing their part to stop the lorry and arrest the driver either in or out of the port. Who could he go to and get such help? Who would now trust him?

There was absolutely not a chance in hell of going to either Kimber or Johnston. Both those dickheads needed teaching a lesson and he would at some stage get around to doing just that, but first things first. He was going to bust this job wide open and get a result and get his job back. He also wanted Ford arrested for causing the injuries he had inflicted on the Customs girl. The Ford brothers were going to pay a heavy price, they just weren't aware of it, yet!

Ridge was asleep as the train passed Gatwick Airport.

Chapter Thirty-Eight

T he three brothers sat around the table in Peter's flat. Paul had called the meeting to organise the final leg of the drugs run into the UK.

Paul had suggested meeting at Peter's flat because it was on the second floor and there was little chance of surveillance on the flat, simply because there were a number of ways into the building and it was unlikely that they could all be covered at the same time. Also, with the flat on the second floor, the only way in to plant listening devices was through the front door. Paul thought that was an almost impossible task, given the high level of security Peter had invested in on the installation of the front door.

Peter poured the drinks and passed the whisky glasses to his brothers.

"Okay, let's talk about eight days' time. Will everything be ready in France, Charles?"

Charles took a quick swig from his glass. "Yes, as you know, I went over there recently to check out the problem on the farm with Andre. The farm is still secure. The lorries are in place and the drivers will go over the water separately and meet up at the farm later in the day. All the lorries are being prepared now and will be finished by the middle of next week and ready to move on the Saturday morning. They will move in two stages on the Saturday morning. The feed lorry obviously goes first, with the others taking a different direction to the port, but arriving there at much the same time ready to board the very next ferry."

Peter said. "What about paying the drivers? We need to keep them sweet, as the last thing we want is for one of them to think he is being hard done by and grass us up."

Charles said, "No problem with the drivers. I've paid them half now, the other half comes once the lorries are parked safely at the farm!"

Paul put his glass down on the table. "Obviously we are going to lose the first driver and the first lorry at the port, is the driver okay with that?"

"Yes, he is being paid the most and we will look after his wife and kid if he gets sent down. He thinks that he will be able to claim no knowledge and walk away from any charges, but we'll see."

Paul laughed."The customs are going to be really pissed off when they later discover that we have had them over." Peter poured himself another drink.

"They will never find out, trust me. If we can just keep this tight and quiet for the next few days, we will be home and dry!"

Paul swirled the last of the amber nectar around his gums. "Charles, have you spoken to your man Ridge yet?"

Charles looked down into his now empty glass and decided to tell them. If he kept it to himself and something went wrong, then he knew he would be forever blamed for whatever happened afterwards.

"Yes, I have. I asked him directly if he had been sniffing around the farm. His reply was: what farm? He genuinely looked puzzled at my question, so I do not think it was him. I reckon I could tell if he was lying to me."

Paul looked at Charles as if he didn't believe a word his brother had said. "So we are none the wiser? Andre saw someone around the farm buildings, but we do not know who that person was. You thought it was likely to be Ridge, but now you are saying, no, it wasn't Ridge! If it wasn't Ridge who was it?"

Peter saw the reaction of Paul and didn't like it. He was always inclined to fly off the handle at a moment's notice.

"Just a second, let's think about this a bit. We know for sure that someone was sneaking around the place. That alone sounds more like police activity than not, they always use that type of tactic because they need evidence to get a warrant. If not the filth, who then?"

Paul thought for a moment. "Nothing has happened since that night. So, I am inclined to go along with Peter's thinking. If it was the French, then I think they would have been all over the place by now. So, yes I am inclined to think maybe it was the filth from over here, which now gives us a problem. He looked at Peter. If it is the filth, then that means it's Ridge and his lot, doesn't it? Mr Ridge clearly wasn't satisfied with one lorry load, he wants the lot!"

Charles felt this was leading in the wrong direction. "I don't think it was Ridge. After all, whoever it was only went to the farm. If it was Ridge, then he would have worked out the plan and covered the flying club where the other four lorries are stored."

"We don't know for sure that he didn't. What we do know," said Peter, "is that on Saturday morning there are two possibilities. One, it could still all go as planned and we come out smiling, or it could all go tits up and we lose the lot and probably get arrested as well!"

Peter filled up his brothers' glasses. "I think," he said, "we ought to go ahead with the job and just cover our backs as we planned to do in the event of an emergency like this cropping up!"

"I agree: I'll set the plan in motion today."

Charles was feeling that he was going to be confronted with something that he didn't like as he watched his brothers exchange some sort of knowing glance.

Peter, the more eloquent of all three brothers, looked at the youngest, Charles. "Charles, the main suspect here is Ridge. Even you have got to accept that. Paul and I thought some time ago that that bastard Ridge might find himself in a position to harm us. So we devised a plan to cover our backs in the event of that happening. It looks like we were both right, doesn't it?"

Charles Ford nodded in agreement. "I suppose so," he murmured. "But I do think he will play it fair with us."

Paul erupted. "Play it fair!" he shouted. "Play it fucking fair! If we get caught with that load of gear at the port, then for sure we will be looking at twenty-five in the poky! Do you want that?"

Charles blanched at the thought of twenty-five years in prison. "No, of course I don't want that. It's the last fucking thing I want!"

"Okay, then," Paul said, "listen up. Everything stays as it is: the job goes ahead as planned." He glanced around and saw two affirmative nods. "Next Friday afternoon we create a diversion for Ridge that will keep him occupied over the weekend period. Without him leading them the Customs will not be sure of anything and that fact alone will mean that we will get through the port without a hitch. After all, it is only the time going through the port that is critical, say two hours tops."

If we have a problem at Dover with the lorries, Ridge will deal with it. We have given him the contents of the first lorry, so that we can slip the other four full lorries through the port without Customs being any the wiser. Even his own brothers were plotting around him, keeping things from him. "What sort of diversion are you talking about?"

Peter picked up the question. "Charles, I know he is your man and that you sort of like him, but we must come first, we are family. Yes?"

Charles nodded.

Peter continued, "We are not going to harm him, just keep him out of the way over the period, that's all. We know that Ridge has a granddaughter who goes to a school near Brighton. If we snatch the kid on Friday afternoon when she leaves school and keep her out of the way, then Ridge can spend his weekend looking for her. That will keep him out of our hair until the job is over. Once were clear of the port, we can make sure that Ridge gets his kid back!"

Charles was mortified. "You think it will be as simple as that? If you go ahead with that plan, Ridge will know who is at the back of it. Once you make an enemy of him, he will be a very dangerous opponent: it's not worth the risk!"

"We have no choice but to cover that risk. If we ignore it, then we are the ones at risk. What's it to be then, it's make your mind up time?" Paul said.

Charles thought about it. "Okay," he said. "But I warn you now, once Ridge works it out, and he will, he won't take it lying down, he will come after us."

Paul raised his hand and pointed his fingers together as if shooting a gun. "Let him fucking come. If he gets nasty, I will deal with him, once and for all!"

Peter showed his irritability. "It's all right talking like that, Paul, but once you have done that, once you have shot a copper, we will have the whole fucking lot of them, Customs as well, after us. They won't rest until they've got us!"

"That's only a last resort, Charles can sort him out and just keep him out of our hair until the job is done, can't you Charles?"

Charles could see the job going down the drain. It was now getting too complicated. Ridge was going to be the problem. He could manage him all the while he was calm, but the moment anything happened to his family he knew Ridge would take no prisoners trying to rectify matters. But it was the best option they had, so he agreed.

"I will deal with Ridge."

"Right, moving on then," Peter said. "Now, that's sorted let's talk about the plan. I will go over to France on the Friday morning and tie up with Andre. I can make sure the drivers are on the ball for the Saturday morning run to the port to catch the ferries.

"The first lorry will leave the farm in time to catch the first ferry at eight-fifteen. The other four lorries will leave the flying club via a different route to the port and catch the nine-fifteen ferry. We know that the whole Customs team have been set to catch the first lorry. Once they have become involved in doing that, their whole port staffing plan goes to the wall for the rest of the day. They will have no one to cover the ferries for the rest of the day. The other four lorries just board the ferry at Calais and come off at Dover Port and all four will be out of the port within thirty minutes. The drivers know the route to the farm, so I do not expect any deviation from that.

"Paul will stay at the farm to see the lorries in, while Charles stays at his place to be the link man. If I need to telephone Paul with anything at all, I will do it via Charles. That way there is no direct traceable body contact between the three of us, but we all know what is going on. Any questions?"

Charles, thinking he was being sidelined again, finished his glass. "Why can't I go to the port at Dover, I can then watch the lorries leaving for the farm and let Paul know they are on their way?"

Paul jumped in. "No, it's better you keep on the end of a telephone. Especially if your man kicks off! He will ring you first; you stall him and then let me know. I have a couple of reliable boys on standby!"

Charles knew that if he was going to keep Ridge out of it, then what his brothers said made sense. "Okay, that's fine."

The brothers, Charles and Paul, finished their drinks and after a bit of banter left the flat and the building by separate exits.

Peter closed the door and locked it from the inside. He went into his bedroom and lifted out of the drawer a small polythene bag containing a large quantity of white powder. Going into the lounge he sat down and pulled the coffee table towards him. Tipping most of the white powder on the glass surface he then separated the powder into two neat lines.

Chapter Thirty-Nine

Detective Sergeant John Snow was at his desk, playing with a metal paper clip, bending it backwards and forwards between his fingers. Like Ridge, he was very much a ferret, happiest out on the streets talking about crime to those committing crime. That was how detectives got to arrest villains, rather than sitting in an office twiddling the keys on a computer keyboard.

The trouble, as Snow appreciated, was that it was now an unfashionable exercise to work informants in a quiet and secretive way. Every Tom, Dick and Harry in the intelligence game wanted to know the name of the informant, particularly if he was seen to be a successful informant. It was also fraught with danger for the brave ones owing to the risk of criticism just waiting to be exercised by the myriad of office dwellers sitting at their desks, all benefiting from the 20/20 vision of hindsight.

Whilst computer information was essential to a detective, it was often being in the right place at the right time and the old-fashioned gut response that came about as a result of a twitching nose. You couldn't buy that or train detectives to be like that; it came about as a result of spending time out on the streets getting your hands dirty, so to speak.

Snow was not very happy. He had a lot to lose by the removal of Ridge from duty. They all had a lot to lose. In fact, if the truth were known and spoken out loud, the job would not go ahead because it could not. If the job was to have any chance of succeeding, it needed Ridge back on tap, driving it forward.

Snow found difficulty in supporting the action of Ridge's supervisors. He considered the two men as absolute tossers to suspend a working detective like Ridge so close to the endgame of what was a massive importation of drugs. If they wanted to suspend Ridge, why not wait until the job was over? At the back of Snow's mind he detected shades of jealousy coming from those two. Without a doubt, they wanted to take over the running of the job without Ridge's presence or input. Now, there they were, all of them, up the fucking creek without a paddle!

Peter Jameson glanced out of his window and saw Snow at his desk twisting the paper clip. He recognised the signs that Snow was pissed off. He smiled as his view took in the entire office staff. It was a funny thing, but watching thirty people at their desks, he could identify those who were desk workers and those fretting at their desks, trying to expedite matters in order to get out of the office. Snow was always amongst those trying to get out of the office, except for today. He seemed to have had the stuffing knocked out of him.

Jameson got up and walked over to Snow. "What's the problem Jon?"

Snow looked at him. "Guvnor, without John Ridge this operation is well and truly fucked. We simply cannot move forward without Ridge! All we can do is wait until the Ford family import their drugs and then try and pick up the pieces. If that happens the opportunity of snaffling millions of pounds worth of drugs is almost certainly lost to us! This is the best job that SOCA has had all year and we are going to let it slip through our fingers because of Ridge's dopey supervisory officers! We are now so close to not only closing this drug team down once and for all and taking a lot of gear off the market, but also arresting Charles Ford for what he did to that female Customs officer."

Jameson, laughing now, sat down and leaned close to Snow. "You are a devious bastard Jon. Are you suggesting that I ought to write to those tossers' bosses in Sussex and explain to them that it is rank bad manners for them to suspend one of their officers from duty whilst he is, in a manner of speaking, attached to SOCA? Tell me Jon is that what you expect me to do? Risk my career just to clear up a drugs job?"

Snow looked up at his grinning boss. "Well, it would be a start!" he said, now grinning like a Cheshire cat. "Seriously though, we cannot move this forward without Ridge. I know he is a cunning bastard and goes his own way a lot, but he is getting the results that we cannot get."

Jameson presented a straight face to Snow. "I'm sorry Jon, you're too late." He paused and looked away so that Snow could not see him stifling a smile.

"Why is that Guv?" Snow asked.

Jameson could not hold his smile back any longer, his entire face creased into laughter lines. "Because..." he stopped, watching Snow's face, "I typed a suitable e-mail to Sussex yesterday, following that embarrassing conference. I am waiting for a reply. That's why I have been in the office all day. Why have you been in the office all day you wanker? Get out and do some police work! Also, I have decided not wait for a reply, it might never come! Secondly, you try and get hold of Ridge; we want him back on-line now, not fucking tomorrow or the next day. Whatever you do don't ring his office; find someone else to talk to, but get him, understood?"

Snow sat there with his mouth open for a moment. "Sir, who was it who said that all detective inspectors are bastards?"

Jameson walked back into his office, sat down and looked out at Snow, sticking up two fingers at him.

Snow refreshed his plastic coffee cup and set to work.

Chapter Forty

Emil Kimber was not a happy bunny. He punched in the door code and entered the back door of the police station. He took the lift up to the first floor and made his way to his office. He had made up his mind: he was going to give his detective inspector a piece of his mind. Please or offend, he was not going to be treated like this. Kimber had decided that he was not going to carry the can for the lazy bastard, just because he was the inspector. No, he was going to have to pull his weight if they were going to get on in future! That fucking embarrassing rebuke at the conference was the last straw. He was not having it.

Kimber got up, walked the short distance along the corridor to Johnston's office, knocked on the door and waited.

"Come," he heard through the door. Entering the office he saw Johnston sitting behind the desk. He did not look very pleased to see Kimber and did not ask him to be seated. Kimber stood and folded his arms across his chest in a show of defiance.

"Emil, is there a problem?" Johnston asked, aware from Kimber's body language that there was.

"Yes, there is," Kimber replied petulantly, but trying to speak in his authoritative, slightly deeper-toned voice.

"I went to the conference with SOCA and Customs yesterday and got the fucking blame for Ridge not being there. I was called upon to stand up and account for his absence which I did to the best of my ability. But I still seemed to get my bollocks chewed off by everyone there."

"So what Emil? You are my detective sergeant and in my absence you accept the authority to act on my behalf. You cannot just have the perks of the job, sometimes you have to take the shit as well. Is that understood?"

"I understand what you are saying, but it is not very nice when it happens to you. Everybody there thought that I had suspended Ridge and that without him the job was as good as dead." He paused letting the last comment sink in.

Johnston tapped the desk a few times before he replied. "Emil, you must accept your part in this plan. If you recall, I asked you to get in touch with the informant and take over as the handling officer as soon as we had removed that bastard Ridge from the scene. Did you do that? No you fucking didn't," Johnston said, answering his own question. "All you fucking did was to allow the informant to put the phone down on you and then you gave up!"

"What else could I do?" Kimber said. "I can't make him talk to me!"

Johnston sat up straight. "Well, Emil, it looks as if you have failed in your role as a supervisory officer with Ridge, which I think is why you reported him to me in the first place. Secondly, it was obvious to me that you could not control Ridge's activities with Ford, which is why I removed Ridge from the scene and left you in charge, hoping that you would get a grip of the informant and move things on. I do not think that you have taken this job seriously. This informant is at the centre of a national, multi-agency investigation and you tell me the man won't talk to you! What am I to think? That you are out of your depth and cannot cope? Thirdly, Emil, you supported me in suspending Ridge, partially, I suspect, because you wanted to get your own back on him for regularly showing you up to be the fucking duffer you are! Do I need to go on?"

Kimber was shaking with anger as the realisation that he was the fall guy in all of this became apparent to him. He had been soundly beaten by his inspector's crafty decision to cover his actions in the way he had.

Watching Kimber's reaction, Johnston saw that he was unlikely to get much support from him in the future so he pressed on determined to put Kimber well and truly in his place.

"Emil, you must get a grip on this job and move it forward, otherwise there will be further complaints that I may not be able to ignore. It's down to you to show us all that you can deal with this man Ford. After all, he is just a fucking criminal!"

Kimber firmed up. "I want to be taken off this job once and for all. I don't want any more to do with either Ridge or his informant or this job. That is an official request, sir."

Johnston was now really pissed-off with his deputy.

"Emil, you are well and truly stuck with this. Now go and get on with it. If you do not make the most of it and fail to get a successful result with the other agencies then I may have to refer to it in your annual appraisal. Now, Emil, get out of my fucking office!"

Kimber did as he was instructed and left the office. As he walked along the corridor to his office, a form of dread was seeping into him. Johnston had him by the balls and he knew it. In one move he had removed Ridge because he was jealous of him and secondly, worst of all, the cunning bastard had worked it so that any blame for failure would rest on his shoulders. He felt tears forming and then tumbling out down his cheeks dripping on to his stained rugby shirt.

Eventually, Kimber realised there was only one way out. He picked up the telephone and dialled Ridge's home telephone number. Marie picked up at the other end. "Hello Marie," Kimber said, recognising her voice, "can I have a word with John?"

Marie bristled. She knew Kimber and had never liked him, seeing him for what he was. This was the second time that he was present and connected with the suspension of her husband. She hesitated momentarily before saying, "No," and putting the telephone down.

Kimber looked at the silent telephone in front of him. How dare she put the phone down on him? Maybe Johnston was right. Perhaps he was too easy with people. If he was, then that status was going to change in the very near future. There was only one person now left to call. He could feel himself sweating as he dialled the number and waited.

Ford picked up the telephone but did not speak.

Kimber panicked. "Listen to me Ford, you must speak to me I need your help." He heard the telephone slammed down onto its cradle.

Kimber sat at his desk for the rest of the morning wondering what on earth he could do; he thought of all the options and discarded all of them bar one. The more he thought about the one remaining option the more he believed it could succeed. If it did succeed, then the success of it would blow Johnston out of his chair and have the others sucking up to him at the next conference. Yes, he would give it a go!

Now smiling, he stood up and walked out his office, whistling as he went. He filled his car up at the nearest service station and then made his way to the bottom of the A23 motorway system. He settled back in his seat, switched on his favourite CD and then drove north to London, smiling in anticipation of a change in his fortunes within a short time.

Chapter Forty-One

Jon Snow sat in his office still twiddling his thumbs. Two days he had sat watching his telephone, waiting for Ridge to pick up. He wondered how much longer he could give it, just waiting for one particular person in the whole world to ring him back.

He guessed that Ridge was seething at his suspension from duty and was probably reluctant to speak to anyone connected with the police service. He could understand that. The last time he had been suspended he had felt nothing but anger for those responsible. Once reinstated, he had taken a long time to get over it. It had created a bitterness that remained to this day. But you do have to move on! Secretly, Snow was relying on Ridge's inquisitiveness. Once Ridge looked at the caller's name, he would be drawn to wonder why he was being called. He would not resist the call for much longer. Snow got up and went across to the cold water fountain to replenish his plastic beaker. He was halfway there when his telephone rang. Sliding back across the top of his desk scattering paperwork everywhere, Snow plucked the telephone from its cradle and identified himself to the caller.

"You called me?" Ridge snapped. Just that, no introduction and an assumption Snow would recognise his voice.

"Thanks for calling John. I know what has happened to you John, but the truth of the matter is we need you. We are fucking dead in the water with this job if you are not pushing it. One way or the other, we at least must meet and get the ball rolling again!"

"I can't," Ridge said, "I am suspended from duty because I stood to close to the edge on this one. Because I thought we were all in the same job, I opened my trap at the conference and those two dopey supervisors of mine were waiting for an excuse to fuck me, and I gave it to them!"

"John, listen to me. Your man Kimber got his bollocks bitten at the last conference. I also know that moves are being made to change your current status, so be patient on that score. In the meantime, I see no reason why you and me could not meet for just a drink and natter about old times, yeah?" Snow crossed his fingers and waited.

"You mean bastard, Snow. You could at least offer a filet steak to go with the drink!"

"Okay, you're on," Snow said, now the happiest man in the country. "Just for your information, there is a letter in the mail to your Assistant Chief about the circumstances surrounding your suspension from duty. Be patient and things will happen. However, the one thing that would really endear you to one and all is to get this job dealt with in a successful way. Do you think we can move it on?"

"Jon," Ridge said, "I can't afford to be stabbed in the back again. What if you were setting me up just like those two wankers I work for, we both know it would finish me?"

"Ridge you tosser! If I was going to do that to you, would I waste my hard earned money offering to buy you a filet steak? Get fucking real!"

Ridge grinned down the other end of the telephone. "Okay, you bastard, let's give it a whirl! The job is on for this coming Saturday morning, so let's meet, say, tonight and get things up and running, yeah?"

"You won't regret this John," Snow said, now pleased as Punch that the job was again up and running. "Where shall we meet?"

Ridge thought for a moment. "There's a *Little Chef*, halfway between us, close to Croydon, do you know it?"

Snow laughed. "Yes I know it, but I can't recommend the steak. Sometimes it's a bit chewy."

Ridge smiled. "Trust me on this Jon, it's fine dining all the way at these places nowadays!"

"Right on!" He put the telephone down and punched a high five into the air and let out a scream that echoed down the length of the office causing people to look up.

Jameson grinned as he watched Snow's antics. He guessed what it was about but did not ask. He was content to leave everything to his subordinate. Snow could cope.

Snow tidied up in his office and spent a few minutes talking with Jameson before he jumped into an unmarked car and headed south. His usual practice when meeting someone, anyone for that matter, was to be early so that he could have a look around and just make sure it was secure. Apart from the *Little Chef* building, which he knew he could not do much about, he wanted to look at the entrances and exits.

Sometimes being able to either get in or get out could be important and he always liked to be first to arrive and pick a seat where he was able to watch the car park entrance and exit for movement. Satisfied, he parked the car and walked into the restaurant. He saw Ridge already there and tucked into a corner seat watching the car park and doors. They grinned at each other realising that they each had the same thought. Snow sat down across the table from Ridge. They shook hands. Snow noticed Ridge's powerful grip. He liked the man immediately. A working dick, who knew how many beans made five!

287

Snow waited for the coffee to arrive before he spoke. "John, I believe if we at least keep talking we can make this job work!"

"I couldn't agree more," Ridge said, now delighted that he was at last talking to a kindred spirit. "Let's deal with this fucking Ford family once and for all!"

They chatted between themselves about the job and its direction until their coffee cups were empty. The two friends then shook hands and agreed to meet again.

They left the car park and went in their different directions.

Chapter Forty-Two

Emil Kimber cursed himself. It was 9.45pm and turning just a little on the cold side. He had not thought of the cold, well, to tell the truth he hadn't anticipated being there that long. A quick trip up to the Smoke, identify Ford's house and an even quicker spot of obs', until he caught Ford either entering or leaving his house. The bastard would then not be able to put the telephone down on him. Oh no, Mr Fucking Ford, this time it was going to be different. The boot was going to be on the other foot this time. His fucking foot! Whether he liked it or not, Mr Fucking Ford, was going to be dealing with Detective Sergeant Emil Kimber in person.

He was also getting hungry and thirsty. Kimber had contemplated stopping off somewhere just for a quick bite on the journey up, but a few problems with the satnav put paid to that idea. He would stop on the way back to Brighton, after he had dealt with Ford.

Unfortunately for Kimber, Charles Ford lived in a detached house in a small cul-de-sac. That meant that he could not simply park his car in the street and watch Ford's front door from a distance. He would soon be spotted by either Ford or one of his fucking nosey neighbours. It was going to be a foot job, no other way of doing it. Kimber abandoned his car some distance from the cul-de-sac and walked around the area seeking a suitable spot for what he had in mind.

Immediately opposite the entrance to the cul-de-sac was a large children's park containing swings and roundabouts and an office building of sorts. From the very centre of the park, Kimber had a good full-on view of Ford's house. The downside was that there was no obvious point of cover nearby. A row of four foot high bushes around a poorly maintained lawn offered the only option, but it required him to be on his hands and knees on the damp grass. He maintained this location thinking that his position would improve as darkness increased. As the coldness increased he found himself getting stiff so he moved from the hedgerow to the small children's roundabout and sat on the metal centre piece. He could still maintain a good field of vision on the house, although to anyone looking he looked like an oversized child stopping out late. Kimber found his vision improved a bit when the street lights came on and from where he was sitting he could easily see the newspaper halfway in Ford's letterbox.

The cold was now getting to him and penetrating his damp jeans. To warm up a bit he walked around in small circles and did a few press-up exercises on the roundabout.

Fuck this for a game of soldiers, he thought, and then said it out aloud, "Fuck this for a game of soldiers!" He was comforted by the sound of his voice because he was not used to being on his own in the dark for any length of time. "I should have brought someone with me, that way at least we could have talked to each other!"

Something made Kimber aware that he was not alone in the park. He looked around and eventually spotted an elderly dog walker standing in the shadow of the office building watching him. The man walked off leaving Kimber to continue talking to himself and resuming his exercises.

Ford's house was still in darkness and when houses either side of his switched their lights off and went to bed the whole area, now in darkness apart from a streetlight, became a little on the spooky side.

Kimber resumed his exercises and began talking to himself as the car, without lights, drew up alongside the park railings and came to a stop. The two men watched Kimber for a few moments, then quietly left their car and converged on him from different angles at the same time. The man closest to Kimber rugby-tackled him to the ground. The second man reached down and seized hold of one of Kimber's arms and began twisting it against the joint as Kimber started kicking out at him.

"Stop struggling or it will be the worse for you!" he said, twisting the joint even more.

Kimber ignored the instruction and increased his kicking at the man as well as shouting abuse. Suddenly, he found himself turned over and a large and heavy knee pressing deep into the small of his back. The first man seized Kimber's hair and began rubbing his face into the damp grassy surface. He then pulled Kimber up on to his knees and, holding his head backwards, moved around towards him and kicked him in the testicles.

All resistance from Kimber evaporated as he took the full force of the blow and began to cry in pain. He was dragged to his feet and handcuffs were placed on his wrists.

"Right, you dirty little perv," shouted one of the men, "you are under arrest. Now stop struggling, unless you want some more?" He raised his foot as if he was going to kick Kimber in the testicles. Kimber tried to cover his groin by placing one of his legs sideways thereby protecting the area. He then saw for the first time that both men were wearing the uniform of the Metropolitan Police.

Recovering from his abuse at their hands, Kimber said angrily, "You can't arrest me I'm a police officer!"

One of the officers grabbed Kimber around the throat and squeezed until he began to choke. "Yes, and

I am the Sugar Plum Fairy in charge of the park! Now let's go to the car, and then continue this conversation at the police station!"

With that Kimber had his wrists forced up his back and was then pushed on his toes to the stationary police car and thrown into the back on his front. His legs were bent double to force him into the car. One of the officers went around the car, opened the rear door and sat on Kimber's neck and shoulders keeping him pinned down for the short duration of the trip to the police station.

In the custody block, the duty sergeant listened impassively to the officer's account of the circumstances surrounding Kimber's arrest, beginning with the dog walker's complaint to them of a strange man in the kids' park, who he heard talking to himself.

The officer looked at Kimber's bloody face and continued his account by saying that when he and his colleague approached the man he was indeed walking around in small circles talking to himself. When they spoke to him he became violent and had to be subdued. It was a simple as that!

"Bollocks!" screamed Kimber. "I am going to make a complaint against these two officers at the highest level, and what is more, I want to see the duty solicitor, right now!"

"Do you now?" the duty sergeant soothed, as if he was speaking to a mentally challenged child.

Turning to both the arresting officers, he said, "I believe this man is too upset as a result of consuming too much alcohol, to process at this moment in time. Strip him of his clothes and personal belongings for his own safety and place him in the drunks' cell until the duty solicitor arrives and interviews him!"

On that instruction Kimber was dragged out of the office and along the corridor. His clothes and personal possessions were removed from him and he was then pushed into the smelly drunks' cell joining two other unfortunates already there. The cell door was then slammed shut after him.

Chapter Forty-Three

John Ridge woke up and reached out for Josie only to find she had gone. He glanced at his watch and found that it was nine-fifteen. No wonder she wasn't there, she was probably at her desk dealing with whatever problems had occurred overnight. He smiled as he thought of the warmth and encouragement she had bestowed on him since his suspension from duty. Josie had identified the problem and provided him with the answer to it. He knew he was now on the way back thanks to her.

To fill in his day, each day whilst Josie was at work Ridge was training with long runs along the seafront and back. He wanted to sharpen himself up after his drinking binge. He mentally ran over his conversation with Snow. He liked the bloke very much. A down-to-earth guy he could and did identify with.

With Snow's help the job was back on track. He needed Ford to ring him with something that would set the whole business on the move to the conclusion. It was a funny thing, Ridge thought, how something started as a lump of raw intelligence that was open to interpretation, sometimes in a number of ways, and then it grew to the point where it became factual and required careful planning to bring it to the boil.

This was the bit where expertise was required because the job and the people involved would be at their most dangerous. Ridge loved that feeling of being involved with people's lives to a point where he knew he could make a difference. However, for the moment he would need to tread warily and be patient. He knew Snow would bend over backwards to get his suspension removed and him back into harness over the next few days. He just had to keep his head down and wait and see.

Ridge's mind wandered to Marie and the family. He knew he should have taken more care over his out-of-office activities. Ridge had treated Marie shabbily over the last few years and was now paying the price for it. If matters within his job worked out for the better he would try to rebuild his lost relationship with Marie. Best to let sleeping dogs lie for a few weeks, let it all calm down and then he would make his move. Josie was a wonderful girl and a real trouper in and out of bed, but it was Marie that he loved.

His telephone rang. It was Ford.

"John?"

"Yes, it's me!"

"Just thought that I would bring you up to date. The driver of the lorry is a South London heavy by the name of Joey Serrif. He's from Catford. He knows what's on board. But, be warned, he's a nasty bit of work. Just make sure that he is arrested at the port. The last thing I want is for that bastard to get away scot-free!"

"Charles, is there anything that you haven't told me that I need to know to avoid one almighty cock-up taking place on the day?"

"No, John, I've told you everything that I know. This will be a nice little tickle for you and your lot, believe me!"

"That's fine then, Charles. I will start to get my lot organised, give me a ring in the week?" Ridge put the telephone down and began making notes of the conversation.

Ridge sat and thought about Ford. There is something funny going on, but sooner or later I will know. He picked up the telephone and spoke to Jon Snow about Ford's conversation. Snow was delighted.

"Well done, John, we are now underway again. Do you want to come to the port on the day of the race or what?"

Ridge declined, saying that if he remained centralised he would be better placed if things went wrong or something needed his attention. He then told Snow again about the gut feeling that he wasn't being told everything by Ford.

Snow pursed his lips for a moment. "We can only act on what we know. If that sneaky bastard wants to play his own game as well, then we can devote a bit of special attention to him afterwards and he can take the same fall as his friends, yes?"

"Sounds good to me Jon," Ridge said as he put the phone down.

Chapter Forty-Four

Detective Chief Superintendent Crispen Stoneheart was aptly named. He had the reputation throughout the Force of being a first-rate detective who had proved his ability time and time again. His one major downside, although it had not stopped his progression through the ranks, was that he did not suffer fools easily. Stoneheart was currently head of the Special Units in the Force. He believed in giving the detectives under him total support to achieve results in their chosen field, but he was not a man to be trifled with.

Stoneheart sat in his large office chair and looked down his half-frames at the two men standing in front of him, Detective Inspector Roland Johnston and Detective Sergeant Emil Kimber. Johnston was smartly turned out in a dark grey suit although he was unnaturally white about the face and noticeably breathing shallow, short, sharp breaths, a bit like a pregnant woman near her time. He was clearly very nervous of the man behind the desk.

Detective Sergeant Emil Kimber stood alongside his inspector. He was dressed in the same scruffy attire that he had worn the previous day when performing his surveillance at Ford's house. His rugby player's shirt looked as if he had been living in it, which of course he had. His trendy blue jeans were grass-stained and also looked as if he had been sleeping in them. The part of him that drew most attention was his face. First impression was that he had not slept very well, there were bags under his eyes, one of which was half-closed. His hair looked unkempt as did his two-day designer stubble. But it was his swollen lips and bloody nose that drew most attention together with the dried bloodstains still in place around his chin. All in all, Kimber looked a mess and a very unhappy officer standing before his senior officer.

Stoneheart allowed his gaze to wander to the two e-mails on his desk in front of him.

He looked up.

"Before I get down to business can either of you tell me, am I missing something here?"

Johnston glanced at Kimber and then back at his boss. He thought that it was probably best that he gave the account rather than leave it to the imbecile by his side. Much better for him to give a sanitised version of events the previous night than allow Kimber to witter on and drop him in the shit as well.

"Well sir, yesterday Sergeant Kimber decided that as one of the detective constables on the Unit is currently suspended from duty, thus creating something of a void in available operational manpower, he would take up the slack, so to speak, and perform surveillance himself on a major drug target that we are currently targeting." Johnston paused, desperately trying to get his breath. "I have to say, sir, that although I did not authorise Kimber's actions and knew nothing about it all, I do think that what followed later was a little, how shall we say, a little unfortunate." Again he stopped.

Stoneheart glared at him. "What was a little unfortunate?"

"Well, sir, whilst Sergeant Kimber was deployed on surveillance duties, it appears that he was reported to the Met Police by a local dog walker out in the park, who thought that Sergeant Kimber was some sort of pervert." Johnston paused, again sucking in oxygen in small amounts and exhaling in short puffs.

By now, Stoneheart's eyes had settled on Kimber who was visibly shaking.

Johnston continued. "It appears that two local police officers went to arrest Sergeant Kimber when some sort of scuffle broke out between them, ending up with Sergeant Kimber being arrested and taken to the local police station and detained."

Johnston again paused, this time for his final piece. He wanted to get this bit right just to show how professional and competent he had been in dealing with the matter. "In the early hours of this morning, I was summoned by the Met and went immediately to the police station where Sergeant Kimber was being detained." He stood up straight and squared his shoulders at this point. "I was able to smooth over the problem with the Met Duty Inspector. Apologies all round, sort of thing, and get Kimber's charges dropped. We travelled back to Sussex in the early hours, which to some extent explains Sergeant Kimber's state of dress. I have had little or no sleep whilst Kimber has not had time to have a bath or change! I have, of course, spoken to Sergeant Kimber about last night's tactics, and suggested to him a better way, the next time he goes out on his own!"

Stoneheart sat back and wafted his hand across in front of his face. "Yes, I can tell that one of you at least needs a course in personal hygiene. Do I understand right, Sergeant Kimber, that you assaulted police officers from another Force?"

Kimber was hoping the ground would open up and swallow him whole. He was on his own here and he knew it. "It's not quite as simple as that, sir," he muttered. "I was the one who was assaulted."

"Who won? Who came out on top?" Stoneheart asked.

Shamefaced and muttering through his swollen lips Kimber said, "I suppose they did, sir."

"Yes, I thought you would say that!" Stoneheart replied, now looking at the e-mails in front of him. "If this sorry little saga wasn't bad enough, let's move on to something connected to it but which in my estimation is infinitely more damaging to the reputation of my department and even the Force's reputation."

He glared at the two men.

"You go first, Roland. Please explain to me very slowly, why you suspended Detective Constable John Ridge from duty when he is, or rather was, clearly deeply involved in dealing with a very dangerous informant in a ongoing situation?"

Roland Johnston felt faint. He knew at the time that he listened to Kimber about his complaint, that Ridge wasn't telling him everything and that it was going to come back and bite him up the arse at some stage.

"Sir, I suspended Ridge following conversation with Sergeant Kimber, who said that Ridge was again doing his own thing and not seeking authorisation from either of us in relation to his activities with this informant!"

Stoneheart had listened to this pompous diatribe for long enough. He put one hand up to his forehead as if unable to grasp Johnston's words.

"Roland, permit me to say this to you, this is not the first time that you have suspended Ridge from duty is it?"

"No sir, it's the second time. Ridge must learn to do as he is told, so that we as a unit can move forward as one, not as individuals."

Johnston felt quite pleased with the way that he phrased that explanation. That would show the boss that he at least was thinking ahead and running a tight ship, so to speak.

"Roland, John Ridge is probably the most productive detective in your department. Dicks like that do tend to be the ones who live a bit on the edge; it's what makes them so good. Without people like Ridge, an intelligence unit cannot function properly as we can witness by last night's fiasco involving him!" Stoneheart pointed disparagingly at Kimber. "When I put you in charge of the unit, I expected some creative thinking, followed by action that would boost the competitive teamwork of your unit. Some of the detectives in the unit adopt a different approach to intelligence work and just collect paper intelligence within the office environment. Ridge is not like that. He goes out and gets his hands dirty talking to people. Others can learn from that approach. You can learn from that approach! Do you understand me?"

"Yes sir, I completely understand you."

"Good, so far so good Roland. I think we are now beginning to sing from the same hymn sheet, yes?"

"Yes sir, we are."

Stoneheart picked up the two e-mails from his desk. "Roland, I have here two e-mails: one from SOCA and one from Her Majesty's Customs and Excise Investigation Service. They are both singing from the same hymn sheet, as us! Like me, they cannot understand, Roland, why when an international drugs investigation is in the final endgame stage you suddenly take it into your tiny fucking mind to suspend from duty the lead officer. They have gone further, Roland, they have said that, without Ridge, the operation is a dead duck in the water! Now Roland, here is what I want you to do. Are you listening?"

Johnston nodded his head. "Yes sir."

Stoneheart parted his lips as if he was going to smile but then changed his mind. "You, Roland, will leave here and go back to Brighton where you will remove the suspension from Ridge. You will contact him immediately and reinstate him. I want him back on the job as soon as. Kiss his arse if necessary, but get him back, now, is that clear Roland?"

Johnston nodded. His mouth was dry and he had difficulty forming the words. "Yes sir!"

"Roland, from now on I will be taking a personal interest in the development of this ongoing job. Leave Ridge to work as he does best. Do you understand?"

"Yes sir."

"Good, now you can get out of my office!"

Johnston, visibly cowed by the withering exchange from his boss, turned and left the office.

Stoneheart looked at Emil Kimber.

"Emil, I believe that there is more than a little jealousy going on in your mind over Ridge's ability to deal with informants. You have heard my comments to your detective inspector. I want Ridge back as part of the team, if that is the right phrase to use. I want you to make it work, do you understand? It is also apparent to me that after last night's fiasco you need further training in surveillance techniques. I will arrange for that to take place after this job has run its course.

"In the meantime, Emil, let me say you have embarrassed yourself and you have embarrassed the Force, as well as jeopardising the job in hand. If your name crops up again in any matter to do with Ridge, I will take a close look and decide if your time would be better spent looking after the day-to-day duties of the traffic wardens in the town. Do you grasp my meaning?"

Kimber felt his knees knocking together. "Yes sir."

"Now get out of my office you fuckwit!"

Kimber turned and made for the door. He was almost in tears as he saw any chance of promotion disappear from view. He got to the door when Stoneheart stopped him. "Sergeant Kimber?"

Kimber turned to his boss. "Yes sir?"

"Get a shower soonest, there's a good chap!"

When Kimber had left his office Stoneheart tuned into his computer and sought out Ridge's mobile telephone number. He listened to it ring for a few moments before it was picked up.

"Ridge, Chief Superintendent Stoneheart, I have just finished speaking to your inspector and his sidekick. I can only apologise for what has gone on in the recent past. We are all now singing from the same hymn sheet. Your suspension from duty has been revoked and I want you back on side as soon as possible. Get the balls rolling again, ASAP, got it?"

"Yes sir," Ridge replied, feeling surprised and grateful that his most senior officer had taken the trouble to ring him and reinstate him.

"Good man," Stoneheart said, and put the telephone down.

Chapter Forty-Five

It was a bright sunny afternoon when Snow left the Underground and walked along the road towards the Old Customs House near Tower Bridge. After the usual preliminaries of signing in at the front of house and then ringing through to the department concerned, he was escorted through the building and up to the second floor and to an office occupied by an undercover team of the Cocaine Intelligence Unit, known as the Hunters. The team consisted of four male investigators led by a senior investigation officer. All the team members were well trained in the difficult arts of surveillance and intelligence gathering. The team leader was normally kept advised on all large scale importation of drugs jobs and was always available to offer advice or assistance in the event of it becoming necessary.

Snow, who had never met the team before, was introduced to each member in turn. He noticed but did not comment on the fact that he was given only the Christian name of each member. Even amongst friendly investigative agencies there was a tendency to be security conscious when it came to identifying team members.

Coffee was served to all those present allowing the usual round of inconsequential chit-chat to take place.

Snow was the first speaker: he briefed the meeting with all the information at his disposal including a scathing account of the politics surrounding Ridge. It was Snow's belief that nothing should be held back. If you knew something you should say it. In the world of intelligence gathering it was not uncommon for the greater struggle to take place inside the job, sometimes placing the success of the job at risk. No secrets, no fuck-ups was Snow's view!

The team leader listened carefully to what Snow said and then offered his advice and assistance. He said that two of his team would be at Calais first thing on Saturday morning to watch the lorry loading. They would identify the vehicle and driver and any passengers that might be with the driver. Those details would be radioed through to the temporary command post at Dover.

Once the driver had parked the vehicle and moved to the upper deck for the duration of the sailing, the team would have a discreet look at the lorry and fit a tracker device to it just in case some unforeseen factor cropped up at Dover.

At the port, a further team would see the vehicle off the ship and join the queue of vehicles going through Customs checks. Once the vehicle was stopped, a casual check by a passing dog handler would indicate something untoward on the lorry. A full search would then be requested in the presence of the driver just to give him the impression that it was a lucky strike rather than a pre-planned operation.

It was hoped that the drugs hidden on the vehicle would be found at this point and the driver arrested. All those present at the meeting agreed to this plan as the best way to deal with matters. As a safety measure it was decided to roll the job over to the Sunday in the event of something cropping up and preventing the lorry sailing on the Saturday ferry. Again, that was agreed.

Snow brought the meeting to an end by asking all present to recall the six pees. Seeing some blank faces, he elaborated, "Perfect planning prevents piss poor performance!"

As they laughed Snow went on, "Don't forget, we have been told that this lorry has a large secret compartment across the back of it containing something like sixty kilos of cocaine. A rough calculation gives us drugs worth nearly two million pounds. That is base value before the drugs are cut and then hit the streets. We are then talking of a street value that could increase a hundred fold. Let us stop this lot fucking-up thousands of people's lives!"

★ ★ ★ ★

At the very time that Jon Snow was briefing the Customs team, Peter Ford was catching the Thursday evening ferry from Dover to Calais. He planned to drive from Calais down through France and be at the farm for early evening. Ford was driving a hired Disco not wanting his own Range Rover checked by some nosy Customs official. He assumed that he and his brothers tripping in and out of the country would be of interest to the authorities and that was something he wished to avoid this close to the day of the race. Why make it easy for them?

On the ferry he saw Joey, the gun, Serrif waiting for him. He didn't like Serrif. He was far too quick at going off at a tangent, hence his name. Serrif was likely to blow up at the least provocation. He was just hired muscle and no brain.

Paul had chosen him because they were birds of a feather, so alike it was unbelievable. The two of them were old-style, across the pavement robbers, who like many had turned to drug smuggling because it was easier.

Although Ford didn't like the man he thought it a good idea to have Serrif on the job with his brother Paul because together they acted as insurance men for the job. There was no honour amongst thieves and there was always a real risk that someone else would become aware of a large amount of drugs on the move and feel that their entitlement was greater. Joey and Paul would frighten off most contenders.

Ford acknowledged Joey with a nod, but did not speak to him throughout the journey. Again, Joey would have come to the notice of the Customs. With his previous convictions they would have wondered why he was on the ship; in fact they were probably watching him now. Ford glanced around but could not identify any likely watchers. He went and got a meal and sat at a table that provided him with a view of most of the restaurant. He could see most of the goings-on without moving.

The announcement came for drivers to return to the lower deck and rejoin their vehicles; Ford finished his coffee and made his way down the stairway. He could see Joey ahead of him. Reaching the Disco, Ford unlocked the doors and climbed in. Moments later Joey climbed in the back and lay down on the seat, pulling a large car blanket over him. With the dark privacy glass on all the Disco's windows Joey remained unseen from the outside. They drove off the ferry and began their journey to the farm.

Chapter Forty-Six

Paul Ford woke up in the strange bed at 8.30 on the Friday morning and wondered where he was. He looked around the room and guessed that it was a hotel room somewhere, but where? He knew that in the not too distance future he was going to have to come off the shit that was fucking with his head. Cocaine was doing his head in. He was taking more and more which, while nice at the time, meant that, like now, he didn't know what day it was or even where he was. Gaps in his memory were becoming more frequent often causing him some embarrassment.

Earlier that year he'd woken up in some bed alone and couldn't work out where he was. He telephoned a friend and had to be helped home from Holland where he had been on a bender for four days. The four days were completely lost to him. Since that time he had vowed to himself that he would reduce his intake and, to be fair, he had. This was the first time since then that he had suffered a memory loss.

Ford turned over in the bed and realised for the first time that he was not alone. His naked companion was still asleep beside him. The boy had his back to him and was curled up in a ball. Ford's memory began to return. He had found the boy near Victoria Station, plying his trade. When he first saw him, the boy was attempting to attract motorists as they left the station precincts. Ford had simply driven around the road system again and picked him up. The boy was up for anything providing it paid ready cash. Ford took the boy for a meal and then booked into the hotel for the night. As his memory returned, Ford smiled and turned towards the boy. He stroked the boy's spine and woke him up. The boy turned towards him and Ford noticed his erection. He began to stroke the boy who pulled back.

"The night is over," he said. "If you want any more then you will have to pay for it!"

"You cheeky bastard," Ford said, grabbing the boy by the hair and pulling him forward. The boy tried to pull away and was met by Ford's fist full in the face. He punched the boy two or three times causing the blood to flow freely over the sheets and the boy to start moaning in pain. When the boy lay still, Ford turned him over onto his stomach and spread his legs open. There was something about a boy's naked body, he thought, it was a real turn on for him! Now that he had punished this boy for his insolence, he was going to have his money's worth!

Afterwards, Ford showered and dressed. He was feeling much better now. There was work to be done so he couldn't hang about this hotel, enjoying himself any longer. After making sure that he had left nothing lying around that would identify him, he paused and looked at the unconscious boy. Picking up the boy's trousers, Ford rummaged through his pockets until he found the money that he had paid the boy. The boy was going to learn a valuable lesson today. Never take the piss out of the punter! Asking to be paid twice, well, whatever next, cheeky bastard!

Let him complain to the filth if he wanted to. See where that would get him. Ford picked up the hotel telephone and dialled an outside number. A woman's voice answered.

"Where are the boys?" Ford asked, devoid of any courtesy.

"Jimmy's here!" He could hear some conversation in the background.

"Put him on then!"

A gruff voice came on the telephone. "What do you want Paul?"

"Take Alan with you this afternoon and go and pick that kid up at the school. Make sure that there are no problems with the pickup, got it?"

"Yeah, that's fine. Still take her to the farm and keep her quiet?"

Paul thought for a second. "Yeah, that's right. Make sure you get the right kid. She will be wearing small hearing aids because she's deaf. "Whatever you do don't get the wrong kid? Have you got it?"

Paul left the hotel by the fire escape door. He saw no reason to pay for the overnight room. When the kid came round he could pay for it!

Chapter Forty-Seven

Eight-year-old Sasha sat at her desk within the specialist hearing unit at her school, watching the teacher chalking on the board. She looked at her five friends and noticed they were also watching the board with some interest.

Sasha's hand slipped down to her belt and found the on and off switch on the processor. She moved the switch to the off position and lost all contact with the hearing world. She now had complete silence and relief from the extraneous blending of noises picked up by the processor. She didn't need to hear for this lesson, watching what the teacher was writing would be enough. When the teacher had finished she turned so she was facing all the kids in the class and asked each of them to take a turn and read out loud the words on the blackboard. Sasha, watching the lip pattern, quickly picked up the words and waited for her turn. It was hard work trying to make sense of the sounds. Not long, she thought, then I can go home in the taxi!

Sasha was excited about leaving school today because it was her swimming night tonight. She usually went to swimming lessons on Friday nights with a friend from down the road. Sasha had noticed that even though her friend was not deaf, she could not swim faster than her.

The teacher was studying the faces of all the kids looking for clues as to those she had lost in the ongoing lesson. Two of the kids had not quite grasped some of the verbal content and had immediately switched off their concentration level and were looking around for something else to occupy their minds. She caught their eye and frowned slightly which brought the kids back into line. She smiled at their reaction. She knew from teaching children over a good many years that the most difficult part of teaching them was to keep them focused. Deaf children were no different. The moment she turned away from them to write on the board, so most of them would cease to strive to hear and take a brief rest. Some would immediately look for an alternative source of interest. Just because the little buggers were deaf didn't mean their brains were not working. They knew just how far they could go! Not for them the distraction of an outside noise or noise in the classroom, something as simple as the teacher taking her eyes off them would do it.

"Right, Sasha," she said, noticing that Sasha's eyes were going around the room and missing the blackboard. "Can you read the sentence for me, please?"

Sasha saw that she was being spoken to; she focused in on the lip pattern and picked up most of the remaining words. She guessed the complete sentence and looked at the blackboard and did her best to read the words.

The teacher smiled at her. This one was the cheeky one. Of all the kids under her care, Sasha seemed to appreciate the help she was getting and often smiled out of sheer enjoyment when she was spoken to and she immediately picked up the words being used.

The teacher asked Sasha to repeat the reading for two reasons. First, it was the opportunity to talk to her again, which was advantageous in as much as it was always an opportunity to increase the amount of words used on the first conversation thereby increasing her knowledge of longer sentences. Also it gave her a second chance to repeat words that she may have been unsure of.

"Sasha, perhaps you would leave your processor switched on in future. It makes it easier for you to understand what I am saying to you!" The teacher kept a poker face. Deaf children picked up on facial expressions and body language in the absence of hearing words.

Sasha went a shade of pink, knowing she had been caught out. She lowered her eyes. "Yes Mith."

Her voice faltered on the last word which came out as a mith rather than a miss. It caused the teacher to smile. There had been a time when Sasha had no conversational skills. Now, although possessing what would be seen by most as limited skills, she was on her way and that was real progress.

The lesson continued with other children taking their turns until the school bell rang. In spite of all the children being profoundly deaf, they all heard the bell: they listened for that sound without fail every single day. It was time to wind down and get ready to go home. Without waiting for the teacher's instruction the desks were cleared in record time.

The teacher stood up and waited for the children to look at her. Stony-faced she said, "Because you all cleared your desks before I said you could, you will all have to stay at school an extra hour today!" She waited for her words to sink in wondering who would be the first to complain. It was Sasha. She raised her hand and waited for permission to speak.

"Yes, Sasha!"

"Miss, I go swimming tonight."

The teacher smiled. A few extra words from these kids was worth pounds. Thousands of pounds! You simply could not put a value on freely thought out conversation; anything done to create speech was to be applauded. But it was important to quit teaching them while you were still ahead.

"Okay, okay," she said, grinning from ear to ear. "I was only joking. You can all go home."

The children, now hanging on to every word, got the message and screamed out their support as they left the classroom and picked up their coats.

Sasha, struggling into her coat, made her way down to the school secretary's office and sat down on a chair and waited for her taxi. She could see out of through the glass doors and see any car coming up the drive to the office.

As a child with special needs Sasha was taken to and from school on a daily basis in a taxi supplied by the Local Authority. During her wait for the taxi to arrive the school secretary usually kept an eye on her from her open office door. Today was no exception, the secretary saw Sasha come along the corridor and take her seat as usual. Sasha saw the large taxi come through the gates and come slowly up the drive, stopping outside the glass doors. She looked out and saw that it wasn't her usual taxi and it wasn't her usual driver. There was also a man in the back of the taxi. He seemed to be showing a photograph to the man in the front of the taxi.

Her usual driver was a nice lady who often gave her sweets on the journey home. This was a man driver. She saw him wave to her indicating that the taxi was for her. Picking up her satchel, Sasha bounded out of the school and into the rear of the taxi. The man sitting in the back looked at the photograph that he was holding and then at Sasha. He said something to the man in the front and the taxi drove off down the drive and out onto the roadway. The school secretary looked out of her office and saw Sasha getting into the taxi. She also watched as the vehicle drove slowly down the drive before disappearing from her sight. She went back to her computer screen.

Fifteen minutes later than it should have been the usual taxi drove up the school driveway and stopped. The female driver came rushing in to the secretary's office full of apologies. "I'm so sorry that I am late. There was a hold-up on the main road, which is why I'm late. Where is little Sasha?"

The secretary's mouth opened but no words came from her mouth; she just seemed to splutter a bit. Eventually she said, "Sasha was picked up by a taxi about fifteen minutes ago. I saw her get into it and drive off."

They both looked at one another before the secretary asked the female driver for identification. She examined it before passing it back to the owner. The secretary, now feeling the first sensation of panic creeping in, telephoned through to the Hearing Unit. There was no response to her call.

Now feeling distinctly uncomfortable she asked the driver to take a seat and then ran quickly through to the Hearing Unit. Her worst fears were confirmed. The place was empty. She ran back to her office and dialled Sasha's home address. Her mother answered the call.

"Is Sasha home yet?" the secretary asked, trying to keep the panic out of her voice.

"Not yet. Why, is there something wrong?"

"No, of course there is nothing wrong: it's just that Sasha was picked up by taxi fifteen minutes ago, and now another taxi, her usual taxi, has turned up at the school to pick her up. It is probably an error on the part of the contract company working for the Local Authority, but I'm just checking that's all!"

Sasha's mother could feel the secretary's defensiveness coming down the telephone. "If Sasha was picked up fifteen minutes ago, then by rights she would be here by now, it does not take that long for her to arrive home."

The secretary was feeling embarrassed. It was probably an error on the side of the company supplying the taxi but she wasn't sure. She rang the company who confirmed that only one taxi had been sent, her usual taxi with her usual female driver.

She rang Sasha's mother. "Has she returned yet?"

"No, I am now getting worried. Is she doing a round robin drop-off at a number of houses first before she arrives here? She did that a few weeks ago and was later than usual getting home."

The secretary was now considering the unthinkable. "No, it cannot be that. The taxi supplied for the journey is here now, waiting to pick Sasha up. It is her usual driver as well."

"What's happened then, have you made a technical error again?" the female driver asked, impatient to get away if she wasn't required.

"No, I haven't made an error. But, I will have to report this whole matter to the headmistress. Turning up late is simply not good enough. Now, I suggest that you go about your business until you are required again." With that the secretary stomped back into her office and slammed the door shut.

The taxi driver glared at the back of the retreating secretary. She heard the door slam shut and took the hint. She returned to her car and drove off.

The secretary sat in her chair for a moment composing her thoughts. She then telephoned the headmistress and relayed the circumstances of Sasha's collection.

"Not to worry," she said, "I'm sure it will sort itself out. You go home, you have wasted enough time on this; I don't want you charging me overtime, do I?"

The secretary, now reassured, replaced the telephone in its cradle, put her coat on and went home.

★ ★ ★ ★

Sasha, seated in the rear of the car with the strange man next to her, did not quite understand what was going on. Normally when she first got into the taxi the lady driver always turned around and watched her put her seatbelt on. She made a fuss every single time and would not move the taxi until she was completely satisfied that the seatbelt was fixed. So far, nothing had been said to her by either the driver or the man beside her. She looked out the car window and saw that she was going home by a different route to the one she usually went by. She didn't understand that either.

Neither of the two men spoke to her, although she could hear some sort of conversation going on. She was not concentrating on what was being said between the men so the content of the conversation was little more than an almost static noise.

Sasha's mum watched the clock. Her daughter was now forty-five minutes late, which was very unusual, in fact it had never ever happened before. She was now worried. Tamara, did not want to panic, but late was late and Sasha to some extent was a vulnerable kid. She picked up the telephone and dialled her mother. Aware of the discord between her mum and dad the last thing that Tamara wanted to do was to add a problem to a difficult time for either of them. However, her mother, bless her, was the fount of all knowledge and would know what to do in a crisis like this.

Marie listened to Tamara's worried voice coming down the telephone line. She assessed the situation quickly and went straight to the obvious solution.

"Tamara, you must ring your father, immediately. You know what he is like about Sasha. He will know what to do."

Marie kept the worry out of her voice as she spoke to her daughter, but the more she thought about it, the more uncertain she became.

Tamara now regretted ringing her mother. Her problem was now shared with her mother and she advised her to ring her father, which increased the number to three and might be a catalyst for bringing her parents into conflict when that was the last thing they needed at this time. Marie, sensing her daughter's reluctance, decided to act herself.

"Stay by this phone Tamara, I will ring your father. He would never forgive me if I didn't." She put the telephone down, and then thought for a moment before picking it up and dialling her husband.

Since the bust-up between them, neither had spoken to the other; both were licking their wounds. Unpleasant things had been said, things not necessary and not really relevant but hurtful nonetheless.

Ridge took the telephone from his pocket and saw that it was Marie's name blinking on the small screen. He looked at it for a moment, unsure whether to answer or not. The last thing he wanted was an argument on the telephone, enough had been said already.

He pressed the button to acknowledge her call. "Marie," he said, waiting for a response that would indicate how the call was likely to go.

"John…" Marie hesitated for a moment, "…there is a problem with Sasha."

Ridge's heart fell to the floor at the thought of something wrong with Sasha. "Wrong, what's wrong with her?"

Hearing the concern in his voice, Marie then told him everything that Tamara had said. When she had finished she waited for her husband to respond. Ridge didn't like what he had heard. The bit about an unknown taxi disturbed him. Something not right there! It appeared as if she was with someone else, she had been picked up by someone else! Why? Who?

"I will ring Tamara now!" he said and clicked off.

He rang Tamara who repeated the conversation she had had with her mother. "What I can't understand, Dad, is that Sasha was clearly picked up by a taxi. That cannot be right. What other taxi would know Sasha? It came to the front door of the school and picked her up. Sasha got inside the taxi without a problem and off it went! Where is Sasha, Dad?"

Ridge could hear the panic in his daughter's voice. "Okay Tamara, let's think about this. Who at the school last saw Sasha?"

"I suppose it was the school secretary, she was the one who rang me. She has probably gone home by now, but I do have a telephone number for the on-duty staff member, do you want it?"

"Yes please," he answered, not sure what use it would be to speak with someone uninvolved in the matter.

327

"Dad," Tamara's voice had changed. She had gone from being panicky to fearful.

"Yes."

"I have just had a thought. Do you think this is anything to do with those two men seen near the school in the last few weeks?"

Ridge's blood went icy cold as he thought of the possible scenarios if that was the case.

"No," he lied. "I expect that was no more than a couple of dad's watching the young girls, that's all."

"Dad, I'm really worried now. Please get Sasha back for me."

Ridge could hear his daughter crying.

"Don't worry kid, I will sort this out for you now. In the meantime stay at home, because I believe that there is a simple explanation for all of this and someone will deliver Sasha back to you shortly. I mean, who else wants a spiky kid like Sasha under their feet all day?"

Tamara smiled at her father's sense of humour. "Okay, I will let you know when she walks through the door."

Ridge called the police officer he had spoken to about the men seen outside Sasha's school. The officer was clear. He had seen nothing.

Ridge called the on-duty staff member at Sasha's school and explained that he wanted the secretary's home telephone number. The woman initially refused to give out the number because it was against the Data Protection Act! However, once Ridge warned of the dangers associated with not assisting the police in a serious criminal investigation, she quickly changed her mind and passed the telephone number to him.

Ridge dialled the school secretary and spoke to her straight away. She confirmed all that Ridge knew. She became upset about matters when she realised that, perhaps, she should have been more inquiring at the time instead of just going home. Ridge put the telephone down on her. A nasty suspicion was now forming at the back of his mind.

He called Tamara. "Any news yet?" he asked, crossing his fingers.

"No, she still hasn't returned, Dad. I am now getting worried!"

"Right, just to be on the safe side, although it is early days yet, I think you ought now to report Sasha missing. Ring the nick and speak to the duty inspector. Tell him you are my daughter and explain the full circumstances to him. Be guided by what he says. In the meantime, I will also ring him. Tamara, this is just a precaution so don't go thinking things that are not relevant!"

"Okay Dad, and thanks. I will do that now!"

Ridge then telephoned Marie. "I have just told Tamara to report Sasha missing. I think it is early days, but just to be on the safe side!"

"John," he could hear the firmness in her voice, "Tamara mentioned those two men seen lurking near Sasha's school. Is Sasha missing connected with that, or worse, is it connected with this drugs job that is tearing us apart?"

Ridge guessed that Marie would soon work through all possibilities and come up with the obvious reason as he had.

"Marie, I honestly don't know. But, trust me, I am going to find out!"

"John, we have had our difficulties recently, but promise me two things?"

"If I can I will."

Marie was on the verge of tears. "Just get our Sasha back, and you come home. I want you here. Forget about what I said earlier, I want you home, do you understand John?"

"Yes." Ridge put the telephone down before the change in his voice betrayed to Marie the fact that her words had just had a profound effect on him. He was almost unable to speak. Ridge gave himself a few minutes to recover and then rang the duty inspector at the police station. He explained that he thought Sasha missing might be attributable to a drugs job he was currently working on.

The inspector's ears pricked up. "This puts a completely different perspective on it then John. No longer is she just a missing kid likely to return home within a short space of time. Uniform are at your daughter's house now, are they aware of what you have just told me?"

"No, I have just become aware of this possibility. There is no need for the family to know at this point, is there?"

"Not at present no, but we cannot keep them in the dark for long can we?"

Ridge conceded the point. "If we go along with the theory that Sasha has been kidnapped because of my work, then two thoughts come to mind immediately. There is no point to this line of action by the drug perpetrators, unless I am made aware that it has happened and who is responsible! So far, that has not happened. No demands have been made of me for whatever reason.

"Secondly, where is Sasha? If she has been kidnapped, then she must be being cared for by someone, somewhere safe. That means that she will be kept safe by whoever is responsible for at least the immediate future. That gives me a bit of a breathing space."

The inspector listened to Ridge. "For the immediate future only, and I am talking twenty-four hours only, I will keep the lid on this just to give you a chance to make some headway in view of the circumstances you have outlined. If anyone out there is involved with Sasha, then I would think you must hear from them soon. The one thing I will do is circulate

Sasha's details nationally on the off chance that something will turn up from elsewhere. We need to cover our backs on this John, and also we may end up needing all the help we can get. Agreed?"

Ridge agreed and thanked the inspector for his help.

★ ★ ★ ★

Josie was not at home, which was something of a relief. He changed into his outdoor gear and drove to the place where he always began a jogging session. He needed a bit of solitude to think over recent events and decide the best way forward.

Ridge liked to run; he always had, especially along the top of the Downs towards the ancient Roman campsite overlooking the sea. From the very top he could look down and watch the sea traffic as it left the Marina and stretched out across the dappled water to France. The sun was setting and casting a peaceful reflection across the hillside. No sabre tooth tigers or woolly mammoths, presented themselves. No Roman centurions keeping watch for intruders in boats: but Ridge knew it had happened once. All he saw now was a kid of about thirteen on an unlicensed trials bike swerving erratically up the pathways to the top of the hillside.

His mind was racing over the possibilities with Sasha. The more he thought about it the more he was inclined to think that he was right to associate it with the Ford family. It could account for Ford's sweaty hands and the clear impression that he had got from talking to him that there was something that he was not being told. It was a gut feeling only, he knew that: not proof by any standard, but he was going to go with it.

Ridge began to jog back the way he had come when his mobile rang. It was Tamara.

"Dad, Sasha is still not home, have you heard anything?"

"Not a single word yet," he replied, in two minds whether to tell his daughter what he thought was happening. He decided to tell her, at least she would then be aware and make her own mind up. He recounted to Tamara everything that he thought was relevant.

"Do you think Sasha is safe and well?" she asked.

"Yes I do, in fact I am waiting for a call sooner rather than later that will settle matters once and for all. Then I will know for sure!"

"Dad, please get her back?"

"I will, don't you worry about that." Ridge heard the line disconnect.

Ridge sat in his car wondering if he was ever going to recover from the mounting problems now surrounding him. He thought it was strange really. When his problems started it was being suspended from duty that hurt him. He considered himself a good cop, generally speaking, although he knew he was sometimes a touch singular when dealing with those two wankers in the office. Now it was his wife and Sasha who troubled him most of all. Could he get Sasha back and go back to Marie with the past being ignored? Somehow he doubted it and it filled him with dread. It would destroy him, he knew that.

Chapter Forty-Eight

Ridge drove back to Josie's flat. He saw the lights on as he parked his car. He really did not want to talk to Josie just now. Too much was going through his mind. He let himself in and found Josie pouring him a glass of red wine. She passed the glass to him and saw that he was troubled by something. "What is it, oh warrior?" she asked, sipping from her own glass.

Ridge took the glass and sat down and told Josie everything. Josie looked at Ridge. Her heart went out to him. She loved him so much, but knew she could not hang onto him. He belonged to Marie and eventually they would get back together again, she knew that and she was happy to help achieve that if she could. She gently touched his arm.

"John, I think you are right and it is the Ford family behind this business with Sasha." Josie hesitated when it came to using the word 'kidnapped', but that is what it was. "I am becoming concerned for you John. Firstly, you are suspended from your job, then your wife throws you out and now, it seems, your granddaughter has been kidnapped; it's as if someone is out there trying to destroy you! The thing is how do we prove it and move forward?"

She paused and he saw the tears in her eyes.

He reached for and cuddled her. "Josie, I know what you mean. In truth, if I could set the clock back I would. I am missing Marie and the family, and this business with Sasha is the final straw. I must get her back whatever else happens. The trouble is I don't feel in control of everything, or anything for that matter." He then told her of his reinstatement to office.

Josie kissed him on the cheek. "That's great, that's just the sort of news you wanted to hear. The fightback has started then. Let's think how we can move it on. Somehow we have got to seize the advantage. How can we do that?"

Ridge paced up and down the small lounge. It had not escaped his attention that Josie had included herself in the fightback.

"I know what to do!"

Josie saw the old sparkle come back into his eyes. "What?"

Ridge sipped his wine. "I need your help."

He then explained to Josie what he had in mind. "You cunning old bastard!" she said, now grinning from ear to ear. "Let's go get them!"

★ ★ ★ ★

Ridge placed the box of tricks in the back of his car and with Josie alongside set off north towards London.

Ninety minutes later they pulled to a stop just around the corner from Charles Ford's house. Ridge left the car and wandered around and saw the lights on in the house. He noted that both upstairs and downstairs lights were on. After a few minutes he walked back to where Josie was setting up her telephone equipment and watched her as she programmed in Ford's home telephone number. The dials on the machine fluttered from left to right and then settled showing that the number had been accepted.

"Okay, let's see what Mr Ford gets up to!" She grinned at Ford. "Keep your fingers crossed!"

Ridge smiled, and walked back down the road to the local telephone box and dialled Ford's number. He waited thinking that it was not going to work and then Charles Ford picked up the other end.

"Charles, I'm speaking from home, what the fuck are you playing at?"

"What the fuck do you mean?" Ford said, taken aback by Ridge's aggressive tone.

"My granddaughter is missing, that's what I am talking about. She has been kidnapped!"

Ford went cold and silent.

"Charles, are you still there?"

Ford regained his composure. "Yes, I was just thinking over what you have said. I have no knowledge of anything to do with your granddaughter."

"Listen to me Charles. I am holding you responsible for this, whatever you say. If anything happens to her, you will be the first person on my kill list. Do you understand me?"

"John, will you stay where you are! I will make a few phone calls to see if I can find out anything. Then I will ring you back."

"Charles, I am on my way up to you now. You had better have some answers by the time I get there!" Ridge slammed the telephone down and hurried back to Josie.

"That should get some action. I recorded your conversation with him, to make sure that the machine is locked into his number. Now let's see what he does about it! If he makes a call from that number we will know about it!"

Ridge looked at his watch. It was now eleven-thirty at night. At six in the morning the guys would be on the plot waiting, watching and hoping for things to go as planned. The team were totally unaware of this development. Josie's machine began making noises and produced, firstly, Ford's telephone number on one screen and then another number on the second screen. Dotted lines appeared on the screen as the machine showed the two numbers were now linked. The called number then showed it as being live. Someone, a male voice, answered. "Yes?"

Ridge immediately recognised it as being Paul Ford.

Another voice, Ridge assumed it was the caller, came up through the inbuilt microphone. Josie twiddled a couple of knobs and improved the sound quality.

Charles Ford screamed down the telephone at his brother, "What the fuck are you doing? I warned you about taking Ridge's kid. He knows she is missing and is on his way up to see me. I need to have some answers because, take it from me, my life is now on the fucking line!"

Paul Ford laughed. "So now you know about it. Who told you, big brother Peter?"

"You stupid bastard!" Charles Ford shouted, realising that he had been duped by both his brothers. "Ridge has been on the phone to me. He is very angry: I know what he is like, so I am going to be the first to get it in the neck when he arrives. There's no way I can convince him that I don't know anything. Where is the kid anyway? What the fuck am I going to do?"

Paul Ford was fast losing his patience with baby brother.

"Listen, Charles, I took the kid as a bit of insurance in case Ridge got difficult on Saturday morning at the port. Our future depends on those lorries getting through the port. It's a shame he has found out this early but the plan stays. Once I know the gear is safe tomorrow, I will let the kid go. She is at the farm. The moment the gear arrives safe and sound at the farm she can go. Got it?"

"I don't think Ridge will swallow that, for fuck's sake it's his granddaughter, not someone else's kid. He will go fucking mad and take it out on me!"

"Bollocks, he has no choice in the matter. If he starts kicking up a fuss I will deal with him. There's too much at risk for the next twenty-four hours. Make him understand Charles! Ridge needs to know his fucking place!"

"Paul, listen to me. I'm telling you, you are underestimating Ridge. He is very resourceful and doesn't really give a toss for anyone. He won't take this lying down! He is a fucking fighting machine on his own, not counting the fucking thousands of filth waiting to back him up. Why risk everything now at this late stage?"

"Phone him back now, and tell what the score is! Also, tell him that he is to stay at home tomorrow and not interfere. If he does that, then I will have the kid dropped off near her home on Sunday evening. That's his only option!" Paul slammed the phone down.

★ ★ ★ ★

John Ridge sat in the car with perspiration dripping down his forehead. He used a large tissue to wipe the moisture from his face. It was the old primeval response. His body was adjusting temperature to prepare itself for a fight or flight scenario. Ridge knew it was going to be a fight situation. Unscrupulous people had kidnapped an eight-year-old kid, his kid, and they were going to pay a heavy price for that.

Josie was just switching her system off and recovering the CD ROM. "These bastards are almost above the law. Whatever were they thinking of, kidnapping my granddaughter. What value do they think she has? Let me listen to that CD again, there were a couple of things I did not quite grasp!"

Josie passed the CD to Ridge and watched him as he placed it in the car entertainment system and pressed play. He made notes on a piece of paper from the glove box. He replayed it, twice, making sure that he missed nothing. He sat there thinking about what he had heard. It was clear now that they were playing some sort of game with him.

Josie looked at Ridge and saw the way that he had come back to life. He was now a force to be reckoned with. He was on the up, and heaven help those responsible for taking his granddaughter. "Did you get all that conversation?" she asked.

Ridge smiled. "At least we know what has happened to Sasha. She is being kept at the farm, which means she is safe for the time being. The other thing of interest is that Paul referred to 'the lorries'. That is more than the one lorry we were promised. Before I drop in on Charles, can you recover the address of the farm from your magic telephone interceptor?

341

Josie handed Ridge a piece of paper containing the telephone number and address of the farm where Sasha was being held. Ridge looked at the paper and mentally calculated the distance to the farm.

"Josie, I need to drop you off at a taxi rank. I don't want you involved from this point on. It is going to get nasty and I can't involve you in any of it, do you mind?"

He looked enquiringly at Josie and noticed her disappointment and the tears in her eyes. He knew she liked the rough and tumble of working with him, but this was different, this was very personal and likely to be dangerous and he didn't want her anywhere near where she could be hurt.

"You selfish bastard: I've been waiting for you to say something like that. I understand what you are saying, but I really wanted to be in on this!"

"I know, but I will work better on my own in these circumstances. I would be worried to death with you near me. These are dangerous people who will resist arrest to say the least. I believe they will fight to the last man: I couldn't bear it if you were injured!"

Josie smiled. "I understand what you are saying and I don't want to get in your way. Give me a call when you have sorted this lot out... and be careful!"

Ridge kissed her. "Thank you for all you've done. Without your help I would be finished, we both know that."

Ridge took Josie to the nearest taxi rank and dropped her off with her bag of tricks. She leaned back into the car.

"When this is over and done with, go back to Marie, she needs you!" With that, and not giving Ridge a chance to say anything, Josie gave the driver instructions and drove off crying.

Ridge returned to the area near Ford's home. He looked at his watch. It was still too early for him to have travelled from Sussex to Ford's address, so he still had the element of surprise on his side. He parked the car and checked out Ford's home. The lights were still on and the place looked quiet.

Ridge walked quietly up the footpath at the front and listened at the door. He rang the doorbell and heard it echo through the house. He heard Ford come down the stairs. Clearly he was not expecting Ridge at this early time. As the door opened Ridge threw his weight at the door. It sprung back and struck Charles Ford on the face knocking him backwards across the passageway. Blood from a small cut on his forehead oozed out as Ridge hit him, breaking his nose. Ridge followed up by seizing him by the lapels of his jacket, smashing his foot forward against Ford's ankle and sweeping him high up into the air before crashing him down on the floor.

Ford just lay where he had been thrown, the pain, shock and force of the throw vibrating through his body. The depth of the carpet had to some extent cushioned the force of his abrupt contact with the ground, but he was still stunned at the sudden and unexpected violence.

Ridge bent down and inserted a bent knuckle deep into a nerve centre on his face and applied aggressive pressure to the nerve. Ford suddenly screamed and jerked his body in some sort of effort to avoid the pain.

Ridge increased the pressure and the pain levels and then released his hold before immediately reapplying the pressure again. Ford continued screaming until Ridge let him go. He then pulled Ford up into a sitting position and banged his head against the nearest wall a couple of times. Ford raised both his hands in surrender. "Stop, fucking stop! You're hurting me!" he screamed.

Ridge let him go and then put his hand around Ford's neck and squeezed until he went red in the face and displayed signs of choking.

"Now, Charles, let us talk about my granddaughter! Where is she?"

"I don't know," he gasped, drawing air into his system.

Ridge reapplied the hold to his neck and squeezed until Ford lost consciousness. He waited a minute and then slapped him around the face a few times to stimulate the supply of blood to his brain. Ford opened his eyes and focused on Ridge in front of him.

"Okay, I'll tell you. I was going to anyway."

"Where!" Ridge barked.

"She's at the farm." Ford rubbed his throat to ease the pain. He spluttered out the address and lay back breathing heavily.

"I want the telephone number to the farm!"

"I haven't got that," Ford lied.

"You have had your chance. Fuck you Charles. I don't need you now!"

Ridge picked Ford up off the floor and kneed him in the groin. As Ford doubled over he then kneed him again this time in the head. Ford passed out.

Ridge rummaged about in Ford's garage and found a box of plastic tie-ups. He secured Ford's hands behind him and then tied his feet together before he dragged him to his car. He did not want Ford to recover and then blow the whistle on him.

Ridge looked at his watch, time was getting on. He needed to be in place before alerting the team to what he now knew. He was going to get one chance only to rescue Sasha. He drove across London towards the Essex countryside with Ford in the passenger seat still unconscious.

Chapter Forty-Nine

Josie got into Brighton an hour and a half after leaving Ridge. She had slept fitfully in the taxi for most of the journey. After paying off the driver she went into her flat and straight to a wardrobe and removed a box of photos. The time for pussyfooting about was over. It was now time for action to help Ridge.

She hunted about for a few minutes and found what she was looking for. In the lounge she sat down and picked up the telephone and dialled Sussex Police using the three-nines number. "I need to speak with Superintendent Glyn Bostock. It's an emergency!"

There was a very pregnant pause before the female operative sarcastically replied, "You do realise what time of the day it is?"

"I've told you, I need to speak with him as soon as possible, now please connect me."

"I'm afraid the superintendent does not work on the weekend, could you ring back at a more sociable hour on Monday?"

Josie lost her patience with the delaying tactics.

"If you don't connect me I will continue to ring the treble-nine numbers until someone does listen to me and, what is more, I will then make a formal complaint about your behaviour."

The woman capitulated. "Please give me your number. I will see if the officer wants to talk to you at this time of the morning."

Josie supplied her telephone number and waited. She thought back to her last meeting with Glyn Bostock. He was an inspector then and they were on the same surveillance course. During one after-dinner drinking session Bostock had touched her up in an embarrassing circumstance witnessed by another police officer. She had resisted his advances and did not make a fuss, something Bostock was grateful for. They both ended the course on a friendly relationship basis, but it went no further than that. But she did retain his card. She felt sure he would help.

Glyn Bostock rang her back within five minutes. "Josie, how are you? What can I do for you?"

Josie explained the whole course of events as she knew them; leaving out the part she had played with her telephone interceptor which she had dumped in the flat corridor on her return.

Bostock was now wide awake. "Are you seriously telling me that later this morning, John Ridge will take on a group of international drug smugglers single-handed?"

"Well, not quite single-handed. He has some Customs people helping but they are not yet aware just how much things have changed in the last twenty-four hours. Because of the problem with his granddaughter being kidnapped, Ridge is diverting his attention to the informant's house in London to get the rest of the answers he feels he needs. Then he is going to go to the farm in Essex and recover his granddaughter. He will be on his own there with no backup so, yes, he does need help, a lot of help and quickly. Can you do anything Glyn?"

"Josie, leave it with me. I will make some calls now and get something off the ground straight away. Give me the telephone number and the address for the farm."

Josie supplied the number and address to him. "Please hurry Glyn; Ridge will be overwhelmed by sheer numbers alone if he doesn't get help soon!"

"Leave it to me, Josie." Bostock replaced his telephone and then called his boss Chief Superintendent Crispin Stoneheart and explained the circumstances of Josie's call.

Stoneheart didn't hesitate. "Glyn, I want the troops called out! Maximum number of armed officers available. If we haven't got enough, go to Surrey Police and borrow some of theirs. I want armed response vehicles to that farm once you are sure you have identified its location. Liaise with the Met and get all the assistance you need from them. Don't take no for answer. I want Customs told of Ridge's diversion to this farm. They will need to stay sharp until it becomes clear what direction this job is going in! This is a high priority from now on. Let's get on with it. Any problems call me."

Stoneheart put the telephone down and got dressed. He then picked up the telephone and called the duty inspector at Headquarters, asking for the police helicopter to be made available to him on the pad at Shoreham as soon as possible. He felt that it was his direct responsibility to support his officers on the ground by being there.

Chapter Fifty

Earlier that evening Sasha had awoken from her sleep in the car when it came to a stop at a major road junction in Essex. Although she had no idea where she was, she was in fact about two miles from the farm. She looked at the man beside her. He smelt. His eyes were closed and he seemed to be asleep.

Sasha looked out of the window but still failed to recognise the roads or area that she was in. The other man, the one driving, kept on giving her a glance through the rear view mirror. She didn't like his face. He seemed grumpy.

Sasha reached down and switched her digital processor on. As neither man could see what she was doing she then picked her telephone out of her school bag and began to text her mother. This telephone was her lifeline. It was Sasha's equivalent to actually talking. She was trying to think of the right words to use when the man next to her reached over and snatched the telephone from her. He wasn't asleep after all. He then studied her processor and took that from her, without understanding the function that it performed. Because it was to all appearances some sort of listening device, that was enough reason to take it from her.

She looked quickly at the man's face and didn't like what she saw. He seemed angry at her. He started talking to the man driving, but because of the angle of his mouth she could not lip-read. Sasha needed a full-on look at the face to do that. She decided she wasn't going to talk to either man. Now she couldn't hear what was being said and without her telephone she could not text her mum. She sat still and thought about it. She didn't like it one little bit. She now wanted to text her mum more than ever.

The man beside her nudged her. She looked at him. "What's your name?" His face looked better, not so angry, but she still wasn't going to talk to him. She looked away. He said it again, although Sasha did not hear him and did not see his lips move because she had returned to looking out of the car window.

Unknown to her the driver had heard his friend attempting to talk with Sasha. He looked in the rear view mirror, caught his friend's eye and said, "No good talking to the kid. She's stone deaf. She can't hear a word you're saying. Just ignore her."

"It's okay, I was just testing her, because she was trying to use her phone. I stopped her before she could send anything like a message! The man showed his friend the telephone and then picked up her processor

351

and showed it to the driver. "This looks like a bleeding tape recorder!"

Sasha caught the gist of the conversation because she was watching the rear view mirror and had picked up most of the lip pattern from the driver. The driver's lips were easier than his friend's lips to understand. Sasha missed the man's comments because she was looking out of the window. She could hear something was being said but had decided that she was not going to help these men by listening to them. She just wished her granddad was in the car. He would know what to do. The driver was thinking about his colleagues remarks. "No" he said "it's not a tape recorder, I think that it is part of her hearing aid."

The driver turned off the main road and continued driving on a much narrower road for about two miles before turning left in through a large set of wooden five-bar gates.

The man beside her got out and opened both gates and let the car through. While he was out of the car, Sasha pressed the door opening switch. Nothing moved, the door did not open, it was locked. Sasha did not move. She would wait for some other opportunity to present itself.

A very big man with a dark skin and long black hair came out of the house and walked towards the car. Sasha didn't like him. He held his arms out like a big monkey as if he was ready to hit someone. When she looked around she saw the old Land Rover, what she called a farm car, parked near the front of the house.

She realised for the first time that she was now on a farm.

The big man stopped by the driver. "Did you have any problems?" he asked.

"No, it was fucking easy-peasy!"

"What?"

The driver looked at him. "No problems!"

The big man walked back towards the house.

Sasha felt hungry. She did not know what the time was, but she was sure that if she were at home, her mother would be cooking something nice for her, something that she could smell cooking. She liked that.

The man who had sat beside her opened the door and indicated that she was to get out. Sasha took no notice. He reached in the car and grabbed her by the arm and pulled her along the seat until Sasha put her feet down on the rough ground outside the car. She stood there glowering at the man. He was worse than the driver.

Still holding her arm, the man led her into the kitchen and made her sit down at the end of the kitchen table. He then went to a cupboard and took out a loaf of bread and some jam and made a bread and jam sandwich which he passed to Sasha. She picked up a corner of the top slice and looked at the jam. Strawberry! It was her favourite jam. Sasha dropped the corner back in place and pushed the sandwich away from her.

She saw the driver look at his friend and saw him say, "Stubborn bitch!"

Sasha knew the first word. She recalled seeing and hearing her granddad use that word when she refused something or other, she couldn't remember what. Her mum and granddad had laughed when he had used the word. This man did not laugh, in fact he looked angry. Sasha looked around the room, anything but look at the man. A cup of tea in a plastic beaker was passed along the table to her. There was no sign of a spoon, so she knew there was no sugar in the plastic cup. She pushed it away from her. Sasha did not like tea without sugar. She was not going to drink it. The two men looked at her. She saw the driver say, "Leave her alone. She can sit there until she is hungry or it is time for her to go to bed."

Sasha picked up most of those words although she gave no indication that she was aware of anything. She just stared at the two of them.

The big man and another man carrying a long gun came into the kitchen and each picked up a mug of tea. The big man with the long hair spoke, "We are all ready now. First thing in the morning the lorries in France will leave the farm for the port at Calais, yes?"

"Yes, that's right," said the man with the long gun. "Not long now."

The big man looked at Sasha. She stared straight back at him. "Why is the girl here?"

"She's insurance. We are using her relation who's a policeman to get us through the port without any problems. If there is a problem then we can bargain with the kid as a hostage. There's a lot at stake here. I have covered all bases, just to be sure." Sasha watched their lips moving; the big man had a strange lip pattern and was difficult to understand. He kept his lips together when he spoke making it hard for her to fully understand what he was saying.

The big man thought for a moment. He did not like Paul Ford at all. He did not trust him. It wasn't his decision to use Ford. He would have preferred to kill him instead. "Tell me again what is going to happen. And say it slowly!"

Ford looked at the big man. He could kill this bastard as soon as look at him. He had not forgotten Cartagena. He owed this big bastard plenty and not in a good way!

"Tomorrow morning the first ferry is going to leave Calais for Dover with the first lorry on board. Customs investigators will be waiting to check the lorry because they have been told that it has a false compartment on board holding about sixty kilos of cocaine. The driver of the lorry will fuck the Customs people about for as long as possible before they arrest him. They will then take the lorry to pieces looking for the drugs. That will take them all day to do that" As Ford left the farm; Andre walked back to the barn and rechecked the lorry for any sign of interference. He did not want anything to come back and bite him.

"Go on!"

"One and a half hours later the next ferry will be carrying the four lorries containing all the cocaine. Because Customs will still be busy, none of those lorries will be checked so the whole two hundred and forty kilos of cocaine will arrive here at the farm untouched. Then our pet chemists can start to work cutting the gear before it goes on to the market. If it goes wrong on that ferry, we have the girl to bargain with!"

Paul Ford looked at the big man, hoping that once they had the gear safely stashed at the farm he would get the chance to kill this bastard, just to teach the fucking Colombians a lesson.

Sasha sat still, watching the men talk. She was going to tell her granddad about these men. She did not like any of them at all.

Twenty minutes later the driver man got hold of her arm and led her into a small bedroom on the ground floor. He looked around and then walked out shutting and locking the door as he went. He never said another word to Sasha. As soon as she was left alone Sasha got to work. She was looking for a way out of the room. She was determined to get out and tell her granddad.

Sasha went to the window in the bedroom and moved the curtains. It was getting dark now so she knew that she needed to be quick. The windows were locked. She tried moving the white handles on each of

the windows but found them both locked and
unmovable. There was no way that she was going to
escape from this room. She then went into the small
bathroom. Her eyes lit up as she spotted an open toilet
window just above the toilet. It was a small window,
but she thought if she could push it open a little more
she could get out.

She put the toilet lid down and climbed up on top
of it. Lifting the metal handle she gave a little push and
the window moved open a few more inches. She stuck
her legs through the gap and smiled as she pushed
backwards and squeezed out through the narrow space
and dropped to the ground. Sasha was now at the back
of the farmhouse.

She ducked down and followed the path until she
reached the gates. She waited until the road was empty
and then crossed making for the adjoining field. She
felt excited by what she was doing and thought of the
two men. They would be so angry.

Sasha crossed a couple of fields and kept going. She
was feeling a little hungry and wished she still had the
strawberry jam sandwich. Her shoes were getting wet
in the grass. They were her best school shoes and she
thought her mum might be cross if they got too wet.
She slowed to a walk but continued on. She knew she
had to find someone to talk to: she felt her eyes well
up and began to feel a little frightened as the darkness
closed in.

Almost an hour after she had escaped from the
room, Sasha was still going strong. She had got a little

frightened of continuing to walk inside the fields. She wasn't sure if there were any big animals left out overnight so she had climbed over a gate and was now walking along a road. Her shoes weren't getting any wetter either but it was getting cold. When she got back to school she would tell her teacher, Mrs Grey, what had gone on. She would like that and she would probably ask Sasha to tell her class about her adventure. She checked her school shoes again.

Sasha saw the car headlights coming towards her. They were a long way away, but they might belong to the two men. They might be looking for her. She ran across the roadway and scrambled over a big gate and fell into the field and hurt her ankle. She couldn't get up and run because of the pain in the ankle, so she just laid there in the long grass and hoped the car hadn't seen her.

The big car stopped near the gate and two men jumped out and looked over the gate.

Sasha kept her head down in the wet grass. The grass smelt very smelly and she wanted to lift her head up, but she didn't. She kept perfectly still until a large hand touched her causing her to look up. She dreaded the thought that it was those two men. What would they do to her? A torch was shone onto her body. By its light she could see the man's face. He was smiling at her. "What are you doing here in the dark?" he asked.

Sasha saw the other man getting over the fence. In the light of the car's headlights she could see that he was wearing what she thought was a policeman's uniform. She looked again and then looked at the man closest to her. He wasn't touching her, but he was still smiling. That was a good sign. Sasha stood up and looked at both men. They were both wearing the same type of clothes, a policeman's uniform.

"What's your name?" the first man asked.

By peering at him, Sasha could just make out his lip pattern. "Sasha," she said.

The second man climbed back over the fence and went to the car. He sat down inside for a moment and shuffled amongst some papers. He found what he was looking for and got out of the car and climbed the gate again.

Using a torch he showed Sasha the A4 piece of paper in his hand.

"Is that you?"

Sasha looked at the paper and saw her picture underneath lots of words. One of the words was 'missing' in big letters.

Sasha smiled. She liked that photo of herself. Her granddad had taken it with his big camera. The other man looked at the photo and read the words. He held the photo up against Sasha's face and shook his head. "No, that's not you!"

"Yes!" She started to look worried. "Me!" she said and pointed to herself. Both men then began to laugh. Sasha realised then that the men were playing a joke. She laughed with them, seeing the funny side of it.

The first man said something to the other man and then turned to Sasha. He looked her full in the face and slowly said, "I think we should take you with us in the car to the police station. Then we can telephone your mum. What do you think?"

Sasha picked up most of the words. She was really pleased. "Yes, please," she said. She knew she was now safe from the other men.

In the car, one of the men used the car's handset to seek advice. Sasha had seen this take place before. Some of her granddad's friends had cars and telephones like this.

The man on the car phone reached over and put his hand near Sasha's head and parted her hair. The brown hair-colour-matched, magnetic plastic receiver was still in place. He smiled at Sasha. "You are deaf aren't you?"

She nodded her head, wondering why he had asked.

"Have you ever been to Cambridge Hospital?"

Sasha new the word Cambridge. Following her Cochlear Implant operation three years earlier, she was now on a course of speech therapy at the world renowned hospital. She had a lot of friends there, all of whom helped her adjust to the many changes needed to understand the technology involved.

Sasha raised a clenched fist and began chanting, "Cambridge, Cambridge, Cambridge."

They all laughed together.

The police officer sitting in the passenger seat smiled. He knew he was on the right track the moment he had heard Sasha talk; he recognised the flat tonal sounds of her voice. He didn't know much about it but he knew enough to start getting help for the kid. He pulled out his personal telephone and found a number he was looking for. Turning to his colleague he explained that his sister was a nurse at the audiology unit at that very hospital and in all probability could help. His sister picked up and he then explained to her what the problem was. He listened and then said, "Thanks, see you soon." He replaced his telephone in his pocket and then looked at the two sets of eyes watching him.

Speaking slowly for Sasha's benefit he said, "It is now three o'clock in the morning." He showed Sasha the time on his watch. She nodded. "The hospital is closed, but my sister is going in to open up the department and wait for you." Again Sasha nodded. "You need the rest of your equipment so that you can hear again. My sister can sort that out. Okay?"

Sasha liked this man. He was kind and he had a nice smile. She nodded. The man turned to his colleague, the driver. "This time of the morning, it's a quick run to Addenbrooke's, let's take her there and she can get sorted. After the night she has had she needs to see friends and be in a place she is familiar with until her parents can collect her. The nick is now trying to contact Sussex and get the parents updated."

The car moved off towards the motorway. Sasha sat back in the car seat, exhausted after her trek across the countryside. Within a hundred yards of moving off in the car she was asleep.

Chapter Fifty-One

Ridge was on his way across North London making for Essex. He had punched in the address of the farm and was now looking at the screen map. The farm was set just outside a small place called Havering.

It was now three-thirty a.m. He was tired, but any chance of sleep was out of the question. He needed to press on and get Sasha back before he could ring Snow. Ridge was looking for the junction that would get him on the M25 when his mobile rang. He switched on the car speaker and listened to his daughter.

"Dad, Sasha has been found. The police found her wandering about the countryside somewhere in Essex in the early hours. She is being taken to Addenbrooke's at Cambridge now. Dad, she is okay, she is not harmed in any way."

Ridge pulled in to a bus lay-by and stopped. He felt an immense relief at the news. He glanced at his watch

and did a quick calculation. "I am halfway there. I can shoot up the motorway and see her now. I can be there in thirty minutes. Can you pick her up once I am satisfied she is okay?"

"Of course I can. I am with mum now, we can come now, together. What are you doing?"

Ridge paused. "I'm running about all over the place!" he said without giving anything away.

Marie came on the line. "John, be careful and come home safe!"

Ridge clicked the telephone off feeling a lump in his throat. He drove on looking for his turnoff.

Forty minutes later Ridge drove into Addenbrooke's and parked his car directly outside the audiology unit. Charles Ford had woken up and was trying to get his bearings. Using a couple of plastic ties, Ridge looped through his wrist ties and secured the additional ties via the metal seat framework. Ford wasn't going anywhere. Ridge then ran along the corridor and down the stairs to the unit. He burst in through the doors.

Sasha was sitting talking to the nurse who was writing notes on a single A4 sheet, information that Sasha was giving to her. Seeing Ridge bearing down on her the nurse stood up and held out her hand. "You must be Sasha's granddad?"

Sasha had seen Ridge coming and jumped up and reached towards him.

Ridge picked her up and kissed her, before introducing himself to the nurse. He looked at his watch, it was four-twenty now. Customs investigators would soon be arriving at the port for the final briefing before taking up their positions.

He satisfied himself that Sasha was okay. The nurse indicated that Sasha ought to remain in the unit until the nuclear scientists came on at nine o'clock. They could then remap her sound system and replace her missing processor. She would then be good to go!

Ridge and the nurse took Sasha to the WRVS canteen for breakfast. They were the first customers of the early morning. While they were waiting for their orders to be cooked, Sasha took the written notes from the nurse and passed them to Ridge. Ridge looked at them. It was a bit like looking at shorthand. Key words were present but a number of the joining up words were missing from the sequence.

The volunteer lady, pleased to see customers at that time of the morning, brought the hot drinks over to the table. The nurse had tea with no sugar, Sasha had a hot chocolate and Ridge had his normal Americano. As Ridge's drink was placed in front of him, he watched the coffee slurp over the rim of the mug and trickled across the table and onto the floor. He pretended he had not seen it occur. Sasha had watched the coffee spill and she gave her granddad a special smile. She was aware of his thing about coffee.

Ridge was still looking at the notes. He saw 'second ferry'.

He looked at Sasha, pointed to the words and raised his eyes. He wanted Sasha to tell him using her own words.

Sasha bent across the table. "Nasty man, more dogs, second ferry!"

He showed the word to Sasha. "Are you sure?"

"Yes," said Sasha, clearly attempting to recall the words used by the man.

"Lots more dogs. Lots of money!"

The nurse joined in. "I couldn't understand that either. First of all, I thought Sasha had said drugs, but then she used the word again and I thought she meant dogs!"

Ridge read the words again making the adjustment. Second ferry, more drugs. He reread it and then smiled.

He showed the page to Sasha and pointed to the word 'dogs'.

Ridge formed an exaggerated quizzical look on his face. "What's that?"

Sasha looked at the word and focused both her eyes and her memory.

Her eyes lit up. Sasha held one hand up as if she was holding something. Then she made as if unscrewing a lid and tipping something into her hand. Picking up the imaginary contents, and using her thumb and forefinger, she put the contents into her mouth forming a downcast as she did so. A few seconds later she beamed a large smile at the nurse and Ridge.

The nurse smiled. "Sasha was just illustrating taking an aspirin from a capped bottle and taking the pill. So she did mean drugs not dogs?"

Sasha grinned, lip-reading the words used by the nurse.

Ridge picked up the papers and threw them into the air and laughed out loud. His granddaughter had just spiked the Ford's drug importation plan. Answers to the problem that he was desperately trying to find had been provided by his eight-year-old granddaughter and neither she nor the nurse had realised the significance of the words.

The nurse looked at him smiling.

"What!"

Ridge sipped his coffee. It was awful, but at this moment he would have drunk water from the toilet and enjoyed it.

Ridge told her and Sasha about the words on the paper. The nurse's eyes widened as she appreciated the gist of her notes. Sasha knew she had done something that her granddad was pleased with. She smiled in a shy way. She had such a lot to tell her mum. Her mum would be pleased with the way that she had tricked those nasty men. Sasha looked down at her school shoes, muddy and scuffed from where she had climbed out of the bathroom window and walked through fields. She had a spare pair of school shoes at home.

Ridge glanced at his watch. It was now five-thirty. They would be in place now at Calais waiting for the lorry to drive into the port and book in. He had to ring Jon Snow and update him.

Chapter Fifty-Two

John Snow and the entire Customs team, now updated by Ridge, were in position and watching the ferry come into the port. They saw the front of the ferry lower its doors to the open position and come to a stop with a slight bump as it connected with the dockside. Ten minutes later the first of the vehicles began rumbling down the ramp and towards the exit.

The team members at Calais port from first light had identified the vehicle they were waiting for as it boarded the ship. They waited until the ship was underway and all the vehicle drivers were upstairs enjoying a breakfast, before they began a check of the vehicle. Only a brief outside check was made using one of the Customs drug sniffing dogs. Although everything that could be done to assist the dog was done, the dog did not indicate the presence of drugs.

The information was then radioed to the team at Dover. Snow listened to the result coming through.

He turned to the dog handler sitting at the table drinking coffee.

"Why didn't the dog pick up?"

"Theoretically, he should have done if there is gear on the vehicle. But down in the hold of the ship, it's very enclosed and there are lots of other intense smells down there, so it's anyone's guess."

Snow looked at the man. "When we pull this vehicle, you and your growler will do a casual check and hopefully your dog will make a positive identification. The question is: what are we going to do if he doesn't sniff the coke?"

"Do we need a result from the dog to make it all work?" The dog man asked.

"Yes, we do, otherwise they will know they have been set up!" Snow said.

"Right then." The dog handler grinned. "Rest assured you will get the indication you require, if I have to bark myself. One way or another, one of us will bark!"

He looked at his dog and bent down towards it. He said something close to the dog's head. The dog's ears laid back and he began to bark excitedly at his handler.

Snow grinned back. "Great stuff. That driver and that lorry are not getting out of the port today, that's for sure."

* * * *

The investigator standing in the roadway let three small cars go through and then raised his arm and waved a large lorry into the side.

A number of other investigators casually wandered out from their static positions and took up places close to the bay that the lorry was pulling into.

The lorry stopped in the bay. The investigator walked to the driver's window and spoke to Joey, the gun, Serrif. "Handbrake on and kill the engine mate. I am just going to do a quick check to make sure that you are fit for the road."

He was halfway around the vehicle looking at straps and buckles on the vehicle when a dog handler with his dog casually walked down the length of the vehicle as if he was going on to some other destination.

Joey the gun watched the performance through the wing mirror. He smiled. The dog handler reached the end of the line when he appeared to have forgotten something. He turned about and walked back the way he had come. He was halfway down the length of the lorry when his dog became excited and started barking at the lorry.

The investigator still checking the outside of the lorry and taking his time walked up to the dog handler and spoke to him. He watched the dog barking for a few moments and then walked around to the driver.

"Sorry mate, but the dog is indicating something on your lorry, are you carrying drugs or anything that you should not be carrying?"

Joey Serrif could not believe it. There was nothing on the vehicle that he was aware of. All it contained was thousands of mangos, yet the fucking dog was barking. He could see it barking.

"No, I am only carrying mangos."

The officer walked over to the office and spoke to another Customs man watching the scene unfurl. The dog handler walked over to them. The dog was still barking. Snow looked at the dog and then the handler. "Well that was as clear a signal as you could wish for, right?"

The dog handler had his back towards the driver. "The dog didn't pick up at all. I would say that there is nothing on that vehicle!"

Snow kept a poker face. "Why did the dog bark then?"

"He is a very obliging dog. He wants to please. So when I asked him to bark, he did!" The man was trying hard not to smile.

Snow considered the situation. This was make or break time for him as the lead officer. No evidence at all to suggest that this lorry or its driver were committing any offence at all. Should he let the driver and lorry pass or should he detain them? He thought about Ridge's updated briefing a short time previously. Snow then slowly walked over to the driver.

"Get out of the lorry sir and come into the office with me. I intend to search you and your vehicle for illegal substances."

Joey was now worried. He had been assured that there was nothing in the vehicle. It was a wind-up for the Customs. It was all designed to keep them busy, so the other lorries would get through. But the fucking growler barked. Why would he do that if there was nothing there? The bastards must have put something on the vehicle just to make sure that he was arrested. Why would they do that?

He stepped down from the cab and suddenly made a run for it. He covered about two hundred yards when he saw the dog handler take his dog off the lead. Joey stopped and raised his hands in the air. He was handcuffed and taken to the detention room close to the office.

Snow called the team together and explained that in spite of the negative result from the dog, a full search of the vehicle and interview of the driver would go ahead. And, as now planned, surveillance would be maintained on the rest of the ferries for that day hopefully to locate the additional vehicles on the next ferry.

A long stop was immediately placed on the road outside of the port in the shape of two investigators dressed as workmen digging up the road. The cameras they had carefully positioned on the temporary barriers whirred into action two hours later and dutifully recorded the four large lorries, one behind the other as they left the Eastern Docks heading in the direction of the motorway.

The Customs men in the examination shed had almost finished their work on the vehicle in the bay. In view of the news from Ridge, a much speedier search of the vehicle was made. The lorry was quickly emptied of its load of mangos and then searched. No special compartment was found and no drugs of any sort were found.

Joey Serrif was quickly interviewed. He denied everything and asked to see a solicitor. He made his views quite clear to the investigating officers. He was not going to be fitted-up, least of all by the Ford brothers. If the worst possible scenario prevailed and he was charged with any offence, he thought it more than likely he would turn Queen's evidence. He was not going to take the can for something he did not do.

The investigative team then left the port almost a full hour after the four lorries and raced towards Havering and the farm.

Chapter Fifty-Three

John Ridge waited at Addenbrooke's with Sasha whilst Tamara and Marie hurried northwards along the M11 towards them. The nuclear scientist had come in early after talking to Sasha's nurse on the telephone and made Sasha first patient of the day. He checked her over and reprogrammed her sound levels and then linked them to the new processor.

Although this procedure had taken place many times before, today for Sasha it was very special. She wasn't sure what was going on but she knew that she was the centre of attention and she quite liked that.

When her mum and her nan arrived it was a bit like her birthday. There were kisses all round. Both her mum and her nan were in tears, but she thought they were happy tears. Then they both stopped crying and laughed a lot with her. Sasha noticed that when her granddad left to go somewhere by himself, her nan cried a lot more.

★ ★ ★ ★

Ridge left the hospital and drove for a couple of miles on the M11. He found a suitable place to stop, stopped the car and got out. He then cut the ties holding Charles Ford and dragged him out of the car. Ford fell onto the ground because his feet were still held by the foot ties. Ridge cut those free and then picked Ford up and slammed him against the side of the car. Ford looked very worried knowing that he had transgressed the line with Ridge.

John Ridge seized him by the throat and began to exert pressure on Ford's carotid arteries. "Charles, I am giving you a chance because I have a lot to do and I do not want to waste my time with you. Go away from here and lose yourself. Do not contact your brothers at all today, is that understood?"

Ford was going red in the face and found that he could hardly speak. "Yes, I'll do that, I promise you. I'm sorry John that it's worked out like this. I didn't know it was going to happen like that, I really didn't. They had me over as well!"

"That's why you are still alive!" he said. "Now go while you still can!"

With that he pushed Ford away from him.

Ridge got back into his car and drove back down to motorway. He knew that he should not have simply dropped Ford off, but he needed to prioritise. He did not have the time to take Ford to a police station. He would have been delayed for hours explaining Fords injuries to a grumpy station sergeant. Of course, there was a small risk in the time left that Ford would contact his brothers, but somehow Ridge didn't think that was likely. Ford was more likely to be making himself scarce knowing that his brothers were going to be arrested for the drug importation within hours. Ridge saw the turn off for junction 29 and then followed the sat nav until he was close to the farm address.

Once sure that he had not been noticed he crept around the fence area until he could again see the barn and the farmhouse and squatted down in the long grass and watched the goings-on. A number of men were gathered outside the front door of the farm, clearly waiting for something to happen.

Thirty-five minutes later four large lorries drove in through the gate and stopped alongside the first barn. The gates were then closed and a large metal chain was tied around the two gates at its centre point.

Ridge watched the drivers shaking hands with each other, obviously delighted at something. Ridge was just outside listening range. He watched as two men began unloading the first lorry and removing a large quantity of what looked like mangos from the back of the lorry. They were simply chucked on the ground to one side of the lorry and left. When that had been done one of the men got inside with a tool kit and began prising away at a panel running the back length of the vehicle. The other man went inside the barn and returned with a sack barrow. After a few minutes the man inside the lorry pulled back a large panel and began emptying the contents from behind the panel. This time he was unloading what looked like kilo sacks of something onto the sack barrow.

Ridge guessed what it was. After a few minutes the two men took the sack barrow into the barn and were gone from sight for a few minutes. They reappeared and repeated the same procedure with several more loads. When they had emptied the compartment they gave the sack barrow to one of the other drivers and walked back towards the house.

Keeping to the fence work, Ridge followed the perimeter until he could cover the open ground out of sight of the house. He needed to look at the sacks in the garage. He made the short distance without being seen and found the sacks. Using his penknife he made a slit in one of the sacks at the bottom of the pile. A very fine white-coloured powder began to trickle out. He tried another sack and got the same result.

At last, all the evidence he needed. He checked outside. No sign of life. The man with the sack barrow was still standing alongside his lorry talking to one of the other men. He was some distance away. Ridge crept on and hid behind the last lorry. He now needed John Snow and his team as quickly as possible. He dialled John Snow's number.

It rang and Snow quickly answered, "Yes John, what is it?"

"I am at the farm with the four lorries. One of the lorries is being unloaded now. It's full of cocaine. If the other lorries are the same, we have about four times the amount of coke that we thought we were getting. How long are you going to be getting here?"

Snow looked at his watch. "I reckon about ten minutes or less. Just keep out of the way until we arrive. You can't take this lot on by yourself, it's too dangerous. As well as us burning rubber, there is also a team of Sussex's finest hot-footing up the M25 towards you. Just hang on!"

Ridge laughed. "You must be fucking joking. This lot have been taking the piss for far too long. Added to which, they kidnapped my granddaughter. They are going to pay for that before they get arrested!"

"John, just don't do anything silly; just lay low until we get there!"

Ridge listened for a few moments before disconnecting.

Snow was a man whose friendship he valued. Normally he would do anything the man said, but it was too late for that now. Once again he was on his own: he was determined to right a few wrongs with the Ford brothers and anyone else that got in the way.

★ ★ ★ ★

John Snow connected with the Sussex Police Force helicopter and Detective Chief Superintendent Crispen Stoneheart. They were out of Sussex air space and entering the air space of the Metropolitan Police. They were literally a few minutes away from the farm, as were a number of armed response units. After listening to Snow, Stoneheart contacted the lead response unit vehicle and in no uncertain terms told the senior officer to put his fucking foot down.

The officer replied, "Yes sir." He looked at his driver. "Do you want me to drive this poxy van faster or what?"

★ ★ ★ ★

Ridge replaced his telephone in his pocket and looked around the front of the lorry. He looked down the drive at the front gates onto the property. They were closed and looked as if they were locked. First things first, he must get those gates open. When the cavalry arrived within the next few minutes they would not be pleased to find they could not enter the property because the gates were locked. Ridge crept along the length of two lorries and made a dash to the gates. Fortunately the gates were not locked; they simply had a large metal chain wrapped around the two gates keeping them together.

Ridge removed the chain and swung both gates open. Still no sign of life! He retraced his steps back to the rear of the lorries and squatted down getting his breath back.

Just when he thought he was safe, he saw the big man watching him. The man was enormous. He must have been at least six foot six tall and about twenty stone in weight, but he looked strong with it. Dressed in a black suit and his long black hair tied in a pony tail he looked a formidable adversary. The man was holding both his arms outstretched like a wrestler and was looking at Ridge as if he wanted to kill him. He began walking towards Ridge ready to seize him. Ridge saw that as the big man moved forward towards him, he seemed to limp slightly on the left leg as if he had a knee problem.

Ridge knew he had no choice. His way out was blocked. He was going to have to engage with this man. The big man was about ten feet away from Ridge and still coming forward towards him.

Ridge sprinted towards him as fast as he could, turning at the last moment so that he was slightly to one side before turning back in towards the man and leaning forward under his outstretched arms as he smashed his left foot directly into the man's knee cap, pushing the joint inwards towards the other leg. The knee joint already weakened and damaged was completely dislocated knocking the big man to the ground screaming in pain. He tried to recover immediately and rolled back on to the other knee and struggled to regain his feet. Ridge face-kicked him, fracturing his nose and jaw. This time the big man fell on to his back, blood spilling from his mouth. He was finished. He lay where he had fallen.

Ridge turned towards the house. The noise of the big man's screams must have alerted others in the house, because a number of men came out of the house and were now facing Ridge.

Paul Ford was in the front of the group. He had watched his Colombian minder destroyed by Ridge. He felt angry that he had been deprived of the pleasure of doing the job himself, but that was life. He pointed the old *Smith & Wesson* at Ridge and waved it at him to make him step away from the big man lying on the ground.

Ridge stepped aside as Ford stepped forward and kicked the big man in the face. Once he had the attention of the injured man he bent down and shot him in the throat. Blood pumped from the wound as the man died glaring hatred at Ford.

Ridge covered the short distance to Ford as the Colombian died. He was almost on top of Ford, when the bullet tore into his stomach wall.

Ridge's foot technique connected with the side of Ford's head and knocked him over causing Ford to drop the gun. Ridge moved in close and chopped him across the throat before grasping his hair with one hand and underneath his chin with the other hand. He swiftly turned Ford's head to one side and snapped it back in a vicious semicircle until he heard it break. He let Ford's body fall to the ground.

In the background Ridge heard the roar of car engines as the Customs team came through the gates. He looked down at his stomach and saw the blood flooding out of the gunshot wound. The pain was starting to affect him now and he was feeling faint and disorientated. Men with guns were running about around him and he could dimly see more cars coming through the gates and skidding to a stop near him.

Dust and dirt was being blown into his face by the helicopter landing as he sank to his knees. He was feeling cold now, all he wanted was a bit of peace and quiet, surely that wasn't too much to ask. He felt someone grasp him by his lapels and pull him up. It was Jon Snow.

"Ridge, hang on, I'm going to sort this lot out. The helicopter will take you to hospital, and you will be all right!"

Ridge looked up at Snow. His eyesight was fading and he felt weak. He tried to lift his arm but was unable to control the movement.

"Bollocks," Ridge muttered and closed his eyes.